Six Skene Street

Alison Morant

An Original Publication From Alison Morant

Six Skene Street
Written and published by Alison Morant
Formatted by Frostbite Publishing
Cover by VilaDesign
Copyright © 2016 by Alison Morant

***

This novel is a work of fiction. Names, characters, and locations are either a product of the author's imagination or used in a fictitious setting. Any resemblance to actual events, organizations, or people, living or dead, is strictly coincidental.

All rights reserved. No part of this publication may be reproduced, distributed, or transmitted in any form or by any means, including photocopying, recording, or other electronic or mechanical methods, without the prior written permission of the publisher, except in the case of brief quotations embodied in critical reviews and certain other noncommercial uses permitted by copyright law. For permission requests, send an email to the writer at the following address: alisonmorantauthor@gmail.com. Thank you for respecting the hard work of this author.

***

www.alisonmorant.com

Dedicated to myself

...for persevering!

Part One

Chapter One

Launceston, Tasmania, Australia

June 1963

The rhythmic slapping of his shoes on the wet footpath was just audible above the rain drumming on the corrugated iron rooftops. Raising his head a little as he ran, his eyes automatically squinting against the stinging rain, Dash quickly gauged the distance before jumping the low front fence. Navigating around shrubs and neat flowerbeds before having a clear run, with a couple of bounds he was up the verandah steps two at a time, before skidding to a stop at Mrs. Connolly's front door.

'Crikey ... I'm glad I'm out of that ...' he panted. 'It's as cold ... as your mother-in-law's kiss.'

White, foggy breath punctuated his words as water

trickled down his face and neck. Cupping his hands together, he hurriedly blew warm air to and fro across his icy fingers. Then, after giving his hands a quick warming rub, he knocked firmly on the wooden door. Twenty seconds later a leadlight window set into the front door was illuminated, followed shortly by the door itself being cautiously opened. Wide-eyed, he watched as a large shape, silhouetted against the interior brightness, came into view. The welcoming glow of the front porch light then chased away the shadows, revealing a kindly looking woman dressed in a man's, red tartan dressing gown.

'Dash, what are you doing here at this time of the morning? It's only five-thirty,' Mrs. Connolly exclaimed, her outstretched arm still on the light switch. 'Come in come in, before you catch your death of cold.'

'It's okay Mrs. Connolly ... I can't stop,' he shivered, 'Mum's run out of Aspros ... she's not feeling too good ...' Dash paused again for breath, then went on. 'She said she's had a headache *all* night ... and if you've got some could she have them ... just 'til she can get to the shops later.'

'Of course of course, but come in while I get them. You can't stay out there.'

Deciding quickly, Dash stepped into the warmth of the welcoming hallway, carefully closing the door behind him.

'Why haven't you got your raincoat on you silly boy?' the elderly woman asked over her shoulder as she bustled her way into the kitchen.

'I lost my last one ...' he called back, momentarily transfixed by the array of beautiful pictures on the walls. 'And Mum said she wasn't getting me a new one 'til next year ... so I'd learn to look after my things better,' he ended matter-of-factly.

He'd just noticed that the hallway light was shining through into the adjacent lounge room, and his feet followed his eyes of their own accord. Peeking through the doorway he saw a fluffy black shape, tightly curled up in the warmth of an open fire. The smouldering wood was flaring with every fitful gust of wind, throwing dancing shapes along the walls and ceiling. Dash's eyes widened, taking in the wondrous jewel colours of the wallpaper and furnishings, while his nose was tantalised by the mixture of wood smoke and rose blooms which hung in the air.

Not daring to enter such a beautiful room while he was dripping with water, he leant forward a little to take in as much of the interior as he could see. Then, quickly closing his eyes, he inhaled deeply, trying to imprint deep into his memory all that his senses were experiencing. He wanted to be able to remember as much of it as possible – it would be something new for him to daydream about the next time his mother sent him to his room for the day.

'Mandrake's got a good spot there,' Dash said, smiling at Mrs. Connolly as she made her way hastily back to the front door.

'Yes, he's a very spoilt cat. Now, here's a packet of Aspros. Tell your mum there's no rush to replace them and if there's anything else she needs to let me know.'

'Okay,' he said, stuffing the pack into his wet pocket. He turned to open the front door when Mrs. Connolly continued in a softer voice.

'And here, you can borrow this old umbrella. This downpour might wash you away otherwise.' She smiled at him as she passed it over, all the time thinking how hard Kathleen was on the young boy.

'Gee, thanks Mrs. Connolly.' Dash's face lit up with a big smile – he'd never used an umbrella before.

'You can bring it back tomorrow. And be careful you don't poke anyone in the eyes with it,' she cautioned. 'How's your leg now?' she then asked kindly, still feeling bad about having phoned his mother.

'Oh, it's okay,' Dash replied, surprised that she'd mentioned it. 'I'd better get going now – Mum will be mad if I take too long.'

Watching him racing down the driveway then jumping over the closed gate, all the while holding the big umbrella just above his head, Mavis again regretted telling his mother what he'd done. Sighing, she slowly shook her head and shuffled her way back inside.

'No good going back to bed now,' she decided, 'may as

well make myself a cuppa.' Mavis partly filled a worn but still shiny kettle and placed it onto the old combustion stove, then bent down and poked a few more pieces of wood into the glowing square of heat. After carefully latching the door she automatically went about the business of preparing a pot of tea, all the while thinking about the last time she'd seen young Dash.

It'd been last week – the first day of spring and a bitterly cold morning. She'd popped outside to retrieve The Examiner from her front lawn and was briskly heading back inside, newspaper in one hand, the other one clutching the top of her good pink dressing gown up against her chin. Just as she'd put one foot onto the first verandah step she'd caught sight of Dash running through her front garden.

'Hmph ... he must be taking a shortcut to Terry's again,' she'd said grumpily to Mandrake, who'd followed her outside, 'jumping over my fences as usual.'

Terry was Dash's best mate and lived directly behind her in the next street. Rather than running half-way around the block, Dash had a habit of cutting through her large, peaceful garden, scaling her back fence, then dropping over into Terry's backyard.

Mavis had been frowning as she watched him sprint across her manicured lawn, when all of a sudden she'd been startled when he let out a surprised shout – his foot had slipped on a frosty patch of grass. The next thing she'd seen was Dash landing in the middle of her flourishing Lovelight camellia.

Her arthritis had been giving her curry for days and she'd woken up in a terrible mood, so seeing him sprawled there amongst the broken branches; large, white petals scattered everywhere, she'd instinctively gone right off at him. Dash had scrambled out as quickly as he'd been able to before tearing off again; blood trickling down his leg.

The sight of her favourite shrub being reduced to a misshapen mass of foliage had Mavis on the phone to Kathleen straight away, complaining heartily about what Dash had just done. But then, listening to Kathleen emphasise how she'd give Dash a good belting when he got home and what a damn nuisance he was, Mavis had remembered seeing blood on the poor kid's leg. Being a usually kind-hearted person, she'd at once felt sorry for him saying, 'No no, don't do that, it was just an accident. I'm feeling a bit crabby at the moment with my arthritis, but I've settled down now.'

'*No*, that kid's more trouble than he's worth,' Kathleen had snapped. 'He's always causing trouble *somewhere* – a decent belting will do him good.'

The soft whistling of the kettle brought Mavis's thoughts back to the comfort of her homely kitchen. A sudden gust of wind rattled the window and she glanced out into the darkness, hoping that Dash was safely home again.

Chapter Two

The street lamps were transforming the rain into glistening darts of light, not that Dash noticed. He was blissfully unaware of everything except for his feet as they splashed straight through any puddles that were in his way. Loving it under the umbrella, he smiled when he became aware of the steady tattoo of raindrops bouncing off the thin, overhead covering. He suddenly started running again, knowing that he had to hurry. Dash was a fast runner and loved the feel of the air rushing past him, but he'd love it even more when he could ride his bike again. His mum had said he couldn't ride it again though, until *she* said so. It was part of his punishment for when he'd accidentally run into Mrs. O'Reilly, when she'd come tearing out of her front gate about six weeks ago. She'd gone flying one way, landing with a thump on her backside on the damp nature strip, while Dash had then hit the front fence with his bike and arm before coming to a wobbly stop.

Apparently Gus, her young cocker spaniel, had gotten loose after she'd taken him for a morning walk and she'd been trying to catch him. Dash's stepdad, Reg, had seen it all happen as he was driving up the other side of the street. He'd immediately pulled his car over against the curb and scrambled out, hurrying straight over to help.

'Are you all right love?' he'd asked Mrs. O'Reilly anxiously, hoping she wasn't too badly hurt.

'Oh … I think so,' she'd tentatively replied, sitting there looking a bit stunned. 'If you could just help me up … I think I'll be all right.'

Reg had held Mrs. O'Reilly's hands and gently pulled her to her feet, all the while making a big fuss over her. With one arm around her waist, he'd then carefully helped her as she'd gingerly limped her way inside her house. Dash had thought she couldn't have been too badly hurt because of the big smile he'd seen on her face.

After eventually managing to get Gus inside the front gate, Dash had then quickly shut it behind him. The silly dog had run round and round, excitedly wagging its tail and barking at him through the gate. He'd torn the sleeve of his school shirt on the fence, which was how his mum had found out about the whole incident. As usual, she'd blamed Dash for everything, even though Reg had explained that it wasn't really Dash's fault. She wouldn't listen though, giving Dash several good whacks while telling him again that he was more trouble than he was worth, before exiling him to his room once more.

Doing an abrupt right hand turn, Dash ran up a dark, overgrown driveway. Bending over slightly to avoid brushing the umbrella against some low branches, he then jumped up two steps at a time into the shelter of the back porch. Not knowing how to close the umbrella, he carefully propped it up in the corner before removing his wet shoes. Then, after a couple of deep breaths, he reluctantly opened the back door.

Making his way through the untidy laundry, he then entered the equally untidy kitchen. His mum was sitting at the new Laminex table she'd been so happy to get just a few months ago, an untouched cup of tea in front of her.

Scrutinising Dash as he stood there dripping water onto the floor, Kathleen scowled then asked in an accusing voice, 'What took you so long, the old biddy only lives six houses up the street?'

'It took her a while to find them,' Dash quietly replied, pulling the now damp packet of Aspros from his pocket.

'Well, don't just stand there making a mess on the floor, give me the damn things then go and get the mop. When you've finished cleaning up all that water you can go and chop up the kindling. Now hurry up!'

Without saying a word, Dash reached over and sat the

packet on the table, then turned around and quickly walked back into the laundry. He found the mop as fast as he could – it was propped in a bucket against the wall, just visible behind the old wooden clothes horse full of damp clothes. He grabbed it and returned to the kitchen, carefully mopping up the small pool of water. Thankfully, *she* wasn't there anymore.

His mum had been extra cranky for a while now, and he'd been doing his best not to upset her by keeping out of her way as much as possible. Checking that the floor was now dry, he put the mop back where he'd found it and made his way outside again, quietly closing the back door behind him. Cursing under his breath as he struggled to push his feet back into his sodden shoes – made difficult because of the dampness of his socks – he turned his attention to the early morning sky.

The wind had eased a little and the rain had now stopped, but it still felt just as chilly. Dash noticed a few stars twinkling far above him in the heavens, and he stood and stared at them until they were once more concealed by the rolling storm clouds.

Suddenly remembering the umbrella, he couldn't help but smile when he turned and saw it standing in the corner. Picking it up again he positioned himself on the edge of the top step, then holding it high above himself, he jumped as high as he could. Thinking he might slowly float back down, he was quite disappointed when he landed with a thud. Sighing loudly, he walked towards the woodshed, angrily stomping through every puddle that he saw. He'd just remembered he'd have to get up early again tomorrow; it was his morning to work with Reg.

Ever since his tenth birthday, eighteen months ago now, Dash had been helping his stepdad with the newspaper run three mornings a week. His mum had said that it was about time he started earning his own keep. Getting up when it was still dark had been fun and exciting at first, but he was tired at school most days now and had been getting into trouble for 'not paying attention'.

When his mother woke him, usually by yelling something derogatory at him, he'd robotically get out of bed and pull on some clothes, often still half asleep. Walking out the back door towards the station wagon the cold would slap him in the face, waking him instantly and making his eyes momentarily water.

After picking up the prepared newspapers from Mr. McIntyre's place, he and Reg would then drive slowly along the dark streets; Reg expertly throwing the papers onto his customers' front lawns while driving with one hand. Dash would sit in the back with his pile of papers and throw them out through his passenger side window, always trying his best to get them over the fences.

There was usually little traffic at that time of the

morning, and Reg had taught him how to drive some time ago, but Dash had still been surprised when one morning a few weeks ago Reg had said, 'I'm just going to drop in and have a quick cuppa with Mrs. O'Reilly, to see if she's recovered from her fall.' He'd then instructed Dash to deliver the papers in that street by himself and to take his time. Since then, Reg had done the same thing at least once a week.

But Dash didn't mind; he loved driving the old station wagon. Turning around at the end of the street was the best part – he'd quickly pretend he was a racing car driver as he swung the wheel around. Then, about two weeks ago, he found out what was really going on with the 'cup of tea' business.

It had been a Saturday afternoon and he'd been on his way to the local picture theatre to see 'Jason and the Argonauts'. He loved movies and it was a rare treat for his mum to have allowed him to go. She must have wanted him out of the way for some reason but he hadn't cared – he'd been out of the house as quick as a flash, not allowing her a chance to change her mind.

He'd been puffing slightly by the time he'd rounded the last corner and seen the flashing sign of the picture theatre, just down the street. It was then that Dash had literally run into Billy Dickson and a few of Billy's mates. Billy was the oldest brother of his best mate Terry, and they just happened to live next door to Mrs. O'Reilly.

The boys hadn't been impressed when Dash had unexpectedly ploughed into them; forcing them to scatter. Billy had managed to grab hold of him by the back of his jumper and happily gave him a few good whacks on the back of his head, all the while telling him that if he didn't watch out where he was going, next time he'd have a size ten boot up his arse.

That being sorted, Billy, who actually didn't mind young Dash, asked him how he was going. Dash had grinned his familiar grin and said, 'You know mate – same shit, different day.'

'You young smartarse,' Billy had grinned back. Then suddenly remembering what he'd heard he said, 'Hey guys, did you know Dash's dad's been screwing Mrs. O'Reilly?'

'Fair dinkum?' one of the boys had asked.

'Yeah, no bullshit, I overheard me mum and old man talking about it the other night.'

Dash hadn't understood what Billy was talking about at first, when he'd said that Reg was screwing Mrs. O'Reilly. When Billy and his mates had realised that Dash was quite ignorant about the whole sex thing, they'd been more than happy to tell him all they knew about the subject. Dash had been quite fascinated with all this new knowledge, and ended up missing the beginning of the movie.

Now nearly finished chopping the kindling, Dash took a

quick breather. Leaning on the handle of the axe for a minute, his mind was on his *real* dad, wondering again if he'd ever get to meet him. Knowing nothing about him was hard for Dash – his mother had refused to tell him anything about the man who'd fathered him; not even his name. Dash had often fantasised though that he must look like him, because she'd often yelled at him to 'get out of my sight, you remind me too much of your father'.

That always made Dash smile inside; he treasured the thought that he resembled his real dad. Picking up the axe once more he continued steadily on with his task, only to hear his mum yell at him to hurry up.

'Nearly finished,' he panted to himself as he hefted the heavy axe up and down; slender pieces of wood flying off with each stroke, 'should be done by the time Reg gets home.'

Chapter Three

Reg saw the signal as soon as he rounded the corner. Jeannie's front porch light was glowing invitingly – her husband wasn't home. Reg was running a bit late this morning but was still seriously thinking of dropping in for a quickie; but thinking that Kathleen was getting a bit suspicious of his comings and goings lately made him think twice.

'She's such a bloody harpy,' Reg thought to himself of his bride of five years. 'How the hell did I get myself into this bloody mess?'

It was no good though, going on about it – he knew he only had himself to blame. He'd been too young, horny and inexperienced to have seen Kathleen for what she really was: a young woman desperate to secure her future by securing a husband, and one that would be a father to the kid she'd already had.

Reg had been working at the local newsagency since he'd left school at seventeen. Mrs. McIntyre had needed help in the busy shop, and someone to do the heavy lifting, ever since Mr. McIntyre had accidentally shot himself in the foot on a weekend shooting trip with his mates. The job included delivering the morning newspaper, and the early morning starts had been the worst part of the job, until six weeks ago. That was when he'd met Jean O'Reilly. Smiling, he thought that it was the best thing Dash had ever done, running into her like that.

Thinking again about the lovely Jeannie, and how much she enjoyed their early morning trysts whenever her husband was working away, Reg felt his cock start to harden and all his reasoning powers start to fade.

'If only Kathleen didn't ration out sex like it was some scarce commodity, I probably wouldn't be after a bit on the side,' he rationalised as he turned the wheel of the station wagon towards a dark section of the road, in-between the street lights. Pulling over against the curb he was frantically trying to think of a good excuse for getting home late when Charlie Dickson suddenly poked his grinning head in the window.

'G'day Reg, how've you been? You're not having car trouble are you?'

Reg jumped, startled out of his thoughts. 'Oh! G'day

Charlie ... no ... I was just ... picking up my smokes, they fell on the floor.' His hard on disappeared; he knew there'd be no morning hanky-panky now.

'It's funny, but I thought I saw your car parked here last week,' Charlie continued, still grinning.

Realising that he'd been sprung, Reg grinned back and said, 'No mate, it must have just *looked* like mine.'

'Yeah, righto, if you say so,' Charlie had laughed. 'But you'd better be careful, you know how people talk.'

'Damn that Charlie Dickson,' Reg grumbled to himself as he pulled back out onto the road. 'Oh well, it can't be helped I suppose,' he sighed despondently. A small smile then began to crease the corners of his mouth as he decided to drop by later that evening. As he continued driving down the road, automatically throwing the papers as he went, he thought about the state of his life. And he wasn't happy.

Being the only child of elderly parents, Reg had inherited the family home – a large, old weatherboard house on a good size block – when his parents had died within twelve months of each other. Aged just twenty-two at the time, he'd met Kathleen a few months later and it hadn't been long before they'd been enjoying quite a few nights together. It'd been all too easy to have her move out of the small flat she'd been renting, into his quietly empty house.

Reg had liked the idea of an instant family when Kathleen told him later that she had a young son. Having pictured married life being full of fun and sex, along with the normal ups and downs that life threw at you from time to time, he'd asked her to marry him a few months later. Kathleen had been fun in the beginning, and as eager as he'd been for an afternoon in bed, but now all she craved was something new for the house.

He'd only met Dash a couple of times before they'd tied the knot. The kid had been living with his nan and granddad – 'just till I get myself sorted', as Kathleen had informed him at the time. He hadn't known that the kid had been living there for nearly four years already. The couple of Sundays when they'd driven the hour to see Dash had always been quick visits. Kathleen had never been keen to stay long, always having some good reason which prevented her from being with the kid for the whole day. And Reg, thinking mostly with his dick back then, had been happy to have Kathleen to himself on the weekends.

After they'd become man and wife and he'd adopted Dash, he and Kathleen had then surprised Dash one Sunday afternoon by telling him he was going to live with them from now on. Expecting the little fella to be happy and excited, Reg had been bewildered at first when Dash had just stood there and stared at them. It had become worse when they set off for home – the poor little bugger was distraught and all Kathleen had done was slap him on his legs and yelled at him to stop crying. Reg had seen a whole different side to

Kathleen then, and he hadn't liked it.

Even then, at five, Dash had always been into mischief and always asking questions. He'd been so inquisitive about everything; he'd often end up breaking something while trying to see how it worked. That would set Kathleen off into a screaming fit. She'd give Dash another couple of good whacks and send him to his room for the rest of the day.

Now heading back home for breakfast before starting work at the shop, Reg had pretty much decided that he had to leave his wife. He couldn't help thinking that he was too young to be stuck in a marriage with someone who was always harping and bitching about something. Her constant nagging for more money or new curtains or a new *something* was draining him of the will to go to work.

She'd also shown hardly any interest in sex for quite a while now, especially in the last few months, which was just about the last straw. He'd wanted to have a family of his own since he was a kid. A family where everyone loved each other like you read about in stories and saw in the movies. He'd been sure if you wanted something badly enough, and prayed for it to happen, then it would. Now, here he was, about to turn twenty-seven next month and all he felt was despair and frustration.

If he was honest with himself he'd realise he'd stayed as long as he had because of Dash. He felt sorry for the little bastard – the way Kathleen treated that kid wasn't right. Just because he reminded her of the man who'd taken her virginity at fifteen and then run off, leaving her pregnant, wasn't Dash's fault.

After thinking it all through again, Reg decided what he had to do. He'd face Kathleen today as soon as he got home and get it over and done with. He'd had enough. He was leaving.

Chapter Four

Kathleen had been pacing between the old Chesterfield couch and the tallboy; the latter of which held an array of her special photos. The largest one, of her and Reg on their wedding day, held pride of place in the centre. She stopped and studied it for a moment, remembering the day she'd become Mrs. Reginald Clive McCallum.

Reg had looked so handsome that day – all dressed up in his black suit, wavy blond hair combed straight back, standing there nervously proud. Studying her own appearance in the photo, she was again aware of the look of relief etched on her face. Feeling a bit unsettled, she changed her focus to several photos of her and Reg on their one and only holiday – their honeymoon. The photos showed a smiling couple with snow-covered mountains in the background, her long red hair tucked up under a furry hat.

There was only one photograph showing Dash, and that was placed at the back behind all the others. It'd been taken at school and showed him dressed in his school uniform, standing at the end of the back row in a class photo. The slightly grainy black and white image showed a handsome young boy with a stocky body wearing a baggy school jumper; his strong, sturdy legs protruding from grey shorts. Tousled black hair partly covered his face, but his cheeky grin was unmistakable.

Kathleen hadn't even glanced at that photo though. When her eyes locked onto the ornate silver frames in front of her, the images seemed to taunt her with their aura of happiness. Now, feeling even more desperate, she knew she didn't want to lose everything she'd accumulated.

The four years before she met Reg had been a hard struggle for Kathleen. Only fifteen when she had Dash, the snide remarks she'd overheard from neighbours had made her feel both ashamed and angry. Her boyfriend had left for the mainland the week after she told him she was pregnant, and she never saw him or heard from him again.

She'd held out hope for quite a while, believing he really did love her as he'd said, and that once he found out he had a son he'd be back to look after the two of them. Naming the baby Dash to create some link to his father, Kathleen had waited. But, after seemingly endless months of coping with a crying baby and no job prospects, she'd had to face her reality – he wasn't coming back.

Deciding to move to a larger town to find work, Kathleen dumped one-year-old Dash with her mum and dad, who'd been more than happy to have him living with them. It'd annoyed Kathleen immensely that Dash loved his nan so much; she'd sometimes hated him for it, but wasn't even sure why. After moving once again, this time to Launceston, Kathleen had first set eyes on Reg a few days later.

She'd been checking out the hodgepodge of shops that were in her new area when she'd stopped by the local newsagency and bought her favourite magazine, 'The Australian Women's Weekly'. Right from the beginning she'd set her sights on the quiet, polite young man who'd served her; doing all she could to snare him.

Suddenly catching a glimpse of Dash grinning happily in his last school photo, a scowl dug deep furrows across her forehead and a hateful look appeared in her grey eyes.

'He's such a little bastard,' she thought to herself, 'always getting into trouble. He'll end up in jail by the time he's eighteen, there's no doubt about that.' Not wanting to even think about Dash anymore, she turned her thoughts back to her present situation.

'I'll tell Reg today, as soon as he gets home,' she sighed hopelessly to herself. 'It's no good waiting any longer – I'm getting headaches thinking about it all the time.'

She'd suspected she was pregnant a few months ago, but

she and Reg had been fighting so much lately she hadn't dared tell him. The nausea she'd been experiencing could strike at any time, and she'd been going to bed early and alone.

Often pretending to be fast asleep when Reg came to bed gave Kathleen a feeling of having some control over him. Knowing how much he liked having sex, she withheld it to punish him whenever she felt it was necessary. She just couldn't understand why she couldn't have what she wanted when she wanted it. After all, they owned the damn house; they must be able to afford some decent furniture, not that she brought in much cash each week. In her mind it was up to the man to provide everything for his family, and she thought Reg was definitely falling down on that front.

Working part-time at the local hospital as a cleaner for the last year, it'd been easy for her to see a doctor straight after her shift last week. After having had a chat and a quick examination, he'd confirmed her fears – she was already three months gone.

'Maybe Reg will be happy about it,' she thought with forced optimism as she slowly crossed the kitchen and sat down on one of her new green chairs. 'He said he wanted to have his own kids one day.'

But he hadn't spoken about that for several years now, and she knew things hadn't been right between them for ages. They fought over money constantly – or the lack of it;

there never seemed to be enough for all the things she needed. Now she'd lose her job. How the hell could they afford to even have a baby?

Just the thought of another man leaving her with another baby sent her hormones into overdrive, flooding Kathleen's body with a rush of nausea and panic. Breathing deeply while slowly patting her clammy forehead with her hanky, she tried to pull herself together. At least her headache was now gone and she was able to think more clearly.

Kathleen needed a plan and needed one fast – Reg would be back from the paper run soon and would want his breakfast. Listening to Dash chopping the kindling she frowned and yelled at him to hurry up, then concentrated on getting Reg's porridge ready. Porridge was his favourite and she didn't want it going lumpy today.

By the time she had it just the way he liked it she'd decided what to do. Hurriedly changing into a dress she knew Reg liked, she then brushed her long, wavy red hair, remembering as she did so how Reg had once said that it was her hair that had first attracted him to her. She applied a bit of lipstick, then stood back to gain a better view of her appearance in her new cheval mirror.

The person looking back could have looked pretty if she hadn't had such a pinched expression on her face. But Kathleen never noticed as her mind was now working overtime, going over different scenarios of how she could tell Reg about his impending fatherhood.

Back in the kitchen, just as she was putting a colourful, knitted tea cosy onto the teapot, she heard the familiar sound of Reg's car pulling up in the driveway.

Chapter Five

After chopping the last pieces of kindling and stacking them with the rest, Dash exhaled wearily then trudged into the shed to put the axe away.

'I reckon I could eat the crutch out of a low-flying duck I'm so hungry,' he muttered. He'd picked up many funny old sayings from his granddad, along with quite a few explicit swear words. His nan definitely didn't approve. She'd always been saying, 'Stanley, stop teaching the boy that rubbish.'

Granddad thought it was a great joke though, hearing the little tacker say things like, 'I'm as full as a fat girl's socks', when he'd finished eating his dinner. Dash never swore in front of his nan though. He loved her so much and hated it when he knew she was angry with him, on the rare occasions he could visit her.

With the axe now back in its home behind the shed door,

he grabbed the umbrella and headed towards the house. Hunger and cold had him hurrying up the worn porch steps, but before opening the door he gingerly sat the umbrella back in its previous position in the corner.

Removing his now muddy shoes and socks, he left them to one side of the door; then, with a weary sigh, Dash stepped through into the relative warmth of the laundry. His first reaction was to sniff the air, hoping it might be one of the rare days when his mum had cooked up a hot brekkie.

'Oh well, Weet Bix and toast it is then,' he sighed with resignation, his nose only detecting the odour of lavender Pine-o-Clean.

Struggling a bit with his clinging wet clothing, he pulled his jumper up and over his head, unintentionally dragging his shirt with it. He became slightly stuck with his arms trapped above him and it immediately panicked him. Not being able to see increased his feeling of vulnerability and he jerked his arms up and down to free himself as fast as he could, shaking his head a little as it emerged from the constricting garments.

Breathing a dazed sigh of relief, he dropped his wet tops into the wash basket; immediately followed by his long pants and undies. His body felt hot and chilled all at the same time, so grabbing a towel to cover his private bits first, he then headed for the bathroom to wash before breakfast.

Opening the kitchen door and walking through, he

noticed a bowl of steaming porridge sitting in Reg's place at the kitchen table.

'Mmm ... I hope there's some left over for me,' was Dash's only thought as he looked up hopefully in the direction of the stove. He then saw his mum and Reg standing there, but the weird thing was they were both just staring at each other. Reg had a shocked sort of expression on his face, and his mum looked like she needed to sit down. Dash instinctively ducked his head and quietly continued on his way.

'What the hell's going on there?' he thought to himself as he soaped up his hands in the pink wash basin. The next thing he heard was the front door slamming shut, followed by the wagon being cranked into life and quickly reversing down the driveway. As he listened to it disappearing down the road he finished washing, then quietly went to his room to dress for school, all the while wondering why Reg had taken off like that without eating his favourite breakfast.

As he re-entered the kitchen, his mum turned to stare straight at him. She was tightly hugging her body and gave him a look filled with bitterness.

'There you are you little bastard. You're half the trouble around here. If I didn't have to look at you every day I'd be a lot better off. Why I didn't just put you into a boys' home years ago I'll never know.'

Dash had often wondered that himself but thought that

now wasn't the time to mention it. She stood there glaring at him while he carefully poured himself a cup of tea, into the 'Best Grandson' mug that his nan had given him one birthday, being extra careful not to spill any milk or sugar onto the tablecloth.

As he was about to check the saucepan on the stove, Dash's mum abruptly told him to get out of her sight and get to school, or she'd give him another good belting. Dash didn't have to be told twice. Quickly gulping his sweet tea, he grabbed a piece of dry toast and left the kitchen without looking back.

Dash was tired and hungry but had no desire to be near his mother any longer than necessary. Not knowing what the hell she was angry about this time, he put his wet shoes back on, slung his school bag over his shoulder and headed off into the cold, early morning.

'I'm gunna get away from this place one day,' he swore to himself. 'I wish the old cow would put me in a boys' home like she's always saying; I bet I'd be a lot better off there.'

Kicking an old soft drink can out of his way, he trudged on down the nearly deserted street. The wind had dropped right off now, but a soft, misty rain was falling from the gloomy sky, gradually soaking him through again. Starting to feel chilled to the bone, he remembered the umbrella, but decided not to go back for it. Instead, after hearing laughter coming from the Wilson's house as he passed by, he fantasised about his future.

'I'm gunna work hard and earn lots of money ...' He was close to tears now and spoke softly. 'Then I'll be able to do whatever I like.' He sniffed a couple of times then wiped his running nose on his wet sleeve. 'I'll buy a big car so I can leave this place and never come back.' Thoughts of his real dad filled his head, and he again wondered about him. 'Dad might even come back and take me with him.'

Dash smiled a little, thinking of the adventures they could have together. Feeling a bit better now that he had his dreams to think about, he continued on his way to school, concentrating on the soft, squelching sound coming from his wet shoes, to take his mind off the rumbling sound coming from his empty stomach.

Part Two

Chapter Six

Portarlington, Victoria, Australia
June 1963

Evie was quite content, slowly meandering along the nearly deserted beach. As usual, her eyes were scanning the high tide mark, trying to find just the right shells for her ever-increasing collection. She loved it here in the hot summer months when the small town was bustling with holiday makers and she could swim every day. But then she loved it just as much in the quieter off-season as well – then she could wander from one end of the beach to the other without having to step over people sunbathing, or dodge whizzing Frisbees.

A stiff breeze was blowing in from the south-west, and the ever-present seagulls squawked incessantly above her as she paused and stared out to sea; absentmindedly scrunching the gritty sand between her bare toes. Lost in her own thoughts, she didn't notice that she was becoming damp from the fine mist of salty spray, or that her short, dark hair was becoming stiff with salt and stuck out at all angles.

Even though she was from a large family – she was number five of six kids – Evie was usually left to her own devices. Her three older sisters were now into boys and clothes and were constantly fighting over 'who took my favourite top' or something, and had no time for her, and Douglas, her brother who was two years older than she was, never wanted her hanging about when he had his mates around. Once he even tied her up to a tree in the park and left her there when she'd wanted to play cowboys and Indians with them. That hadn't fazed her at all though, because, being the tomboy that she was, she'd managed to loosen the ropes in no time and proceeded to stalk them for an hour without them knowing. When she'd sprung them smoking a cigarette behind the old scout hall, they'd chased her all the way home. She'd managed to get there before them though, and hung around her mum for a while as if she was going to dob on them.

Her youngest sister was just three years old and didn't interest Evie very much. The baby of the family, 'and definitely the last one at that' (as Evie had overheard her mum say on numerous occasions), Joanne was quiet and shy and quite happy to play at home with her dolls. Evie, however, wasn't the type of girl who liked playing inside much – she preferred climbing trees, swimming or making mud pies to throw at the Yankee kids when they were staying next door in their two-storey holiday house.

Finally starting to feel cold, Evie suddenly realised how late it was getting, so abruptly turned on her heels and headed back along the now deserted beach towards home. The late afternoon sky was rapidly darkening while the gusty wind continued to blow the white caps off the waves, depositing them along the shoreline in discoloured foamy clumps.

'Bugger,' she muttered as she sprinted along the sand and looked up at the sky. 'I didn't realise how late it was. Mum will chuck a fit if I'm late for tea again.'

As long as she was home by tea time she'd be alright; it was the only rule her mother insisted she follow. She could be gone all day long and usually no one would question her about where she'd been or what she'd been doing, but get back late for tea and her mum's usual indifference to her would rapidly change to anger.

Truth be told, it was about the only time Evie received much attention, not that it worried her unduly. What you don't know you can't miss, and Evie knew nothing of the workings of a loving family. To her it was normal to be overlooked in favour of her demanding older sisters and spoilt brother, not to mention little Joanne who was often sick with the latest childhood ailment. However, being the independent little person that she was, she actually liked having so much freedom to do as she pleased.

Not knowing that her dad had been disappointed at having another girl when she'd been born, she'd eventually become his favourite. She was always thrilled on the rare occasions when he had time to take Douglas and her fishing, or to fly the big kite he'd made for them one Christmas. Douglas, on the other hand, would try everything to exclude her from these outings as he wanted his dad all to himself for a change. He was sick of being surrounded by girls and girl talk, and at thirteen years of age he thought girls were the stupidest and noisiest people on earth.

Cutting through the park and past the old scout hall, then quickly running along the main road, Evie could now see the glow of the Peter's ice cream cone above the door of the shop at the end of the street.

She was out of breath by the time she burst in the front door but still raced through the shop, then bounded up the steps into the hallway of the house. Her sister Maureen was helping her dad serve the half a dozen boys who were clustered around the counter, and she gave Evie a withering look as she shot by. Evie was too young to work in the shop and Maureen resented her for it.

'It's not fair,' Maureen whined again to her dad. 'Why do

I have to work in the shop and not her?' she said, pointing to Evie's retreating figure.

'You know damn well she's not old enough, now finish up here and go and help your mum with tea,' he replied tiredly.

Maureen turned on her heels and stomped up the steps into the house. Seeing Evie heading into the bathroom she followed her in; 'accidentally' giving her a good shove into the wall. Then ignoring Evie completely, she stood in front of the mirror and patted her teased hair into place.

Looking older than her sixteen years, Maureen knew she looked good and she was learning how to use her looks to get what she wanted. What she wanted now was to get out of this damn family and start living her own life. Turning from the mirror she looked Evie up and down and taunted, 'It's easy to see you'll never have a boyfriend, you're way too ugly and skinny', before flouncing out, head held high.

As soon as Evie was sure Maureen had gone, she stood on a chair and studied herself in the bathroom cabinet mirror. The scruffy-looking person looking back was very suntanned, nearly as brown as her eyes, and when Evie tried a tentative smile her slightly crooked teeth were revealed. Unruly hair was sticking out everywhere and there was a grimy streak of dirt down one cheek. Looking down at her arms and legs, she remembered hearing her dad say that she had a wiry build, and now she knew that must mean skinny.

Evie suddenly felt a bit sad, thinking that she must be ugly, so stepped down off the chair.

'Oh well, I don't want a boyfriend anyway,' she thought to herself. 'Boys are stupid and loud and bossy.'

Grabbing a comb she tried to run it through her hair but it was too stiff with salt. Instead, she put the plug in the sink and started to fill it with warm water so she could wash the salt, sand and dirt off her grubby hands and face.

Chapter Seven

Jim had shaken his head as Maureen stormed off, thinking again that it'd be nice to have some help in the shop without all the drama. After he finished serving the rowdy boys, he headed outside to get more soft drinks to replenish the drinks fridge.

As he stood surveying the array of wooden crates, each revealing a sparkling glimpse of colour, his mind wandered again to the day he'd decided to move his family to the small seaside town of Portarlington.

He'd originally thought it would be a great idea – getting his boisterous brood out of the rat race of the city and into a more laid back lifestyle near the beach. Growing up inland, Jim had often dreamt of living by the sea. Fishing was his favourite pastime, so when he'd heard about a small business for sale on the coast he'd immediately arranged to have an inspection.

The next day he'd driven the ninety minutes to the real estate office in Portarlington where he'd met Darrel, the agent he'd contacted the day before. After the usual smarmy salesman chit-chat, Darrel had insisted on driving Jim to the inspection in his new EH Holden company car.

By the time they arrived at the business in question – the local milk bar/grocery shop – Jim had heard every enthusiastic statistic regarding the car but nothing in regard to the property he was contemplating buying. As they'd slowed, then stopped entirely to allow an oncoming car towing an old aluminium caravan to pass, he got his first good look at the front of the shop.

The front door was placed centrally in the slightly run-down timber structure, and sign-writing on each of the large, adjacent windows indicated that the milk bar was to the left, and the grocery area to the right. His gaze had taken in the placards on one side of the building advertising Coca-Cola and Tarax lemonade, while Peter's and Streets ice cream signs adorned the front.

Darrel's incessant chatter about the new Red Engine had begun to irritate by then, so Jim had been more than pleased when they finally drove through the open double gates and up a long, yellow gravel driveway.

Stepping out of the car as soon as it'd stopped, Jim took in the large, overgrown backyard with one sweep of his head.

There were several fruit trees in dire need of pruning and a decent size fibro and timber shed, which, he'd been pleased to see, had plenty of room for his small boat.

Jim thought that the property was a little run down but had agreed with Darrel, who'd finally started his salesman pitch, that its position in the main street, opposite a sprawling park and camping area, was a perfect location. He'd also definitely thought it a bonus that there was a house attached to the rear of the shop, saving him the hassle of having to find another one for them all to live in.

Entering through the back door of the residence, he'd glanced at the laundry, kitchen and bathroom as an enthusiastic Darrel had pointed out different features; then after following on past three bedrooms, a study and a lounge room, they'd finally come to a stop at the end of a long hallway. A faded curtain with a tassel partly covered a glass panelled door, and after Darrel had pulled it across and opened the door, he stood aside, allowing Jim entry into the shop first.

Hastening down the worn wooden steps, he'd been transported straight into the milk bar area. But before he'd been able to give anything a proper once-over, his eyes had been drawn to the fantastic view of the bay, framed by the shop's huge front windows. Momentarily mesmerised by the sight of the sun sparkling on the bright blue water, he'd then found himself walking through the shop and out the front door. A cool breeze had sprung up, bringing with it the salty smelling tang of seaweed from the nearby beach. He'd felt both relaxed and invigorated and had fallen in love with the place on the spot.

Jim had bought the business that afternoon, putting the house they'd then owned on the market at the same time. Nancy had not been impressed when he'd told her, but he'd been sure that she'd like it once they moved in and got themselves settled. Unfortunately, later that same year, supermarkets appeared in the bigger towns and most of the locals had been lured by the cheaper prices to shop there instead. What followed were several years of hard struggle, always trying to make enough during the busy summer months to hold them over in the off-season, when they had to rely on the dwindling local custom. Jim's dream had become more and more of a nightmare with each passing year, and he'd been searching for a viable way out for some time. If only his relationship with Nancy had been the same as it had been in the beginning of their marriage, he probably could have tolerated the other hardships. But he knew she didn't love him anymore and that had been the hardest thing to bear. It wasn't just Nancy either. The older girls were way too much for him to deal with en-masse now - all that non-stop talking and fighting drove him crazy. The twins had always seemed to be bickering over something, and Maureen treated him like the enemy these days. Wishing he had more time to spend with Douglas, he also couldn't help wishing his son wasn't such a sulky kid when things didn't go his own way.

'That boy's had it way too easy with all these females around, that's for sure,' Jim thought as he loaded another crate of Fanta onto his trolley. Then, as he turned around to grab a crate of Coke, he couldn't stop a wry smile from momentarily lightening his features.

'Yep ... and here I am ... seven years later,' he muttered to himself. 'Where's the bloody time gone?' Shaking his head a little he sighed, 'Well ... I suppose they do say that time flies when you're having fun.'

Mechanically refilling the Coke machine, Jim's thoughts turned to little Joanne and he felt a wave of sadness wash over him. As cute as she was, he didn't spend as much time with her as he knew he should. He felt bad about it, but he just couldn't help it – his mind had associated her arrival with the departure of what little had remained of his sex life.

His biggest shame though, was the fact that he'd been seeing another woman. Just thinking about Annie gave him a warm feeling inside and produced a soft smile on his face. He hadn't realised how much he'd missed love and affection 'til he'd slowly experienced it blossoming again.

It'd started three years ago, not long after the stork had dropped Joanne off. All he'd experienced from that 'happy' event were feelings of being more of a nuisance than anything else.

At first the older girls had been madly keen to be in charge of the baby and wouldn't let him do anything, shooing him out of the way all the time. Once the novelty had worn off though, they'd begun fighting over whose turn it was; now preferring to do their own things instead. And Nancy – well, she'd become more of a cold fish than ever, often giving him the silent treatment. After having endured a difficult pregnancy and labour with Joanne she'd informed him that he was to never touch her again. She'd certainly left no doubt in his mind; that part of their life was now over.

Even though it had been the September school holidays at the time, business had still been slow. The sun had only appeared briefly during the previous week, and wind and rain had been gusting severely for days. Many of the holiday campers had either packed up and gone home or had been travelling into Geelong for entertainment. His earnings for the quarter had been looking dismal, but Jim thought he'd take advantage of the drop off in business to escape for a while.

Having instructed Maureen and the twins to take it in turns to serve in the shop at tea time, he'd then been free to do the one thing that'd been saving his sanity. Telling Nancy that he'd eat his tea later, he'd headed off with his rod and tackle box straight down to the pier. Often catching enough fish within a couple of hours to feed them all, he knew that

Nancy was never concerned when he went missing for a while.

When he'd seen Annie for the first time she'd been standing on the lower jetty that he usually favoured, throwing in a line of her own. Something about her had attracted him and he'd unconsciously walked towards her without thinking. They'd struck up a conversation and basically didn't stop talking until he'd had to go, two hours later.

Over the next three years their meetings ever so naturally progressed; from talking and trying their luck at catching a good size fish, to having furtive assignations at her holiday house, on the rare occasions that he could get away from home. It hadn't taken very long at all though, for both of them to realise how they felt about each other.

The jangling ring of the shop's doorbell brought Jim out of his private head space. His thoughts of Annie slipped away, along with the small smile that her memory had produced, as a man and woman ushered their squabbling kids into the shop, all the while loudly promising them an ice cream if they'd just behave. Letting out a deep sigh, Jim reluctantly returned to the here and now as he once more attended to his customers.

Chapter Eight

Annie was a widow. Her husband Robert had died exactly one year after having a severely debilitating stroke. She'd met then married him after an exciting whirlwind romance, just before her thirtieth birthday, but he'd been a workaholic for the entire nine years of their marriage, obsessed with finance and making more money. Dying at fifty-two, he'd left her with a multitude of investments, making her considerably wealthy.

Robert had always insisted that Annie was to accompany him on his many overseas business trips, so they'd never had any children. After he'd died she'd felt somewhat lost at first and had become a bit reclusive, spending a lot of time in her beautiful garden. It must have been the therapy that she needed though, because a year later she decided to go back to teaching – a profession she'd enjoyed before marrying. She certainly didn't need the money; it was more the pleasure and satisfaction of interacting with her students that she found so gratifying.

Her favourite pastime though, had always been fishing. Even as a girl she'd loved just sitting there gazing into the water, waiting for that elusive nibble. None of her female friends liked fishing, so she'd begun her habit of packing some food and a thermos of hot, sweet tea and setting off on her own little adventures whenever she could.

After several day trips to Portarlington, where she enjoyed catching quite a few very tasty flathead, she'd decided to buy a lovely little holiday house she'd seen for sale. It was a kilometre or so along the coast from the township, only metres from the water, and she loved it. It was nowhere near as palatial as her house in Kew, an expensive and leafy suburb of Melbourne, but she was soon spending all her holidays and most weekends there.

Meeting Jim that day when she was fishing off the pier had been such a pleasant surprise for her; Annie hadn't laughed or enjoyed herself so much for a long time. She hadn't been interested in any men since Robert had died. Jim had been so easy to talk to though, and always such a gentleman – not like some of the men she'd come across when she'd been socialising with her friends. It had surprised her just how disappointed she felt to find out at that first encounter that he was married ... and had six kids!

They often met on the pier after that, and it wasn't long before they were making arrangements to meet up on a certain day or time. Not wanting any gossip circulating in the small town, Jim often picked her up in his small boat a little further along the beach from her place, at an isolated spot where no houses had yet been built. They'd then spend a couple of blissful hours floating on the blue-green vastness of Corio Bay, just talking, laughing and fishing. Having no intention of ever being a marriage wrecker she kept her feelings to herself for a long time, until the day arrived when all reasoning had seemingly departed.

He'd been helping her into his boat before they were to go for an hour's fishing, and as he'd taken her hand to steady her she felt a tingle of energy shoot through her body. She'd known he'd felt it too because they'd both instantly looked up at the exact same time and stared into each other's eyes. The next thing she knew they were kissing and moving against each other until the boat started rocking and they'd nearly fallen out. They'd laughed and held each other until the boat became stable once more, then reluctantly let each other go.

That had been the day that everything changed. The irrefutable force of their attraction had won, and after they'd somewhat self-consciously walked the short distance to her place, they'd spent the rest of the hour in her bed. Later they'd talked about what on Earth they were to do, until Jim had suggested they could continue meeting discretely until the time was right for him to leave his wife. In Annie's mind though, she'd thought the time would never be right for all concerned.

They'd been meeting surreptitiously now for nearly three years, but she felt that their inability to see each other more often and openly was becoming more and more frustrating, especially for Jim. She thought he'd been quite pensive the last few times they'd been together, and had wondered if he'd had enough of his deception and was going to end their relationship.

'I'm prepared to wait for him, but is he prepared to do the same?' was all she could now think. Mulling it over for a while, Annie eventually decided to ask him tonight when he rang; he always rang her for a quick chat on Sunday evening. If he wanted to call it quits she knew it would hurt her to her core, but she would accept his decision for the sake of his family.

'It'll be easier over the phone too ...' she reasoned, knowing she could hang up if necessary before she cried. Impatient now for his call, Annie was mentally preparing herself to hear his answer to her question.

Chapter Nine

Evie's mum hated everything about moving from her lovely, if a bit small, previous home to this godforsaken house. She was actually quite embarrassed about the whole thing - living in a house built onto the back of a shop of all things, not to mention the come-down in status by having to *serve* people in the shop.

'Whatever was Jim thinking, bringing me to this damn place?' she asked herself yet again. It was no good stewing over it now though. Joanne was unwell and had vomited over all the clean clothes in the ironing basket, and the whole lot had to be rewashed. The stupid wringer was jammed again so she gave it a good, hard whack on the release lever, forcing it to spring undone, then pulled out the troublesome piece of clothing. As she once again fed the wet clothes through the wringer and into the rinse water, she thought about all the chores she still had to get done that evening, and also about the miserable life she now seemed condemned to lead.

Nancy had never been that keen to have kids; the fact that she'd ended up having six both amazed and depressed her. She'd blamed Jim of course; he'd always been at her for sex. The love she'd felt for him early in their marriage had disappeared a long time ago, now she just resented him for the life he'd thrust upon her. Giving birth to Joanne three years ago when she was forty-one had been the last straw. She'd told him in no uncertain terms that he was to leave her alone from then on.

'If Jim works in the shop for a while tonight, I might be able to make some headway with all this housework,' she grumbled.

It was never-ending – cooking, cleaning, washing, not to mention all the work involved in running a business. She was exhausted every night and cranky every morning, and with the continual declining state of the business she didn't know how much longer she could stand it. Leaving the next load of clothes to chug away in the old washer, she called out to one of the older girls to come and hang out the load she'd just done.

'Pamela, would you get off that phone and give me a hand here, we'll never get to eat tea at this rate. And where's Maureen? She better not be out talking to that boy again.'

She knew the older girls were starting to run wild. There

was a steady stream of boys coming in whenever one of them was helping out in the shop. They'd hang around the old jukebox in the corner, drinking their Coke and laughing. Noting the looks that were passing between them she knew what was on their minds and had no intention of having one of the girls getting pregnant – she didn't think she could bear the shame.

Nancy had been mortified when she realised she was pregnant with Joanne. She'd hidden it from the kids as long as she could, not wanting any questions about how babies were made. The trouble was she had very little maternal instinct; her nurturing qualities were minimal, and the thought of actually talking to the girls about sex horrified her. But she knew she had to do something, after all, Maureen was now sixteen and the twins were coming up to fifteen. Jim would be hopeless at it – she knew that for sure – so it would be up to her to somehow give them the information they had to have. But there was no damn way she was having any little talks with Douglas. Jim could definitely handle that one.

She made a mental note to buy a booklet explaining the facts of life to give to the three older girls, and then wearily headed towards the cluttered kitchen. It was time to start serving up the beef stew she'd had simmering on the Rayburn for hours. They used to always have a roast meal on a Sunday night, but she just couldn't afford one this week.

'He can't even provide properly for his family now,' Nancy thought bitterly to herself. She often wished she'd never married Jim and blamed him for everything that was wrong in her life. And tonight in her tired, angry state she thought it would be good if she never had to set eyes on him again.

Chapter Ten

Having just finished washing her hands and face when she heard her mum call out that tea was ready, Evie quickly took her place at the large kitchen table. The delicious aroma of beef stew had her mouth-watering, and as soon as her plate was placed down in front of her she began eating ravenously, having eaten nothing since breakfast time.

She hadn't wanted to come home for lunch in case her mum had said she was to stay at home and play with Joanne in the afternoon, and she had better things to do than that. Hunting for just the right shells for her collection had become a passion to her – a cowrie shell being the ultimate prize; however, little did she know that they weren't to be found in that area.

The muted jingling of the shop's front door bell signalled the latest customer leaving, and looking up, Evie watched as her dad appeared at the kitchen door. He stood there for a moment looking at the scene before him, and Evie wondered why he had such a sad look on his face.

When Jim realised that Evie was looking at him, he gave her a quick wink and a smile and was rewarded with a cheerful smile and a wink in return. Feeling worn out and a lot older than his forty-six years, he then sat down at the head of the table and slowly allowed his lean body to relax into the chair. Everyone at the table was talking a mile to the minute except for Maureen, who was surprisingly quiet for a change.

'I was talking to old George earlier today ...' Jim spoke to Nancy in between mouthfuls of hot stew. 'He said the bay's full of flathead ... we could do with another good feed of fish.'

'Hmm ... well, don't expect me to clean and scale them, I've got enough to do as it is,' Nancy shot back while futilely endeavouring to get Joanne to eat something.

'No, I can do that,' he replied, head down, concentrating on his meal. 'The wind has dropped right off ... I think it'll be calm enough tonight ... so I'll go out later ... about eight.' Hearing this, both Evie and Douglas spoke nearly as one.

'Can I come too Dad?'

'No, not this time ... you two have school tomorrow and I could be out late tonight.'

Douglas started sulking straight away, but Evie just finished up her tea, thinking of how much she'd love to go fishing at night again – it was such fun last time. Maureen startled everyone by abruptly announcing, 'I'm going round to Rhonda's place later. We have a school project to do together.'

'Oh no you're not young lady,' her dad quietly countered. 'I think you just want to go around there to see Vince. Rhonda can come round here if you have schoolwork to do.'

'Oh ... it's not fair,' Maureen yelled. 'Why can't I have a boyfriend? I'm already sixteen.'

'And he's twenty and way too old for you,' her dad angrily retorted.

Maureen pushed her chair back and stormed out of the room, yelling 'I hate you!', as she went. Hearing the bedroom door slam shut, Jim just shook his head in resignation and continued eating. No one took any notice as Evie, having finished her meal, slipped off her chair and placed her now empty plate into the sink. The twins were still squabbling over which one of them looked prettier in their school photo, and Joanne had just pushed her good Bunnykins bowl containing scrambled eggs onto the lino floor, smashing the bowl in the process.

Evie had a quick shower so she wouldn't have to share a bath with Joanne, who sometimes peed in the water, then entered the chaotic mess that was the bedroom she shared with Pamela and Beverly. Drying off, she pulled on her pyjamas before finding the Famous Five book she'd borrowed from her school library. Reading was her favourite pastime – she loved being able to go to another place in her mind every time she opened a book.

Finally dozing off then falling into a deep sleep, she dreamt that she was searching for something important, something just out of reach. But she couldn't seem to work out what it was. She didn't even stir when Pamela and Beverly came in, grumbling about having to go to bed because it was a school day tomorrow and they couldn't watch the Sunday night movie on TV. It was an Alfred Hitchcock movie, 'The Birds', and they'd badly wanted to watch it. They finally shut up, but only after their mum stuck her head round the corner of the door, threatening in a loud whisper that she'd give them both a good slapping if she heard them again.

Sometime later, Evie woke from a deep sleep. Slowly opening one eye first, she then squinted with both when she saw the bright rays of the early dawn streaming in through the half-open curtains. She lay still, listening for a moment as her sleepy eyes focused on golden dust motes as they swirled around in the sun beams; then, hearing nothing out of the ordinary, she wondered what it was that had woken her up.

Evie yawned loudly then rolled over to get a bit more sleep; she could tell that she had at least another hour before having to get up for school. It was then that a sound rang out that had her and the twins out of their beds and running into the kitchen in a flash.

Her mum was sitting on one of the old kitchen chairs, but Evie hardly recognised her – a combined look of fear, panic and shock had completely transformed her face. Another horrible moaning sound rent the early morning stillness, and Evie now realised where it was coming from as she stood mesmerised, watching as her mother's stricken face gradually fell forward, coming to a briefly, silent stop when it encountered the hardness of the kitchen table.

It was then that Evie saw the policeman standing in the doorway. Maureen was crying and Douglas began asking, 'What's wrong, what's wrong?' all the while pulling on the policeman's arm. The twins just stood there seemingly frozen in place, staring wide-eyed at the scene before them. Evie was truly scared for the first time in her life. The policeman was talking again and now his words slowly penetrated through her fog of confusion; finally, horribly, settling in her mind.

Her dad was missing, presumed drowned.

Apparently an early morning jogger had come across his old wooden boat floating upside down near the shoreline more than two hours ago. The jogger had alerted the police and they'd immediately organised a search and rescue team to scour the bay and coastline. His old lifejacket, which he'd never bothered to wear, and his now empty plastic tackle box had been found half an hour later washed up further along the beach ... but nothing else. One of the fishermen on the scene had known whose boat it was by the name written on the side: *The Marilla.*

It seemed that one of those sudden squally storms, common this time of year, had blown into the bay about ten o'clock last night. It'd brought with it wild winds and driving rain, and to all appearances had caused his pride and joy to capsize.

Someone must have phoned Dr. Morrison because he suddenly appeared in the kitchen carrying a shabby-looking leather bag. After giving her mum some tablets with a glass of water, the doctor then helped her to her bedroom. Thankfully it wasn't long before the distressing moans subsided.

Chapter Eleven

Fourteen hours had passed since they'd received the shocking news and the house was now silent. The next door neighbours had all been and gone, offering 'anything we can do just ask', and her Aunty Ivy and Uncle Frank, who Maureen had called as soon as she'd managed to stop crying enough to find their number, had arrived an hour and a half later from their home in the city. They were now sitting at the kitchen table drinking yet another cup of tea. Earlier in the evening they'd gathered all the kids together and reassured them that they'd stay as long as they were needed.

Evie's life seemed to have come to a standstill, even though everything was still going on around her. A fuzzy, numb feeling had infused her body and she couldn't think any thoughts through to their end; it felt like a part of her mind had gone away and there was just a blank, empty space left behind.

It was evening now and the thought of her dad floating around in the darkness somewhere, all by himself, filled Evie with a dreadful feeling of terror and grief. She rolled over and buried her face into her pillow once more and sobbed uncontrollably, her tears soaking into the old flannelette pillow case. It was quite some time before her sobs subsided enough for her to take that last big gulp of air ... and she was then finally able to breathe calmly again.

Now lying on her back on her rumpled bed, blankly staring at the fly-spotted ceiling, Evie desperately tried to make sense of what had happened. Was her dad really dead? Surely he'd come walking through the door any minute now and laugh about all the fuss that he'd caused. Emotionally exhausted, she eventually fell into a fitful sleep. Her dreams were filled with a kaleidoscope of horrors which, thankfully, she wouldn't remember when she woke up.

Chapter Twelve

Evie gave up trying to read her book; she just couldn't concentrate on it. She'd thought that if she read one of her favourites it would stop her from thinking about the funeral, but every time she tried she ended up just staring at words that made no sense. Sitting in one of her favourite places – up in the old cypress tree in the backyard – she was escaping from the throng of people who'd descended on her home after leaving the cemetery.

After adjusting her position a little so she could check her surroundings for any sight of Douglas, Evie then relaxed and ate another cake that she'd just unwrapped from a paper napkin. Earlier, when she'd seen the fantastic array of cakes and sandwiches all beautifully set out on the kitchen table, her eyes had widened. Acting quickly, she'd put together a selection of the yummiest-looking ones before heading for her hideaway.

'Mmm … yum.' Licking the sweet icing from her fingers, Evie wondered if she should feel bad because she'd just come from her dad's funeral service and was now pigging out on cakes. She hadn't gotten her head around the whole 'God' thing yet, having never attended church, but now reasoned that He'd be happy to see her being happy.

Checking for any sign of Douglas again, Evie's good feeling disappeared as she thought of how her brother had been more of a pain than ever this last month – throwing things at her whenever he felt like it or saying things to her like, 'go away you stupid *girl*', like it was a swear word or something. When he'd thrown a Raggedy Anne doll at Joanne, knocking her off her feet, Evie had run over and punched him hard on his arm. Luckily Uncle Frank had come in then and Douglas sulked off to his room.

After re-wrapping the last cake and stashing it in the shade for later, Evie laid back on a thick, comfy branch out of everybody's view. She had a habit of laying up there and considered it to be her place where she could just watch the clouds and think. Today the clouds were few but her thoughts were many. As her eyes followed a lone seagull as it flapped its way across an otherwise clear sky, her mind once more robotically replayed the day's events.

The funeral had been held mid-morning, and while she'd been standing there with the others, only half listening to the constant flow of words around her, Evie had wondered how such a sad event could be taking place on such a beautiful day. Bright and sunny, the cool breeze had rustled through the surrounding trees, bringing with it the faint smell of salt, seaweed and pine. She'd thought that it should have been dark and raining to better suit her mood.

A multitude of people had joined in the search for her dad, looking along the extensive stretch of coastline and also out at sea, but he'd never been found. They'd all congregated instead around a shiny goldish-coloured plaque set into the lawn of the cemetery. She remembered how the minister had spoken for a long time about the sad loss of such a fine man, '...a fine *family* man ...' he'd stressed, and how those words had started many people crying again. Then, after everyone recited The Lord's Prayer, it was finally over.

The house had later filled with people – some who were visibly distressed, some who were cracking jokes with mates they hadn't seen since the last funeral, and others who just seemed intent on getting to the food first. Having finally fled from the sad looks and commiserations directed at her by relatives she didn't know, she'd left them to their tea drinking and reminiscing.

In her mind the previous four weeks seemed to have passed by in a blur of visitors, both family and friends. Several policemen had come to talk to her mum as well, and she'd overheard them talking about something called 'an inquest'. There'd also been a couple of visits from different men in suits, all bringing papers of some sort for her mum to look at and sign. Evie then remembered the shocked feeling that she'd had when she saw her mum really smiling a few nights ago, straight after the last suited man left.

'How *could* she?' Evie fumed to herself again. 'Dad's *missing* and she can still *smile*; it doesn't make *any* sense to me.'

She'd never accepted the belief that her dad had drowned. Instead, she was sure that he'd been washed up on a deserted island somewhere and was trying his best to get back to them again. All she had to do was be patient and wait for him to walk in the door.

Eventually the sounds of people saying their goodbyes cut into Evie's thoughts, but she stayed where she was, finally coming down only after her mum had yelled at her to 'get down out of that damn tree!'

Chapter Thirteen

After the last of the mourners had finally gone and she'd yelled at Evie to get out of the tree, Nancy took a couple of Aspros for her developing headache. She'd completely accepted that Jim was dead, and when she recalled her thoughts of not wanting to see him again, on the night he disappeared, she was filled with mixed emotions; but guilt wasn't one of them.

She was incredibly angry that he'd left her to cope with all the kids and the business on her own, then the anger turned to self-pity, thinking of how her life had turned out to be such a disaster.

'At least he had his life insurance policy; if he'd left me penniless I would have never forgiven him.'

The thought of how much she'd be receiving though, transformed her frowning features into a self-satisfied smile.

She'd known he'd had a policy, but until recently hadn't known that he'd increased his payments about three years ago, resulting in her now receiving a substantial payout.

'It won't matter how much the shop sells for now,' she smiled. 'I've already got enough to buy a decent house again … hmm … I'll go to the estate agents tomorrow and see what they have available. The sooner I get away from this damn place, the better.'

The atmosphere in the house had now settled into a subdued sadness. Nancy was slightly aware that the kids were unnaturally quiet; the twins hadn't been bickering as much as usual, and Douglas, who'd been inconsolable at losing his dad, had been staying in his room as much as possible. She's been relieved at that at least, having no desire to have to deal with his distress.

Even Maureen was quiet for a change. Nancy had become sick and tired of hearing about how the last words that Maureen spoke to her dad were, 'I hate you', so had told her plainly and simply that there was no point worrying about it now and to just forget about it.

Little Joanne had been fretful; not understanding what was going on but picking up on the sombre mood around her. As Nancy tucked the bedcovers over the child's chubby arms she wondered if the day would ever arrive when she would just have herself to please, and no one else.

Just a matter of weeks later, the day came for them to

load all their possessions into the big removal van, and Evie was distraught.

'How will Dad find us if we're not here when he comes back?' she asked herself over and over, salty tears streaming down her face. She asked her mum the same thing but she just told her not to be so silly.

'Your dad's not coming back, you know he's dead. Now go and finish packing up the rest of your books, we haven't got all day.'

Evie went to her room and slumped onto the floor. Her tears had now given way to anger – anger at her mum for not believing her dad would be back. She knew what she'd do, she'd write him a letter explaining what had happened and where they'd all gone and leave it somewhere that he'd be sure to find it. She quickly wrote all the details down on a piece of paper that she tore out of one of her school books, then tried to think of the best place to leave it. Remembering that one of her dad's favourite places was his old shed out the back, she hurriedly slipped outside.

After bit of a struggle, she somehow managed to pull the heavy, old wooden door open enough so she could squeeze through the gap. The shed smelt musty and was gloomily empty except for cobwebs, dust and a few old bits and pieces that no one wanted. There was an old nail stuck in the wall right near the dirty light switch, and she pushed the piece of paper on to it so it wouldn't fall off.

Looking at it one last time, she turned around and squeezed her way back out through the narrow opening. Not noticing the dirt and cobwebs from the door which had stuck to her hair and face, Evie slowly walked back inside to her almost bare bedroom. Now sure that her dad would be able to find her, she was able to set her mind to packing the last of her possessions for the move to her new home.

When she'd taped up the last box of her books and written her name on it with Texta, she closed the bedroom door and slowly sat down, leaning back against it. Staring out her bedroom window she felt sad and alone, even though she could still hear the rest of her family as they were going about their packing. Thinking about her dad again she knew she had to say a proper goodbye to him; for now at least.

Jumping up she opened her bedroom door a little, just enough to enable her to view the passageway. Not seeing anyone, she made a dash for the back door then ran quietly along the edge of the driveway to the front gate. Standing back behind a bushy tree, she saw a huge removal van parked out the front of the shop, and then a man jumping out of the back of it. He then went and helped another man with a trolley load of heavy-looking boxes. Just then, Maureen ducked out of the front door of the shop and took off down the street.

'Hmm ... she must be going to see Vince before we leave,' Evie thought, glancing at her sister's retreating figure. She could hear her mum through the open window yelling at Douglas to get a move on, then at Beverly because she was changing her clothes again.

'But I have to look good when the new neighbours see me,' Evie heard Beverly whine loudly in reply.

Shaking her head in bewilderment at the things the twins worried about, she took one last look around to make sure no one had noticed her, then she was off like a shot. Straight across the road and into the park, she deftly dodged trees as she ran without stopping down to the beach.

By the time she arrived at the place she'd chosen in her mind, she was out of breath. Dropping down onto her bottom just above the high tide mark, she kicked off her thongs, then stretched her legs straight out so the small waves could wash over her feet. Loving the delicious feel of the cold water on her hot skin, she dug her dirty toes into the soft, grainy sand and spoke quietly to herself. 'Hmm ... that feels better.'

It was overcast and quite cold, and with her breath finally under control with one last big sigh, Evie looked both ways to see who else was about. Not seeing anyone to her right, except for a couple of dogs further down the beach trying to catch seagulls, she turned her head the other way and immediately saw a woman walking towards her. She was only about thirty feet away, and Evie idly studied her as she came closer and closer.

The woman was well rugged up against the chill, wearing a blue parka with the hood up and matching tracksuit pants. She also wore large sunglasses which prevented Evie from seeing her face properly.

'Hello there,' the woman said brightly as she slowly walked the last few steps to where Evie sat. 'Do you mind if I sit here next to you for a minute? I'm puffed out from my big walk along the beach.'

'That's okay,' Evie replied solemnly. 'There's plenty of room.'

Turning her gaze back towards the distant horizon, thoughts of her dad filled her head again. Tears began to roll down her grubby cheeks leaving wet streaks until she angrily wiped her arm across her face, transforming them into a grey smear. The woman sat silently beside her for a moment, then began speaking in a gentle voice.

'I do hope I'm not intruding, but I have something here that I thought you might want to have.'

Distracted from her thoughts, Evie turned her head to see what it was; watching as the woman reached into the large bag she'd been carrying.

'I found this hat washed up on the beach the other day and I believe it belonged to your father,' the woman said tenderly as she held it out for Evie to see.

Staring at the green fishing hat she'd given to her dad for his last birthday, Evie initially couldn't move or say a word.

Her eyes widened to their full limit, and the wind caused them to water some more. Wiping the tears away with the back of one hand, she finally reached out the other one and said in an unsteady voice,

'Yes, that's my dad's. How did you know?'

'I looked inside and saw the name Mr. Jim Carpenter written on the edge and 'Happy Birthday Love From Evie'. I was at your father's funeral and remembered seeing you there,' the woman replied. 'You looked so sad.'

Evie could not believe she was holding something that her dad had been wearing on the night he disappeared. A warm glow started to fill her up inside, and she felt a connection with him that she'd been missing so desperately. She couldn't help but to start to smile.

'Thank you,' she managed to get out, just before her mixed emotions took hold and her smile crumpled into sobbing tears.

'It's okay sweetie, there's nothing wrong with having a good cry,' the nice lady was saying. 'Here, you can use my hanky if you like.'

Passing it over, she then put her arm around Evie's shoulders and held her while she cried. They sat together like that on the damp sand for another ten minutes. Seagulls were circling above them in the breeze hoping for some handouts, but neither woman nor child were aware of the birds' noisy presence.

Having cried herself out at last, and feeling a lot better for it, Evie looked up and saw that the lady had removed her sunglasses and was wiping tear streaks off her cheeks as well. As she scrutinised the woman's pretty face, Evie was momentarily transfixed by her beautiful green eyes.

'Why were you crying?' she questioned softly. 'Did you know my dad too?'

'Yes, I ... knew him ...' she hesitated for a moment then took a deep breath to compose herself once more. 'I bought some fruit and veggies in your shop once ... you must be missing him dreadfully,' a look of genuine concern on her face.

But Evie had a new feeling inside her now. She wasn't sure what it was yet, but she felt better than she had for a long time. After thanking the lady once more, she said she'd better get back home before her mum missed her. Scrambling to her feet and quickly putting her thongs back on, she suddenly stopped and looked directly at the bearer of her precious object.

'What's *your* name?' she asked inquiringly, her head tilted slightly to one side.

The woman paused for a moment, then with a sad smile replied, 'Annie.'

'Annie,' Evie repeated slowly, before continuing, 'well I won't see you again Annie, because I'm moving to the city today. That's why I have to get going. Mum will chuck a fit if she can't find me.'

Gazing yet again at the treasure she held firmly in her hands, a smile started to transform her previously worried features. Spontaneously bending forward and flinging her arms around the woman's neck, she inadvertently pushed back the hood on Annie's parka, revealing shining auburn hair. Evie quickly kissed her on the cheek, then said 'Bye Annie ... maybe we'll meet again one day,' before turning and taking off like a startled rabbit.

As she sprinted along the firm, damp sand, Evie couldn't get the smile off her face. She didn't have to say goodbye to her dad after all. A feeling of connection with him had energised her; she truly believed that he'd somehow managed to leave the hat where it would find its way to her.

'I'm not telling anyone about Dad's hat,' Evie thought as she ran. 'I'm going to keep it as my secret.'

She didn't think any of them would treasure it like she would. Arriving back home unnoticed, she hurried straight to her room. Dodging the packed boxes, she pulled the bedroom door towards her and looked behind it. 'Good, it's still there.'

Her red TAA school bag was just where she'd left it. She'd put all her favourite things in there for safekeeping during the move, and away from the prying eyes of the twins. Gingerly removing an old shoebox containing her most prized shells, Evie carefully slid the hat to the bottom, trying not to disturb her bits and pieces too much, then covered it over with her latest Secret Seven book.

Slumping back against the wall she exhaled loudly. Her legs were tired from all the running and she was still puffing slightly, but the smile had not left her face.

'Evelyn, where are you? I need you to watch Joanne. Now hurry up, you know I haven't got all day.'

Even the sound of her mum's harping voice couldn't dampen Evie's spirits. Jumping up, she hurried out into the shop and took Joanne outside and out of her mum's way. She felt relaxed and at ease for the first time in weeks, and was finally able to accept the big move to her new home.

Part Three

Chapter Fourteen

Geelong, Victoria, Australia

February 1995

Dash couldn't believe his luck. Having driven into Geelong that afternoon not knowing a soul, he'd been able to tee up a job and new digs in a matter of hours. Now trying to keep up with his elderly landlord's sprightly pace, he hurriedly followed Jack up to the first floor, glad when they came to a stop on a small balcony. Dropping his swag and big canvas bag down out of the way, he then stood and slowly stretched his shoulders up ... then back. It was then that he was startled to see that he had a fantastic view of the bay.

'Hey ... room with a view. I wasn't expecting that.'

'Yes … damn, I've got too many bloody keys here … yes, it's a great view isn't it …? Damn, that's not them either.'

Out of the assortment of keys he held in his hand, Jack was trying to work out which was the right set for the flat, continuously swearing softly under his breath as he fumbled around with them.

As Dash stood there patiently he thought about the new job he was to start in the morning, hoping it would become permanent so he could stay put in one place for a while. He'd had a good feeling ever since he'd driven into Geelong; there was something about the place that had appealed to him, and now things just seemed to be falling into his lap.

'Damn it, I think I've left them on the passenger seat of the car,' Jack muttered. 'So I could find them quickly.' Turning to look at Dash he grinned. 'I'm going mad, I'm sure I am. I'll just pop back down to the car and get them; won't be long.'

As Jack hurried off on his mission, Dash casually leant against the balcony railing and admired the panoramic outlook. The glistening blueness of the bay had caught his eye, and as he relaxed his stance a little more he watched as the blue briefly darkened as a large cloud passed overhead.

'Hmm … can't wait to have another shower and a good feed,' he sighed, rubbing his aching neck. 'An early night wouldn't go astray either.'

Having left Devonport on the Spirit of Tasmania three

nights ago, he'd pretty much been on the move ever since. After getting off the boat in Port Melbourne he'd soon discovered that the job in Williamstown he'd crossed 'the ditch' for had been delayed for several months, so he'd decided to head to Hastings to catch up with Neville; an old mate from way back.

Nev was a chef who worked very unsociable hours, so Dash had been lucky to find him at home when he'd rocked up unannounced later that day. After spending an uproarious day and most of the night laughing, drinking and relating stories, he'd finally grabbed a few hours' sleep on Nev's comfy old couch.

Next day had heralded a slow beginning for both men. Nev hadn't had to work until later that afternoon so had taken advantage, saying he was going to sleep 'til noon. Dash had dozed on and off after waking early with a wicked thirst which he'd tried to quench with lemonade. Having finally decided it was coffee he'd needed, he'd sat up and surveyed his surroundings. Taking in the sight of several empty pizza boxes he'd grinned, remembering how when they'd become hungry, Nev had declared, 'Fuck cooking ... I do enough of that every day ... let's order in.'

A cold blast of water after a hot shower had done the trick for Dash, waking him fully. After quickly dressing he'd leisurely sipped his freshly ground coffee on the roof-top 'garden', enjoying the early morning warmth before what would be a hot day. Thoroughly enjoying the aroma and taste of *real* coffee, as Nev always called it, he'd considered his options. Knowing he could always get work in one of the numerous mines again he'd soon decided to head back over to Kalgoorlie, but his plans had changed after a phone call he'd made to Enzo.

'G'day Dash, what's happenin' you old bastard?' Enzo had replied to Dash's initial greeting.

'Not much at the moment mate. I'm just about to head out of Hastings,' he'd replied. 'I stayed the night here at Nev's and I'm feeling a bit delicate this morning,' he'd grinned. 'I've decided to head back over to Kal' though. There's fuck all work happening around here.'

'Yeah, it is a bit like that at the moment,' Enzo had agreed. 'But mate, I was just talking to Boggy in the pub yesterday and he'd said his uncle needs riggers and crane operators in Geelong. Drop in mate; mention my name and you should be right. I'd have grabbed it for myself but I'm heading back to Tassie on the boat tonight. Young Ricky's been getting into trouble with the cops and Paula's saying I've got to come back and sort him out.'

Dash had chuckled. 'Mate, if I mention your name I'll probably get locked up.'

'Hey, I've been keeping out of trouble lately.'

'That'll have to be a first for you mate. So, where is this job anyway, and who do I have to talk to?'

'His name's Lou Bogdanovich. His office and yard are in North Geelong.' Enzo had given him the street address, then after telling each other their latest dirty jokes he'd said, 'Hey, guess what Paula bought me?

'What?'

'One of those new-fangled, mobile phones; it's great mate.' Then, chuckling, had added, 'I think she got it for me so she can keep track of me better; she's already rung me three times today.'

'She'll need more than that to keep track of you,' Dash had laughed.

After Dash had written down Enzo's new phone number they'd said their goodbyes.

'Ok then Dash, I've got to get going. I've still got to pack me stuff and catch up with a couple of blokes before I get the car on board. Plus Stewie's dropping by for a couple of beers later, so I'd better get me skates on.'

'Yeah, okay, take care mate and I'll see ya when I'm looking at ya.'

'Well, Geelong it is then,' Dash had thought to himself, hanging up Nev's phone. 'I haven't been there before so it won't hurt to check the place out.'

After catching the car ferry from Sorrento over to Queenscliff, Dash had then driven to Geelong arriving about three o'clock. First locating the site office, he'd been rapt to find out he had a definite start in the morning. His Sigma wagon had been packed with all his basic possessions, so he'd thought he'd better get some accommodation sorted next.

Admiring the many magnificent houses as he'd driven along The Esplanade, Dash had decided to stop and have a beer before he started his quest for suitable lodgings. A small pub had caught his eye, so he'd done a quick U-turn, parked the car, then relaxed at the bar with an icy-cold pot of Melbourne. Being the friendly sort of bloke that he was he'd started chatting to the old fella standing next to him, later offering to buy him a beer. Dash had casually mentioned that he had a new job to start in the morning and was about to start looking for somewhere to stay, when his fellow drinking companion offered him a flat to rent that had just become vacant.

'I've owned the place for years now. Gives me a bit of extra money to play with, plus it's an interest for me,' Jack had said. 'Some people live like pigs though. I've just spent the morning cleaning the place up after the last one left. You can have it for $130 a week. It's got two bedrooms but no beds, there's an oldish fridge and washing machine and a bit of old furniture too. Oh, it also has quite a large garage.'

Dash had taken it on the spot, sealing it with a handshake and another beer. Later, after a quick drive following along behind his new friend's old Rover, Dash had pulled over then parked behind Jack's car; directly out the front of number six Skene Street. He'd been a little surprised at how tidy the block of eight flats had looked.

'Scoring this flat's been a real winner for me. Thanks again mate,' he said to Jack, who'd finally returned with the correct keys. Unlocking the security door first, then the front door of number four, Jack stepped back against the balcony rail to give Dash a clear view into the flat.

'Not bad, is it?' Jack had a certain amount of pride in his voice as he continued. 'I could probably charge more for it, but really, I'm just glad to rent it out to someone stable for a change. I've a few horror stories to tell. You'll find that the gas and electricity are still connected, but you'll have to transfer them into your name – the last guy scampered without paying his bills or having them disconnected.'

As Jack passed over the keys, Dash handed him enough money to cover the bond and one month's rent as agreed, but couldn't help grinning as he said, 'Well, I can't vouch for how stable I am, but I promise not to trash the place.'

Jack looked straight back at him. 'I bet that grin's got you in some trouble at times, but I can tell a genuine person when I meet one. Stay as long as you like, just give me a couple of weeks' notice before you move out if you can.'

Thinking to himself how right Jack was about the grin, Dash replied, 'No worries Jack. Hey, where's the nearest pub around here? I'm going to have a counter tea after I get sorted, and a couple more beers wouldn't hurt either. We could catch up for another one if you like.'

'Thanks Dash, but some other time. I've got to get home now to check on the missus. She's not been too good lately. Anything you've got a problem with just give me a call. Here's my phone number.'

Jack handed Dash a card then turned and headed back down the stairs. 'There's a pub about a ten minute walk from here. Just turn right at the front of the flats and follow your nose – you can't miss it. I'll take a rain check on that beer though,' were his parting words as he hurried off.

'This is a bit of all right,' Dash said, glancing around as he entered the flat. 'Lounge first ... doesn't look too bad, even a couple of armchairs,' he was surprised to see, as he then wandered into the kitchen. He opened the fridge to check that it was going, and was pleased to find that it was, then walked around an old wooden table and had a quick squiz out the kitchen window.

'Hmm ... not a bad view from here either,' he murmured as he continued on through the flat.

Dropping his swag and bag in the middle of one of the nearly empty bedrooms, he grinned and stretched.

'Right, a quick shower and shave first, then I'll check out the local. I'm starving.'

Stripping off the clothes he'd been wearing since the day before, he stepped into the shower and under the steady flow of warm water.

'Ahhhhhh … yes … this feels good.'

He turned the taps on even more until hot water was pounding into his aching neck and shoulder muscles. He wasn't sure how long he stood there – the soothing sensation of the water hitting his head and back had lulled him into another place. Suddenly coming back from where he'd drifted to, he quickly soaped up and rinsed off. After having a quick shave he was then dressed and ready to go fifteen minutes later.

Locking the front door behind him, Dash turned to check out the adjoining flat. There were just the two flats at the top of these stairs and they were separated by a mesh security door.

'Lucky buggers. Look at the size of their balcony compared to mine,' he thought to himself. 'Oh well, can't complain. I'm bloody lucky I got *this* place.'

Wondering now who he might be living next to, he gave it a quick once-over and decided it was either a female or a gay guy.

'They're into horticulture anyway,' he thought as he checked out the assortment of potted plants, all artfully arranged around a couple of armchairs and an old two-seater couch. A bamboo wind chime was hung to catch the breeze, and he quite liked the soft, melodic 'bonk bonk' sound it was making. 'Oh well, no doubt I'll meet them soon enough,' he thought with a smile, 'but there *is* also a chance I regret meeting them at all.'

Grinning to himself at the thought of some of the people he'd run into during his travels, he took one more look at his surroundings to get his bearings, then headed off in the direction of the pub.

When his alarm woke him early the next morning, Dash had a bit of a hangover and it took him a minute or so to recall where he was.

'Ah, that's right,' he murmured as he rolled over onto his back. 'Geelong.'

Remembering he had a job to go to, he clambered out of his swag, got his balance, then slowly made his way into the kitchen to put the kettle on.

'By God that Enzo can drink,' he mumbled, as he then made his way towards the bathroom.

After a quick shower and shave he was feeling more human, and as he pulled his work clothes out of his bag he couldn't help chuckling as his mind replayed the events of the previous night.

He'd found the pub easily enough and had bought and downed his first beer before finding the public phone in the lounge area. It was just as noisy in there as in the bar, but he'd wanted to thank his mate for the tip about the job. Dialling Enzo's number, Dash couldn't help but think that his mate was onto a handy thing with his new mobile phone.

'I think I'll check one out for myself when I have the

time,' he thought, just before he heard Enzo's voice.

'Hello.'

'G'day mate,' Dash had yelled over the noise of the crowd. 'Did you get on the boat okay?'

'No mate, I bloody missed it. I was just about to leave when Chalky walked in. I stopped to have one quick one with him, then by the time I remembered about the boat it was too bloody late. I rang Paula and told her what had happened and she said I was so bloody useless not to bother coming back at all.'

'Mate, Paula's right – you are bloody useless,' Dash had chuckled. 'So what are you going to do now?'

'Well, I've got another berth for tomorrow night but I can't stay here in my digs tonight because I told Stewie he could stay here with his girlfriend while I was away. Have you got room for me where you're staying?'

'No worries mate,' Dash had replied. 'I don't have a spare bed, but there's plenty of floor space.'

Dash had given him the address of the pub and Enzo had arrived an hour or so later by taxi. After they'd both had a good feed of T-bone steaks, chips and eggs, they'd started playing pool and ended up drinking until the pub closed at about one in the morning.

Tying the laces on his work boots in between sipping his coffee, Dash looked at the dishevelled body sprawled out on the lounge room floor. Enzo's curly black hair was sticking out everywhere, his head resting on a seat cushion. Half undressed, wearing only jocks and a shirt, he still had one hand clutching the neck of a Jack Daniel's bottle. Resisting the temptation to wake him up, Dash was still grinning as he headed out the door to go to work.

It was now approaching six in the evening, and after a tiring day at work Dash was nearly home again. The pressure was on at work to have the job finished by the end of the month, so there'd be quite a few ten-hour days until then; not that he minded the overtime money. He knew his body would be back into the swing of work soon, but for now he just felt stuffed.

Looking forward to having a cold beer, Dash slowly drove down the narrow laneway which gave access to the rear of the flats, then parked his car out the front of his garage. 'I'll put it away later', he thought as he grabbed his work bag and wearily opened the car door. He was rounding the back corner of the block when he heard the music to 'Bat out of Hell' being played … loudly.

'I knew that would have to be you, you noisy bastard. I've just moved in here, and now you want to get me kicked out. I haven't even unpacked yet.' Dash couldn't help grinning though, as he went straight to the fridge and grabbed a beer. 'Go on; turn that bloody music down a couple of decibels before I have the neighbours banging on the door.'

Upending the stubbie, Dash drank half of it while Enzo adjusted the volume of the music.

'And where the hell did you get *that* from?' he asked, pointing with his stubbie towards an old stereo system.

Enzo tried to look serious as he said, 'Yeah, and good afternoon to you too mate. Here I go and set you up with some music and all I get is abused.' He couldn't help but smile though as he went and grabbed another beer for himself.

'Cheers mate,' he said before having a quick swig.

'Yeah, cheers mate. So, where did you scam that from anyway?' Dash queried as he finished off the stubbie.

'From your next door neighbour,' Enzo replied, a big smile on his face.

'Oh yeah, and who might that be?'

'Well, I was out on the balcony talking to her for about half an hour. She said her name's Evie, so I said 'Oh, like the song?' She laughed and said that it's actually short for Evelyn but she's never liked that, so as a kid she decided to only answer to "Evie". That worked with everyone but her mum apparently,' he chuckled. After taking another swig of beer he carried on. 'When I mentioned that you'd just moved in and didn't have anything to play your CD's on, she said she'd recently bought a new one so you could borrow her old one, 'til you get a new one for yourself.'

'Yeah, and I bet you were batting your baby blues at her

too, you smarmy bastard,' Dash chuckled. 'So, what's she like then … young, old, good looking or what? 'Dash wasn't sure why he wanted to know, just normal curiosity he supposed.

'She's not bad mate. About our age I'd guess. I'd take her out.'

'You're a married man remember, you degenerate. No wonder Paula's ready to kick you out.'

'Hey, I'm working on that. I've got money in my pocket and I'm going to wine and dine Paula every night until she sees what she'd be giving up. I tell you what though mate, I was lucky,' Enzo continued. 'I was pretty much busted arse broke when she first rang me about Ricky last week. There was no way I could have afforded to buy a boat ticket, so I told her I was getting work done on the car and I'd be over as soon as I could. Then the day before yesterday I put twenty bucks on a trifecta and cleaned up. A couple of bloody roughies came in; I couldn't believe it – nearly three thousand bucks.'

Enzo said he'd shout Dash a meal and a few beers at a pub Evie had mentioned earlier that day. 'She reckoned it was all right. 'The Great Western' I think it was. Consider it my thanks for putting me up here at such short notice.'

'Putting *up* with you is more like it,' Dash said grinning, starting on his second stubbie.

Half an hour later, after Dash showered and had another beer, they headed off, deciding to walk the short distance to the pub. Enzo took his bag with him so that later he could get a taxi straight to the wharf where he'd left his car parked.

They chose steak, eggs and chips again and made short work of it too; even enjoying the bowls of mixed salad. Ordering another round of beer, Enzo then phoned for a taxi before they sat in the quietest corner to drink and chat for a bit. It wasn't long before they heard the taxi beeping out the front, and as they walked outside Enzo offered his hand for a handshake.

'See ya mate. Take care of yourself you ugly bastard.'

'Yeah, you too ya wog prick, and don't go stopping at any pubs on the way this time. Oh, and say hello to Paula for me,' Dash grinned wickedly.

'No way, you bastard,' Enzo laughed. 'She's always liked you.'

They were both still grinning as Enzo's taxi drove off.

Chapter Fifteen

The next day Dash arrived home to a much quieter reception. Because of a delay in receiving the next stage of pipe work there'd been no overtime, so being a Saturday he'd finished at two-thirty and was home twenty minutes later. He'd decided against having a few beers with the boys after work – he knew he'd get stuck there – so he'd said he'd catch up with them about six for a counter meal.

It had been stinking hot again all day and he thought it was about time he kicked back and gave the old body a bit of a rest. All he felt like doing was sitting in the shade with a beer or two and reading more of Stephen Hawking's 'A Brief History of Time'. He enjoyed learning about different things and was quite intrigued by what he'd read so far.

Walking into the hot lounge room he dropped his work bag down behind the door. It was stifling in the flat; he hadn't thought to pull the blinds down in the bedroom or kitchen to keep the afternoon sun out.

'Probably too late now,' he thought as he pulled them down anyway, instantly blocking the dazzling glare, 'must remember to do it tomorrow though.'

Checking first that all the windows in the flat were open, he ducked back down the stairs and out to the station wagon. Sweat started running down the side of his face as he dragged his old folding chair out from under his doona and spare blankets. 'I won't need those in this weather, that s for sure,' he panted, shoving them across to one side.

Back in the restful garden he chose the biggest tree to sit under, the bottom branches of which had been pruned a long time ago, allowing him to position the chair so he'd be in some dappled shade.

'I might get to meet some of the natives if I'm sitting out here,' he thought, studying the block of flats before him. He enjoyed meeting people and didn't mind having bit of a chat himself. Taking two steps at a time up the stairs, he wondered if his next door neighbour was home – he wanted to thank her for lending him the stereo. Her security door was propped open by a pot plant so he decided to give a quick knock on her front door.

'Oh well, I'll catch up with her eventually,' he thought when there was no response. Putting it out of his mind, he turned and walked back into his own flat.

Slowly sitting down on the old chair in the bedroom, he took his boots and socks off first, then stood and stripped off all his clothes, dropping them where he stood. Finding a clean pair of old footy shorts, he pulled them on and headed into the kitchen.

'It's about time I just sat and relaxed,' he sighed, grabbing two beers from the fridge and a stubbie holder off the bench. When he couldn't find the book he wanted to read he picked up a People magazine instead; one that Enzo had left behind. Dash hadn't had the time or the inclination to wash dishes or tidy the flat since his visit. Using one foot to push the door wide open, allowing any breeze full access, he headed outside.

Drinking from one of the beers as he descended the last steps, he paused at the bottom for a moment and took in the whole garden area.

'Someone spends a bit of time on this place,' he thought, checking out the neatly trimmed lawn and flowering garden beds. Strolling over to where he'd left his chair he admired a couple of silver birches and a large bottlebrush tree covered in red brushes. A swarm of small birds were chirping loudly as they hopped from one red brush to another, greedily gorging on the sweet nectar.

Near to where he'd set up his sturdy, if a bit squeaky, canvas deck chair, was a small seat concreted into the ground – big enough for two or maybe three people. Dash sat down in his old faithful chair and let out a contented sigh. Putting his feet up on the seat opposite ... he stretched his legs out ... leant back ... and with a big sigh finally completely relaxed.

Even under the shade of the overhead branches it was still quite hot, but every now and then a slight breeze would flow over him, feeling deliciously cool on his near-naked, sweaty body. The breeze brought with it the unmistakable scent of roses as he idly watched a bee flitting between flowers on a trailing vine.

Finishing his first stubbie he dropped it onto the grass beside him then picked up and opened the next one. Just as he was about to flick through the magazine, a skinny little woman with bright red hair caught his eye. She'd appeared from around the corner of the flats about twelve metres away, carrying a basket full of folded towels. He'd seen the clothesline at the back of the flats yesterday when he'd been checking out his garage area.

'Bugger, that reminds me. I have to do some washing later,' he was thinking to himself when the woman suddenly stopped and looked directly at him. He lifted his hand in greeting, but before he could say a word she gave him a quick look up and down then abruptly turned away and stomped up the stairs at the other end of the block of flats.

'Ah ... wonder what that was all about?' he thought, turning a couple of pages. 'She looked like she'd spent the day sucking lemons,' he grinned, thinking of the woman's tight, unsmiling face.

'Don't think she liked the look of me though. Oh well, wouldn't be the first time – I have got bit of a rough-looking head.' Leaning right back in his canvas chair, the old wooden frame creaked ominously.

'Don't collapse on me now, old girl,' he muttered, thinking he wouldn't have the energy to get up if it did. He slowly drained his second stubbie, savouring every drop, then dropped it next to the other one. Clasping his hands behind his head and with his legs still stretched out on the seat in front, he let his eyes slowly close.

The girly magazine he'd started looking at was spread open across his legs, showing a variety of Home Girls in different poses, but nothing was going to keep his eyes open now. Even with his sunnies on everything had looked too bright for his tired eyes.

'Ahhh ... it's so good to just stop,' he thought as he adjusted his position to a more comfortable one. Thinking that he'd just shut his eyes for a few minutes, Dash was fast asleep within seconds.

Chapter Sixteen

Languidly rolling over onto her back and then sitting up in one smooth movement, Evie was grinning as she spoke.

'Hey, remember I said that I'd met Enzo yesterday; my new neighbour's mate?'

'Yeah.'

'And that he was quite good-looking, except that he knew it.'

'Yeah.'

'I tell you what, he had the most gorgeous blue eyes and curly, black hair I've ever seen ...' Pausing as she remembered the encounter, she then went on. 'Anyway, before I picked you up I stopped by home to get my beach gear and caught a very nice eyeful of my new neighbour. He was asleep in a deck chair under the elm tree. I would have told you on the drive down here but you wouldn't stop bitching about Jason.'

'Oh, forget about Jason, tell me more ... what's he look like?'

Liz, her best friend, was lying face-up on a gaudy, oversized beach towel next to Evie.

'Enzo said his name's Dash, and he hasn't got a bad body actually,' she smiled at the recollection. 'He was only wearing a pair of short shorts, I couldn't help having bit of a perv,' Evie smiled even more, 'but he did look a bit rough around the edges.'

'Hmmm ... unusual name ... but he might be just my type,' Liz smiled lazily. 'How old do you reckon he is?'

'As long as they've got a pulse, they're your type,' Evie grinned in reply.

'Oh rack off,' Liz laughed. 'At least I've got a sex life. You're like a nun these days.'

'Yeah, well, I'm sick of drop kicks, bullshit artists and liars. I'd rather be on my own than with some of the cretins that are around these days.' Evie stopped while she adjusted her position, then leant back on her arms.

'Anyway ... he looked around our age so he'd be way too old for your tastes,' she grinned again, 'you like them younger than you, remember?'

Liz couldn't help smiling at the memory of a couple of her past liaisons. Rolling over onto her back, then awkwardly propping herself up onto her elbows, her large, bare breasts caught the full force of the sun's rays. Looking towards the beach she noticed an elderly couple holding hands and casually walking into the sparkling surf. They were both completely naked and didn't seem to have a worry in the world. A wistful expression settled on Liz's face, watching them frolicking about like teenagers in the frothy, white foam.

'Yeah, well, most men my age aren't much fun. They either have a heap of baggage or they're workaholics, married or gay, as I know only too well.'

'You haven't had your girls out in the sun for a while, have you?' queried Evie, glancing at Liz's white breasts. 'You'd better put some sunscreen on them. I don't want to listen to you complaining about being sunburnt later.'

Unlike her chubby, well-endowed friend, Evie had a reasonably slim body. Looking down, she brushed some sand off her own smaller, tanned breasts saying, 'Pass me the sunscreen when you've finished with it, will you? I forgot to put more on after our swim.'

As she smoothed the cream over her neck and shoulders, she smiled and asked, 'So who did you decide to ask to the party tonight; Adam or Troy?'

'Neither of them, Jase ended up deciding he wanted to come with me – he thought it'd be fun.' Stealthily slapping at a sand-fly that'd landed on her leg, Liz went on, 'He does need some cheering up though. Ever since he broke up with

Simon he's been miserable and driving me mad. Why don't you ask your new neighbour to go with you, it'd do you good. Besides, I wouldn't mind checking him out for myself.'

'I told you before,' Evie sighed. 'I'm going by myself and coming home by myself. You know I'm not interested in hooking up with anyone just now, so give it a rest.'

'Okay, okay,' Liz said as she lay back down, placing her hat over her face. 'Don't get your knickers in a knot.'

For some reason, though, Evie couldn't seem to get the image of her new neighbour out of her mind. After bit of a pause she said, 'He did have a sexy body though – he must do some sort of physical work to get those nice shoulders.' Smiling at the memory, she continued, 'But I don't think he'd really be my type anyway. He'd fallen asleep with a girly magazine open on his knees and empty stubbies lying around ... he's probably one of those guys who only talks about footy and cars.'

'Hmm ... he sounds alright to me,' Liz murmured. 'I think I'll be dropping by your place a bit more often.' Abruptly sitting up again, she wrapped her colourful sarong around herself, tied it in a knot, then awkwardly stood up. 'God it's hot,' she moaned as she bent down and picked up her towel. 'I'd love a cold beer.'

Giving her towel a vigorous shake, her attention was caught by several good-looking guys who were walking their way. She jumped when Evie suddenly yelled, 'Hey, watch out. That's going all over me.'

'Oh, sorry Evie,' Liz giggled. 'I didn't realise.'

'You're bloody hopeless,' Evie said, brushing sand out of her short, silvery hair. Then, reaching into the small esky they'd brought with them, she removed two chilled bottles and passed one over to Liz.

'I'd love a beer too; but here, have a healthy bottle of water instead.'

'Thanks Evie ... hey, can you believe that Linda's forty? She looks great doesn't she?'

'Yeah, absolutely,' Evie replied after having a drink. 'But she works at it all the time. I can't believe I'll be forty-three this year ... time flies when you're having fun I suppose.' she grinned wryly.

'Hmm ... remember what I was like ... just before I hit forty?' After spreading her now sand-free towel out, Liz slowly sat down again.

'Mmmm ...' Evie sat down as well, nodding her head slightly in recollection of her friend's traumatic time.

Wrapping her arms around her bent knees and hugging them tightly, Liz went on. 'I can't believe how much has changed since then. Funny isn't it, how life goes ... up and down all the time? I'm going to make the most of this up-time though, that's for sure.'

They sat silently side by side for a while, remembering how Liz had felt her life had been in a complete shambles.

She'd found out that the new man in her life was gay, then her previous divorce settlement money – which had been invested on the confident advice of a 'friend' – had disappeared, along with the said 'friend' when the stock had dropped disastrously. Then a couple of days after that, Lisa, her daughter whom she loved dearly, had moved overseas to work in London for five years. Liz still missed her every day.

While sitting there, each deep in their own thoughts, they were unconsciously checking out the variety of people enjoying nature's splendours – topless or in the all-together. It was a picturesque spot for a nudist beach. Sheltered from any hot, northerly winds by towering cliffs, it had a sweeping stretch of soft sand leading to a huge rock pool; only revealed at low tide. The best thing though – it was never crowded because of the long, steep walk required to get there from the car park above.

Liz sat with her head thoughtfully leaning to one side; her curly, long blond hair now tucked up under her hat. Sipping some more water, she then spoke.

'I love being the age I am now. I feel so good about myself at last, just the way I am. Actually, I love everything about my life, just the way it is. I can finally do whatever I want to do without having to worry about anybody else. Of course, the finances could be better,' she finished with a grin.

'Yeah,' Evie agreed, watching as a couple of wetsuit-clad surfers tried and failed to catch a wave further down the beach. 'The finances could always be better, but it's good isn't it, being able to do your own thing when you want? I've been doing it for most of my life.' Changing the subject, Evie then said, 'It should be a pretty good party tonight, Linda's been talking about it for ages. She's actually been a bit stressed about it all, you know … the big four-oh thing.'

'Only because she's obsessed with looking young these days,' Liz frowned. 'It's silly. I think she has too much time on her hands now. She hasn't worked since she married Andrew, and what's that … six years ago?'

'I know, but Andrew wanted her to give up work so she could travel with him. It's when she's at home that she gets bored and starts obsessing. 'Checking the time on her watch, she said, 'Come on, let's get going. It's six o'clock already. It'll take you and Jason ages to get ready no doubt, and we're supposed to be there no later than eight-thirty. I don't want to be rushing around in this heat either.'

They picked up their bits and pieces then strolled back along the wide stretch of wet sand; cold wavelets continuously rippling over their feet as they chatted about what they might wear to the party. All talk was cut to a minimum though, as they puffed and panted their way up the steep walking track leading back to the car park.

Chapter Seventeen

Dash woke with a start and glanced around, still in bit of a daze and wondering what had woken him.

'I said ... do you have to leave that revolting magazine lying round like that for everybody to see?'

It was the woman with the red hair he'd seen earlier, standing with her skinny arms placed firmly on her skinny hips, glaring at him with a disgusted look etched on her face.

'You ought to be ashamed of yourself, reading that filth,' she sneered loudly.

'Hey, hang on a minute luv,' he said slowly, still stretched out comfortably. 'Don't tell me what I can and can't read. Don't look at it if it offends you so much.'

'Well, don't leave it lying there on the grass for all and sundry to see,' she snapped before turning on her heels and marching off in the direction of her flat.

Dash just sat there, slightly bemused, his eyes following her retreating figure as she angrily ascended the stairs to the far corner flat.

'Well, not all the natives are friendly,' he couldn't help grinning to himself. He reached down and retrieved the magazine where it had fallen off his lap, thinking that it was definitely time for another beer. Picking up the two empties as well, he slowly stood up, stretching his back muscles from side to side as he did so. He wondered how long he'd dozed off for as he unhurriedly headed back upstairs. Looking at the old wall clock above the kitchen sink, Dash was surprised to see that it was nearly twenty to five – he must have been asleep for about an hour.

Feeling a bit more alert after his nana nap, he put a load of dirty clothes into the big, old Hoover then added some laundry powder. Deciding to leave the washing for now, he stripped off his shorts and threw them in as well, before stepping under the shower.

He'd just dried off and pulled on another pair of shorts when he heard a knock on the front door. Walking across the lounge room he could see through the mesh door out to the balcony. A short, plump woman was patiently standing there holding something in her hands.

'G'day,' Dash said as he opened the security door up wide.

'Oh, hello, I do hope I'm not disturbing you,' the elderly

woman said softly in a pleasant German accent. 'I'm Mrs. Busarny, from number three. But please, call me Hilda. I just had to come and let you know that we're not all like that old biddy upstairs. I heard her screeching at you before, she's never happy unless she's having a go at someone.'

'That's alright luv ...' Dash grinned in reply. 'Water off a duck's back.'

'Anyway,' she continued on, 'I've brought you this as a welcoming gesture; I hope you like chocolate.' The woman removed the lid of a big Tupperware container revealing a delicious-looking, homemade chocolate cake.

'Too right I do,' he replied. 'Come on in. The name's Dash, nice to meet you.'

She seemed slightly agitated though, quickly answering, 'No no, I won't come in, thank you very much anyway. I've got to get back to my grandson now. He's supposed to be doing his homework, but if I'm not there I know he'll be watching some silly cartoons on the television.' Pressing the lid firmly back in place she handed the large container over. 'So, welcome to our little community,' she said with a warm smile, 'and don't worry about Betty, the rest of us are friendly.'

Dash was slightly taken aback by this show of kindness. He'd never had a welcome like this before.

'No worries then Hilda, thanks again for the cake. I'll look forward to having some later.'

With that she beamed a friendly smile at him and turned her plumpish body to quickly but carefully descend the stairs. He watched her for a moment then returned inside.

'What a nice old duck,' he thought as he rearranged a couple of six packs to make room for the sizeable container, 'certainly different to that old, red-headed harpy.'

His characteristic smile was still on his face as Dash put an INXS CD into his borrowed stereo, thinking it was about time he unpacked all his gear.

'Might as well,' he thought. 'It looks like this is going to be home for a while.'

He was singing along to 'Suicide Blonde' while he pulled his wrinkled clothes out of his bag, then roughly folded them to fit on the shelves in his wardrobe. Luckily someone had left a few coat hangers behind so he used them to hang his good shirts on.

That finished, he went back down to his car and unloaded his spare blankets, doona and few other bits and pieces. After sorting through his stuff he finally started the old Hoover washer, then left it to do its thing.

He was singing again as he washed the small pile of dishes he'd used, leaving them to dry on the sink before checking what time it was.

'Six o'clock now ... I should be back here by nine,' he calculated, pulling on a t-shirt and sandals. 'I'll have to get some groceries soon so I can stay home and cook myself a meal,' he thought as he headed off to catch up with his workmates.

Chapter Eighteen

'I love … Southside,' Liz wheezed, finally at the top. 'But the walk back up is … always such a killer.' Stopping to catch her breath, she bent forward and put her hands on her knees for a moment. 'I am so unfit,' she said, straightening up. 'I've *got* to lose some more weight.'

Evie was out of breath as well. Leaning against the fence she stood gazing across at the fantastic weather-sculptured cliffs. When her breath was back to a slower rhythm, she replied,

'Yeah … it *is* a bugger of a steep walk … but it's such a magic place.' Turning around she grinned as she watched Liz checking out a couple of tall, tanned surfer types as they bounded up the last few steps, surfboards under their arms.

'We'll have to come here more often; the walk up and down will do us good,' Evie smiled as she opened her car's boot and unceremoniously dumped all her stuff in.

'Hmm ... definitely,' Liz grinned, eyeing off a few more hunky-looking guys. Stashing her beach bag and towel alongside Evie's then closing the boot, she opened the passenger side door and angled herself into the car, thankful for the sheepskin covers between her and the hot seat.

Less than ten minutes later Evie deposited Liz at the house she shared with her ex-boyfriend Jason in Torquay, then cruised back to Geelong along the busy Surf Coast Highway. She turned the stereo up, smiling as she thought about her crazy best friend.

They'd met when Evie and her family had moved from the shop in Portarlington into their new home in Highton. Liz had lived two doors up and within days they'd become inseparable.

Even though Liz was eight months older than Evie they'd still gone through high school together, usually in the same classes. Both leaving at the end of form four they'd started earning their own money within weeks, then three years later had been each other's bridesmaid within six months of each other.

Laughing and crying together many times, supporting each other through bad times and celebrating the good, their credo had been 'to always be honest with each other, no matter what'.

'I never would have imagined we'd still be friends more

than thirty years later,' Evie smiled as she expertly manoeuvred her car along the narrow one-way street then parked it in front of her garage.

Getting her towel and beach bag out of the boot first, she made sure the car was locked before heading inside out of the sun's glare.

As she opened her front door the stuffiness immediately hit her in the face. 'Whew … it's hot in here.' She hung her keys on a hook near the door then turned on a fan that was sitting rather precariously on a well-stocked bookcase. Dumping her bag, towel, sunnies and hat onto the kitchen table, Evie walked into the lounge room and pulled open the curtains. Then, opening the windows as high as they would go, she inhaled deeply. 'Ahhh … that's a bit better.'

After opening all the other windows in the flat, she picked up her damp towel then pressed a button on her stereo. Santana's 'Black Magic Woman' instantly flooded the flat with its sensuous Latin American rhythm. As its languid beat percolated its way through the flat, she danced in rhythm with the music into the bathroom.

Dropping her beach towel into the dirty-clothes basket before adjusting the shower taps; she then stripped off her bikini and stepped into the cubicle. Giving an involuntary gasp as colder-than-planned-for water streamed over her head and down her body, she turned the hot tap on a bit more then began to automatically shampoo the salt and sand out of her hair.

Evie loved to let her mind wander when she was under the shower – it often surprised her with some distant recollection. Her earlier memories of Liz had stirred up others from that time and she now remembered more of the big move.

Apparently her dad had taken out a life insurance policy on himself years ago, straight after he'd married Evie's mum. When her mum had found out just how much she'd be receiving, after he'd been pronounced dead, she'd been very excited.

Declaring the business bankrupt, her mum had then used the life insurance money to buy a lovely house in a good part of Geelong. The shop sold about six months later for much less than what her dad had paid for it. Evie remembered how she'd overheard her mum and Aunty Ivy talking about it one day over afternoon tea.

The new house had been a much larger and nicer place than the old one; it'd even had a bungalow in the backyard that Douglas had immediately taken over. It'd had a bed, sink and a small, old, electric hotplate, and he'd stayed out there as much as he could, even eating his meals out there sometimes.

Evie had also overheard her mum saying to Aunty Ivy how she didn't foresee any problems with parenting on her own, and, in fact, 'she might be able to turn the girls into ladies yet'.

Needless to say her mum had been completely mortified when just three weeks later Maureen informed her that she was pregnant and wanted to get married. All hell had broken loose, resulting in Maureen packing some things and storming out. She'd married Vince in a registry office in Melbourne a month later and had never come home again.

The twins had regularly been in trouble at school after that, wagging it to meet up with boys in the city. Attracting a lot of attention anyway with their identical blond bouffant hairdos, they'd also been very pretty, something they'd both been well aware of. They'd had a lot of fun driving the boys crazy – swapping clothes to confuse them and always craving to be the centre of attention.

It hadn't surprised Evie at all when they'd married brothers on their eighteenth birthdays in a double wedding ceremony. Following that ostentatious spectacle, they'd then set out to see who would have the first baby – Pam winning that one, having the first of her three daughters eleven months after her honeymoon. Bev had felt slightly vindicated three months later having the son her husband had so much hoped for, followed by two more within the next four years.

Turning the hot tap off completely, Evie stood for a moment under the cold water before turning it off as well. She was frowning slightly as she dried herself, trying to remember when she'd last seen Jo.

'It must be about two years ago now, when Doug got married,' she thought to herself as she walked naked through the flat into her bedroom.

He'd invited the whole family to all of his weddings; that'd been his fourth. She couldn't help smiling when she remembered overhearing the twins at the reception making bets on how long *this* one would last.

Evie's phone rang, interrupting her idle thoughts as she was taking a couple of dresses out of her wardrobe. Laying the clothes onto her bed first, she then pulled on her satin bathrobe as she walked towards the insistent ringing; only stopping to turn the music down first.

'Hello.'

'*Evelyn*, I'm glad I've caught you at home. I was *just* talking to your Aunty Ivy. She mentioned that you haven't let her know if you're bringing a partner to the *reunion*. How can you *possibly* expect the catering to be organised without knowing *how many* are expected?'

'Hello Mum.' Evie's mood immediately dropped a couple of levels.

'You can't expect *her* to have to be chasing everyone up,' her mother continued in her uptight voice. 'And she shouldn't have to be chasing *you* up.'

'I'll call her as soon as I can,' Evie quickly said. 'I'd forgotten about it, I've been busy. Sorry I can't stop and talk now, I was just walking out the door. I've got a taxi waiting,' she lied.

'Oh ... well ... I'd better let you go then,' her mother replied reluctantly.

'Okay, bye then. Thanks for the reminder,' Evie said in a rushed voice.

'Ring me some time', were the last words she heard before she hurriedly replaced the receiver.

Sighing as she walked over to the fridge, opened the door, then peered inside, Evie wasn't aware that she was slowly shaking her head from side to side. Making an effort to distract her thoughts from the negative vibe her mother had imparted, she stood and surveyed the contents.

'Hmm ... just as well I'm eating out tonight, there's not much left in here.'

Mentally adding grocery shopping to her list of things to do tomorrow, she removed a chilled bottle of water from the bottom of the fridge then automatically grabbed a glass out of the freezer. As she walked towards the kitchen window she slowly poured herself a drink.

Mother Nature was showing off. The early evening sky was an impressive blend of orange, pink and red; but for once, Evie didn't notice.

Having never been able to establish a close connection with her mother, Evie had eventually acknowledged that it was okay to feel the way she did; and although she hated lying, she really couldn't handle talking to her tonight.

It was years ago now that she'd come to terms with the fact that her mother had done the best job of mothering of which she'd been able. The fact that it wasn't really good enough for any of them was just unfortunate. Evie would have loved to have experienced that close mother/daughter bond that some of her friends had with their mothers, but it wasn't meant to be. And she knew it irked all of her siblings that her mother always insisted on calling them by their 'proper' names. They were all now known by the shortened versions – even Maureen, who now only ever answered to Reen or Reenie.

She felt sad because her mother was someone who rarely seemed to be genuinely happy; always managing to find something to complain about even if she was enjoying herself. Her mum had also inadvertently constructed a lonely life for herself by thinking only of her own immediate wants and needs. By not having the time or inclination to truly get to know her children and grandchildren, they in turn didn't know her very well either and so didn't visit very often.

Evie had also been quite exasperated with her mother many times over the years, especially when she'd try and put the blame on other people for the bad things that happened in her life, instead of taking some responsibility for her own choices. But Evie also couldn't help feeling some love for her mother, recognising how hard it must have been for her when Dad was no longer around. Raising that amount of kids by herself could not have been easy.

After the twins had married and moved out, the house had become relatively quiet and peaceful. Douglas had done his own thing, as usual, keeping to himself in the bungalow most of the time doing God knows what, and Evie had finally had a bedroom all to herself. Not long after that her mother had joined a few social clubs and was rarely home, often leaving Evie to look after Joanne in the evenings. Moving to the Gold Coast twenty-five years ago with her new husband, Ted, her mum had then decided to stay there after he'd died last year, choosing to be close to her new, small, circle of friends.

Pouring the last of the water into her glass, Evie still felt a bit unsettled as she wandered into the lounge room and over to her stereo. Her happy mood had been quashed a little so she looked through her CD collection for something that would revive it again. Choosing ZZ Top, she turned it up loud before returning to her bedroom.

As she reached for her favourite body lotion, Evie thought out loud. 'Oh well, I'd better decide if I'm going to take someone to the damn reunion or not I suppose.' She knew if she didn't she'd have everyone asking her all day, 'so you're still on your own then?' She also knew that if she did take someone they'd get the third degree about, 'so how long have you two been together then?' A smile transformed her serious expression as she pictured it in her mind, all the while meticulously smoothing the fragrant lotion over her body.

Resolving not to let it bother her anymore tonight she put on her bra and knickers. Then deciding to wear her new silk dress, she picked it up off the bed and slipped the delicate fabric over her head, delighting in the coolness of it as it slid over her warm skin. Turning around she looked at herself in the long mirror that was fixed to the inside of the wardrobe door.

'Not too bad for an old girl,' she said out loud, smiling at her reflection. The mauve colouration of the dress flattered her tanned complexion and silvery hair, giving her a soft, glowing look, while the ice-green splashes along the hemline provided an interesting contrast.

'Now, a bit of makeup and I'll be about ready.'

Evie loved not having to fuss over her hair anymore. For several years now she'd been keeping it really short by shaving it with a number four shaver. Before that it had been long, thick and wavy, but being quite grey she'd had to colour it regularly. Finally getting sick of the time and money she was spending on her hair she'd had it shaved and never coloured it again, quite liking her silvery look. She was lucky in that she had a nice shaped head and ears; people often commented on how much the short style suited her.

Of course there were some people who assumed she was gay because of her hairstyle; she'd even had a couple of women try to chat her up. It had always given her a bit of a grin the way people couldn't help categorising others by first appearance – she was guilty of it herself sometimes.

Makeup finished, she took one last look in the mirror as she put on some earrings, and then she was ready. Glancing at the wall clock as she re-entered the kitchen, Evie was pleased to see that she still had ample time.

'Great. I've got at least half an hour before Liz and Jason get here.'

Deciding to have a drink out on the balcony and just relax for a while, she grabbed a beer out of the fridge, a stubbie holder from the bench, and walked outside.

'Mmm ... that's better.' Sitting right back in the old vinyl armchair, Evie propped her bare feet up against the cool balcony railing. As she sipped her drink she turned her head to the right, trying to see if her neighbour was home. The front door was open but no lights were on, and she was unable to see or hear anything through his closed security door.

'No sign of life there ... doesn't look like he's home again,' she murmured. 'Oh well, perhaps we'll cross paths tomorrow.' Sitting with her head slightly to one side she pondered for a moment, then slowly thought out loud.

'Hmm ... I'm not sure what it is ... but for some reason I feel a bit strange when I think about him.'

Chuckling to herself she decided it was probably just the

hot, steamy weather making her feel horny, plus the fact she'd seen him almost naked except for those short shorts he'd had on. Still grinning, the image of his sprawled out body teased its way around her mind.

Evie had turned her stereo off before coming outside, often preferring to listen to the sounds of nature, and now savoured the peace and quiet of her surroundings. She thought about how much she loved living where she did; having a stunning view, her own fairly private balcony, and it was no more than a twenty-minute walk to buy anything that she needed.

Gazing straight ahead she could see over the roof of the house next door, to the moss-covered slate roof of the two-storey house next to it. Newtown was a leafy suburb. Most houses were quite big and had large old trees in their gardens, and this helped muffle the sound of the traffic from the nearby highway.

Her neighbours were great too ... well, except for Betty. Evie hadn't been able to find out what made that woman so bitter, and now chose to mostly avoid her. She liked Ross and Jazmin though. They lived next to her in number six and were a bit on the 'alternative' side. Several Buddha's decorated their balcony and Evie often smelt a variety of exotic incenses wafting from their windows. Even though there was a brick wall dividing her balcony from theirs, they could still lean forward over the railing and have bit of a chinwag.

Another lovely couple lived in number eight, on the other side of Betty. Lewis and Sharna always had a cheery greeting for her and would often stop for a chat. They hadn't lived there very long but she'd already decided they were into fitness and the healthy lifestyle, often seeing them heading off to the tennis courts or the gym. These two flats were on the same level as Evie's but at a right-angle to hers. Built above the garages, they formed the short section of the L-shaped block.

Downstairs in number one was old Vic Rankin. Evie smiled and shook her head slightly as she thought of old Vic. He kept to himself pretty much, but he did have a passion for jazz and played it loud at least once a week. Not that it bothered Evie, or Christina – her neighbour directly below in number two. Christina was rarely home. She'd happily told Evie that volunteering for a couple of different organisations after she'd retired was the best thing she'd ever done. Between driving for Meals on Wheels three mornings a week and helping out at the Red Cross op' shop, she said she'd never felt fitter. Evie had a real soft spot for her friend Hilda in number three, often catching up with her for coffee, cake and a chat.

Just then Evie's attention was caught by the sound of running feet. Losing her train of thought as she looked down and to her left, she saw young William quickly disappearing around the corner of the flats.

'Oh no, he's off again,' she sighed. 'Poor Hilda, she doesn't need this at her age.'

Five seconds later Hilda appeared. 'Willie, come back here.'

She must have known he was gone though, because she stood silently for a few seconds then muttered something under her breath. Just as Evie went to call out to her, Hilda's phone rang. Sighing, Evie watched as the elderly woman hurried back inside to answer it.

'I'll drop in and see her over the weekend,' she thought as she relaxed back into the chair again. 'It's so hard for her, bringing up a grandson at her time of life.'

Feeling thoroughly relaxed, Evie's thoughts went back to some of the other places she'd lived in over the years. She smiled at the memories of some them. She felt she'd been quite lucky in her life so far; having had to confront and overcome a few unforeseen difficulties along the way had pushed her to grow into the person she was happy to be now. A wry smile appeared on her face as she thought about how gullible she'd been in her twenties. She sighed and shook her head, remembering some of the hard lessons she'd learnt during her ill-fated marriage, and afterwards.

One of the disappointing but necessary lessons she'd learnt was to stop naively believing everything that people said to her. This one had been a hard one to learn, and it'd taken her a couple of relationships to grasp it, but after her whole world had been turned upside down for the second time she knew it would take a special man to earn her trust again. Evie smiled, remembering how excited she'd been playing house for the very first time.

She'd been twenty-two at the time and living in Grovedale, a new suburb of Geelong, and had loved absolutely everything about her life. Her husband of three years had been good-looking, affectionate and had a great job. They'd had a beautiful new house and a fun circle of friends, all they'd needed was a baby to top it all off. The day Evie had befriended Karen, after noticing her moving into the house next door to her and Phil, had been her first error of judgment.

Being a single mum and not too handy around the house, Karen had often asked her if Phil could drop over when he had the time. Evie remembered how Karen had always seemed to have something that needed to be fixed or moved or something. A small, nostalgic smile crept over Evie's face as she sat there recalling how much Phil had loved playing with Karen's little boy, Sam. He was a real cutie, and at two-and-a-half was an unstoppable little dynamo.

Phil had been mad keen to start a family as soon as they'd finally moved into their own home after nearly three years of saving up for a good deposit. When she hadn't fallen pregnant after twelve months of trying, Phil had gone and had his sperm count checked.

Evie remembered how he'd later grinned and told her, 'I'm not shooting blanks baby. In fact, the doc said I've got nothing to worry about. 'He'd had a cheeky smile on his face as he walked over towards her. 'He thinks we could be stressing over it too much and we should just relax and let it happen.' Snuggling up behind her he'd nibbled her ear and then went on. 'I still made an appointment for you to get checked out next Friday though; may as well cover all bases.' Gently turning her around so she was able to see his face, he'd looked directly into her eyes and stated, 'I love you so much honey ... I can't ever imagine being with anyone else.' He'd gently kissed her and went on, 'And I know you'll be the perfect mother for our kids. I can hardly wait to have my own son, then I'll show my old man how to be a proper father.' Holding her close he'd continued excitedly. 'The old man will be over the moon when he knows he finally has a grandson to keep the family name going.' Taking her hand, he'd led her towards their bedroom, smiling wickedly back at her asking, 'Now, how relaxed are you feeling?'

Three months later her life irrevocably changed. They'd gone camping with friends over the Christmas holidays to an isolated spot they'd discovered, just above the sandy shoreline of Lake Hindmarsh. Two days later when they'd been out on the lake fishing from Phil's boat, she started having severe abdominal pains, later collapsing as she'd tried to get into their car. Phil had been drinking and in his panic took a wrong turn resulting in them heading in the wrong direction. Not knowing the area, they'd got lost and it was hours before they finally arrived at the local hospital to eventually discover that she'd suffered an ectopic pregnancy.

Maybe because of the delay in receiving medical treatment, a raging infection had set in, and when she'd finally fully recovered they'd been told that she'd probably never be able to have a baby. Phil had been great at first, assuring her that it didn't matter, but over the ensuing months she was vaguely aware of a distance growing between them. Suffering from depression for several months after hearing the devastating news, she hadn't noticed just how much time her husband had been spending next door.

When he came home one evening a few months later and said that he was leaving her, she'd felt completely numb and emotionless, and had just sat there like a cold, lifeless statue. She'd been unable to properly comprehend what he'd been saying at first, but as it gradually took shape in her foggy thoughts she'd felt herself being slowly sucked into a black, desolate pit of despair.

Feeling a heavy pain in her chest, she'd known without doubt that it was her heart breaking. Tears ran unchecked down her face as she silently watched him walk out the door. He'd been tightly clutching his overnight bag and hadn't looked back.

Two days later when he rang and informed her that he'd moved in with Karen and had been sleeping with her for months, Evie had been livid with both of them, instantly feeling her broken heart harden into a horrible, throbbing anger. It had turned out, though, to be the catalyst that enabled her to drag herself out of her deadening inertia.

She'd thought she'd known everything about Phil, having been with him since she was seventeen, and it had made her speechless with anger when she'd realised just how quickly he'd betrayed her total trust in him. Not being able to comprehend how she could have been so blindly in love with such a cheating bastard, she'd filed for divorce within days, instructing her lawyer to arrange for the property settlement to be dealt with as soon as possible.

Knowing she had to get away from everything and everyone, she'd then packed some clothes and basic necessities into her car and driven off. Both her mind and body felt leaden and she didn't really care at first where she went. She had known, though, that there was no going back.

Evie couldn't remember much of the drive, or of the motels she'd stayed at, but after driving north for four days she'd stopped and found herself in a beautiful little place called Trinity Beach. It was situated about twenty minutes north of Cairns and was an absolute tropical paradise. She'd rented a lovely house two streets back from the beach and ended up staying there for two years. Meeting Dan on a scuba diving trip six months after settling in had been just the tonic she'd needed at the time.

It had been the second time she'd been exploring the wonders of the Great Barrier Reef. This time she'd gone with Natalie, a friend she'd made at work, and a group of her friends. Dan was one of them and had volunteered to be her diving buddy.

He was good-looking, funny and loved life, and being set up financially he could indulge in his passion for adventure. By the end of the day he'd asked her to have a meal and a few drinks at a pub in Cairns where they'd ended up talking and laughing for hours.

Not realising at the time how emotionally vulnerable she was, Dan's abundant charm and attention had made her feel alive and desirable again. He was fifteen years older than her, had never been married and had no children. It hadn't worried him at all that Evie couldn't have a baby; he said he'd never wanted one anyway.

They spent as much time together as they could and it hadn't been long before Evie felt that she'd fallen in love again. A couple of months later when he asked her to move in to his palatial ocean front house with him, she'd been so swept off her feet from his constant attention that she hadn't hesitated.

It had taken Evie quite a while to become suspicious of Dan's assortment of excuses when he began coming home late. Being honest and up-front herself, she'd naively believed his explanations about late meetings or having to entertain an important client. The day Diane and she had decided to have lunch at an expensive new restaurant to celebrate Diane's birthday, her world had crashed again.

Dan had been sitting in a corner booth with a gorgeous young blond, laughing and smiling at her the same way he'd done to Evie. He'd left no doubt in Evie's mind as to what was going on. Diane and she had decided to stay and have lunch anyway and to wait until he noticed them. Sitting there watching him lightly trailing his fingers up and down the young woman's arm, and smiling at her in that intimate way of his, Evie had felt her whole being burning in anger and another small part of her die.

As angry and crushed as she'd felt at the time, the look on Dan's face when he'd finally seen her had almost made her laugh. He'd come over and shamelessly tried to explain it was a business meeting, but he knew she hadn't believed him. Later that night when Evie had finished packing her things, Dan had continued trying to explain that he did love her – he just wasn't ready to settle down with one woman yet.

Standing next to her packed bags, Evie had listened to him in silence, all the while swearing to herself that she'd never again be in a relationship with a man she couldn't trust one hundred per cent. As he stood in front of the naked wall of windows, gesticulating wildly while trying his best to rationalise his behaviour, Evie's eyes had slowly focused on the panoramic view of the Coral Sea shimmering in the moonlight behind him.

She'd finally seen Dan through clear eyes and she'd nearly laughed. He was an attractive, charismatic man, no doubt, but one who'd been over-indulged all his life by pleasure-seeking parents, ultimately rendering him unable to be happy with anything for very long.

Sleeping with much younger women kept him in that place of feeling young and alive, while the thrill of the chase fed his constant need for newness and excitement in his life.

She'd been surprised to realise just how calm she then felt. His complete betrayal of her trust had completely wiped her emotional slate clean. Picturing him at sixty with a fluffy young thing of twenty-something on his arm had made it easy for her to turn around and walk out the door. She'd moved in with Diane for a while, then a few months later, after securing a job in Brisbane, had quit her job at the golf course and moved on.

Just then a car horn tooted, abruptly bringing Evie out of her ruminations.

'Hi Evie ... are you ready?' Liz called, her blond head poking out through the taxi's window. 'I didn't think we'd ever get here. Jase was in the bathroom for more than an hour ... yes you were,' she replied to something Jason had said. 'If we get going now we won't be late, you know Andrew's a real stickler for time.'

Smiling, Evie quickly stood up and waved. 'Okay, I'll just get my bag,' she called back. Feeling ready to party she picked up the small bag she'd left ready on the kitchen table, locked her front door and headed down the stairs towards her noisy friends.

Chapter Nineteen

Dash had just returned home from one of the local pubs after having a few beers, a big steak, and several games of pool with Leon, Sid and Pete. As he dropped his wallet and keys onto the bench top the phone rang, so putting the receiver to his ear he walked back out to his small balcony, the long cord snaking behind him.

'Hello,' he said, stretching one arm above his head and bending his body from side to side.

'G'day big brother, how're they hangin'?'

A big smile immediately creased Dash's face and he dropped his arm back down. 'They're hanging pretty good mate, how're yours?'

'Loose and full of juice mate,' Laurie replied, having a good chuckle. 'So have you found yourself a decent woman yet or what?'

'I haven't even found myself an indecent one yet,' Dash replied, grinning.

They both had bit of a laugh then Laurie asked, 'So how are things going? Got a job yet? All you left on my answering machine yesterday was your address and phone number.'

'Yeah, well, if you were home instead of out carousing we could have had a chat then,' he grinned then went on. 'I actually started work a few days ago; should last a few months too.'

'That's great mate.'

'Yeah, I'm rapt because I'm rigging as well as operating the crane. You know I like a bit of variety.'

By the time Dash had finished telling Laurie most of what had happened over the last week, he'd gone back inside, pulled a cold beer out of its tight plastic noose and had made himself comfortable in his deck chair again.

'So, what have you been up to Loz, still seeing that spunky blond piece?' he asked while swatting at an annoying mosquito when it landed on his leg.

'No, we broke up a couple of months ago. I'm happily single again and loving it.'

Flicking the dead mozzie away, Dash couldn't help smiling as he thought about Laurie's varied love life. Changing the subject, he asked him how *his* job was going.

'Just the usual,' Laurie said in resignation, 'still trying to impart knowledge to my reluctant students.' Being an art teacher working in an under-financed school that put more emphasis on sport than anything else had been very frustrating for Laurie.

'Hey, I entered one of my paintings in a local art show here today, and guess who won first prize?'

'Did *you*? Good on you mate. My brother the famous artist,' chuckled Dash.

'Yeah, right, but I have to say it was a bit of a buzz. I sold it, too. You'll never guess who bought it.'

'What is this, a guessing game?' Dash grinned. 'Okay, I give up. Who bought it?'

'Marley.'

'Marley?'

'Yeah, Marley ... your daughter Marley.'

'I know who you're talking about,' Dash frowned. 'I'm just surprised to hear that she's over there. The last I heard she was still in Queensland.'

'She was. She said that she'd come down here to catch up with you. She was disappointed to hear that you'd left.'

'Hmm ... wonder what's going on there? I haven't seen her for about five or six years. How's she looking?'

'Really good actually, although she looked a bit tired. But she was all dressed up; looked quite snazzy.'

'Oh ... what happened to the hippy look I wonder?'

'Don't know mate. Anyway, she was after your phone number. I gave her your address as well so you'll probably be hearing from her soon.'

'Thanks mate.' Dash couldn't help frowning about the prospect as he finished off his beer. She'd never tried to look him up before; what made her want to do it now? Slowly standing up and walking back inside, he asked, 'So where *are* you anyway; at home?'

'Yeah, I just got home ten minutes ago; heard your message again so thought I'd better call you now. I was out with a mate last night when you rang; celebrating the birth of his second kid. I didn't get home 'til about one. I tell you what mate,' he went straight on, 'I don't think I'll be going down the kid track for a long time ... if ever. I reckon there's too much fun to be had, rather than having little rug rats running around.'

'Yeah, well, these things just happen sometimes,' Dash chuckled.

'Won't happen to me mate, although I know Dad and Jean would love a grandkid because they were talking about it tonight. I've actually just come from their place – they'd asked me around for dinner.'

'You lucky bugger, so you're still being pampered?' Dash teased as he sat down on his creaky deck chair after getting another stubbie. Putting his feet up on the balcony rail he continued on, 'I suppose she's still doing your laundry as well?'

'Fuck off,' Laurie laughed in protest. 'She hasn't done

that since I moved out. Listen, I've got to go, I've still got to have a shower yet. It's been hot here today .. for Launceston,' Laurie said with a smile in his voice, 'and I smell a bit woofy.'

Promising to keep in touch they said their goodbyes. Dash wandered inside and hung up the phone, standing there with a pleased, thoughtful look on his face.

'Good on him,' he then said out loud. He loved his 'little' brother and wished he saw more of him. 'I'd better buy one of his paintings while I can still afford one,' he thought, grinning at the idea.

Still smiling, he returned to his spot outside, leaned back in his chair and put his hands behind his head. Memories of the day he'd come home from an unexpected holiday with his nan and grandpa to discover he had a little brother ran through his mind. He'd been so excited – he couldn't wait 'til Laurence was old enough to play with.

He'd known something had been brewing at home before that, but he'd actually thought his mum and Reg were going to split up, and that was why they'd wanted him out of the way for a while. They'd either been arguing or giving each other the silent treatment for months, with Reg often taking off in the car and not returning 'til the early hours of the morning.

After Laurence had been born though, Reg had always come straight home after work and only sometimes went out at night. His mum had changed for the better too, at least in regard to mothering Laurence. Even though she'd still just tolerated him, the atmosphere in the house had been lifted and Reg had usually had a smile on his face.

When his mum had unexpectedly died four years later of a brain aneurism, Dash had already moved out; sharing a small house with Terry in Devonport. Reg had seemed bereft at the time of her death, but later shocked a few people when he'd married Jean O'Reilly as soon as her divorce had come through twelve months later.

Dash couldn't help thinking about the different upbringings he and Laurie had received. 'What a difference a real mother makes to the equation,' he thought as he stretched his arms up above his head. 'Oh well, at least one of us had the experience.'

When his mother had been alive she'd done all she could to drive a wedge between the two of them, but it'd never worked. Even though there was a twelve-year age gap between them they'd always been close. No one believed they were brothers though, not even half-brothers – they looked nothing alike.

Laurie had inherited his mother's red hair and fair skin and was a wiry six foot two. Not only was his hair carrot-red, it was also tightly curled like springs and some kids had given him hell over it when he was younger. These days he wore it long, usually tied back in a ponytail, and all the girls loved it. Laurie loved being taller than his 'big' brother, and where Dash was interested in all things mechanical, Laurie was interested in all things artistic.

Now feeling tired, Dash checked the time and saw it was ten-thirty. He exhaled wearily, picked up the empty stubbie and stood up.

'Ahhh ... thank goodness I've got two days off,' he muttered to himself. 'I'll have to look to buy a bed soon. I've just about had enough of the old swag.'

Chapter Twenty

The next morning when Evie woke up she felt better than she'd expected. Now glad that she hadn't overdone it the night before, she was out of bed and in the shower by eight o'clock.

Drying off as she wandered into the lounge room, she turned on the stereo hoping to catch the weather forecast. As she put on her robe she thought she could feel a thunderstorm brewing, and as soon as she stepped outside she was certain of it.

It was already very warm and the sky was full of swirling, dark grey clouds. She leant forward against the balcony rail, soaking up the feel of the electricity in the air. Smelling the ozone, she thought again of how thunderstorms had always been her favourite type of weather. She just loved watching the wild, unpredictable elements of Mother Nature in all her glory.

Her eyes were drawn towards the choppy bay, and she noticed a few yachts swiftly heading towards the shelter of the marina. Hoping that the rain would hold off for a bit, she turned around and walked back inside to get ready. She had a nine o'clock appointment on the other side of town and didn't want to be late.

Parking in the street out the front of her destination, Evie picked up a bag containing her compass, pencils and notebook, then stepped out of the car. She was doing a Feng Shui consultation, and as she slowly wandered up the driveway, noticed that several large trees grew at the rear of the house, sheltering it from behind, which usually, but not always, signified support for the inhabitants.

As she studied the beautiful home which was before her, the front door opened and a tall, dark-haired woman quickly stepped outside.

'Hello', the woman called anxiously as she made her way hastily down the winding path. 'You must be Evie.'

'Yes, hello, and you must be Rita,' she replied with a smile. 'Now, you said over the phone that your business has dropped right off since you moved into this house.'

'Yes, that's right. We've been here for just on twelve months now. We only moved here because we needed more room for storage, but since then our turnover has decreased each quarter.'

'Okay, let me have a look around the property first, then I'll come inside,' Evie said, gazing around. 'Did you manage to get a copy of the floor plan and find out the year the house was built?'

'Oh, yes. I've left the floor plan on the kitchen table and the house was built in 1968. Is that good or bad?'

'That makes it Period Six; so yes, that was a good era to have a house built.'

'Well that's something good then,' Rita smiled. 'But why does it matter when it was built? What's that all about?'

'Well, in Feng Shui it's believed that when the roof is completed on a new structure that it affects the energy levels in the structure forever, unless the whole roof is replaced at a future date, which would then re-set the energy to that Period.'

'Oh.'

'Yeah, each Period lasts twenty years,' Evie elaborated, loving the intricacies of her chosen career, 'and as we're now in Period Seven, the energy levels in your home will increase until 2004. After that you'll still have good energy until 2024 when it will then become dead energy for twenty years.'

'Oh ... okay then,' Rita said with a slightly bemused expression on her face. 'So ... you think we should be okay here for a while then, if you can remedy our business problems?'

'How about I get the chart done first so I can then give

you an accurate assessment?' Evie smiled, now impatient to get started.

'Yes, yes, of course. You get started then. Do you want the floor plan now?'

'No, not yet thanks,' she said as she started to make a move. 'I'll check out the house's outdoor environment first to see how it affects the flow of energy into your home,' Evie said, nodding her head slightly she went on, '... which is a very important factor.'

'How long will it be before you can let me know if there *is* a problem with the house?'

'I can come back Wednesday morning if that suits you.'

'Wednesday morning,' Rita had a quick think. 'Yes, that suits me.' She had a rueful smile on her face as she followed Evie towards the left of the house. 'My husband thinks I'm nuts getting you out here. That's why I asked you here on a Sunday – he plays golf every Sunday come what may. I'd love it if you could prove him wrong,' she chuckled. 'I'll go and put the kettle on. We can have a cuppa when you've finished if you like.'

Evie was smiling as she began her inspection of the property. She was thinking of how many people didn't believe in Feng Shui until they'd experienced the results for themselves. Creating a harmonious flow of energy in and around the home or business was the goal; enhancing the positive and decreasing the negative energy was the method used. She'd been intrigued to learn how this method was based on time, direction, alignment, the Earth's magnetic field, and the five elements – Fire, Earth, Metal, Water and Wood – with each element relating to a colour, number, family member and even body parts.

After walking right around the house and ascertaining that the front was the 'facing direction' – the side with the most windows and activity – she then took compass readings from three different areas, all about a metre out from the house. Evie had learnt early on in her studies that any metal fixtures on a house, such as down pipes or security doors, could affect the accuracy of the readings, so three were recommended to establish the exact direction that the house faced.

It had initially surprised her to find that many houses 'faced' the rear of the property, especially those that had a view from that direction. She'd often come across this when she'd done consultations around the Surfers Paradise area where lots of homes were built facing the canals behind them, instead of facing the street view.

'Okay, its 74 degrees north east,' she said to herself, writing her calculations down on her notepad. Having another look around - noting the estimated dimensions and alignment of the surrounding houses, as well as the different features of the landscape - she then headed inside.

Taking her time as she surveyed the interior of the lovely

home, all the while making notes as she went, Evie was finally finished. Having a copy of the floor plan was a bonus, saving her from having to measure the house and each room herself. She had a quick cup of coffee and a chat with Rita, rolled up the floor plan they'd been looking at and, taking it with her, said her goodbyes.

'See you next Wednesday then,' she said to Rita, who'd followed her outside.

'Okay love, I hope you have good news for me. Don will be flabbergasted if this makes a difference.'

Evie smiled and gave a small wave, then hurried back down the driveway. She was just thinking how lucky she'd been that the rain had held off when several huge droplets of water suddenly splattered on her head and onto the paved driveway in front of her. The number of drops rapidly increased, and by the time she was back in her car and on the road, the pounding downpour made it difficult to see.

'At least it's a bit cooler now,' she said to herself as she turned the stereo down, needing all her senses alert to negotiate the busy, wet road. She decided she'd get some groceries then go home and start on the chart before Liz came round later.

Chapter Twenty-One

Finally waking up completely at about ten o'clock, after half waking then rolling over several times, Dash relished the feeling of not having to be anywhere in particular.

'Thank heaven for Sundays,' he mumbled, as his eyes followed the curtains as they blew in, then just as suddenly sucked back against the half-open window again. Lying on his back with just a sheet covering his naked body, he had a good stretch first then leisurely stood up and opened the curtains.

'Hmmm ... I thought I could feel a thunderstorm brewing,' he said to himself, watching the dark clouds as they jostled for position. 'It's going to piss down soon.'

Having decided to have a shower and a coffee before getting his groceries, Dash ambled into the lounge room first, all the while scratching various body parts as only a man can.

Knowing reception would be bad on his stereo during a thunderstorm, he flicked it straight onto CD mode, replaying 'The Loved Ones' CD he'd been listening to the previous night. The intro' to 'Ever Lovin' Man' tickled its way into Dash's head as he continued on towards the bathroom, singing along as Gerry Humphreys' distinctive voice boomed through the flat.

With a towel wrapped around his waist, Dash walked into the kitchen whilst rubbing his wet hair with another towel. Stopping to push the button on the electric kettle he stood for a moment, his attention caught by flashes of brilliance emanating from the rapidly darkening sky.

Five minutes later he was dressed and standing out on the balcony sipping his coffee. Hearing several large raindrops thudding on the tin roof above, he smiled, having always loved thunderstorms and the incredible power they produced.

'Ahh ... here it comes ... wish I could just sit back and watch it ... but ... I better get some groceries, I'm sick of eating out.'

Finishing off his coffee in a couple of quick mouthfuls, Dash grabbed his keys and wallet and headed off.

By the time he'd parked in the supermarket car park the rain was teeming down with such force that it was ricocheting in all directions, creating a knee-high spray of water. He watched people running from their cars to the shelter of the store; hunched over, futilely attempting to stay dry.

'Oh well, here goes,' Dash said under his breath as he opened the car door. He'd parked as close as he could but was still dripping by the time he made it to the sliding doors of the supermarket. Just as he stepped into the air-conditioned refuge, a spectacular flash of lightning momentarily lit everything with an incandescent glow, instantly followed by a massive crack of thunder which seemed to make the very foundations of the store tremble.

Having just put the last of her shopping onto the conveyor belt, Evie was casually standing at one of the noisy checkouts. She was watching a variety of bedraggled-looking people rushing in through the doors every time they slid open, when she suddenly recognised her next-door neighbour heading towards the entrance. Just as the doors slid open again and he stepped into the store, there was an incredible flash of blinding light followed by an enormous, booming, cracking sound. Evie and everyone else around her instinctively ducked, then a couple of seconds later, realising it was lightning and thunder, most people nervously smiled and looked around either in relief or anxiety. The noise level in the store then dramatically increased as people felt compelled to comment on the awesome display of power they'd just witnessed. Checking out her neighbour as he walked through the turnstiles, Evie couldn't help grinning; *his* was the most impressive entrance she'd ever seen.

As the last of her groceries were being scanned she moved forward a bit to see around two women who were obviously catching up after some time. They were stopped in the middle of an aisle, both oohing and ahhing over each other's toddlers, when one of the little darlings decided it was the perfect time to throw a tantrum.

Evie was now able to see her neighbour again through a gap in the throng of people, and watched him struggle to remove a carry basket which was stubbornly refusing to yield its grip from the one underneath. Smiling, her eyes followed him as he slowly wended his way through a line of people patiently waiting in the fast checkout lane.

Still grinning after his mad sprint to the door, Dash finally managed to extract a basket from the wobbly stack, then eased his way through the throng waiting in a long queue. People were still commenting on Mother Natures' incredible light and sound display as he scanned the store looking for the meat section. Something suddenly caught his eye and he turned his head back slightly to see what it was.

His eyes locked onto a woman waiting at a checkout about five metres from where he was standing; next to a tempting display of strawberries which were on special. She was looking directly at him and had one of the nicest smiles he'd ever seen. It'd been her hair, though, that had caught his attention – it was really short and was a stunning silvery colour. A man obscured his view for a moment, but craning his head to the left he watched as she chatted to the checkout girl and paid for her shopping. Someone behind him tapped him on the shoulder and, turning around, he saw that he was blocking the way.

'Sorry mate,' he apologised to an elderly man, at the same time stepping aside to allow the old bloke room to pass.

Evie was still smiling when his eyes locked onto hers, then was distracted when the checkout girl said, 'That comes to eighty-seven dollars, fifteen cents.'

As Evie handed over two fifties the girl was still talking about the thunderstorm. Agreeing with her that it was the loudest thunder she'd ever heard too, Evie took her change and moved forward, pushing her trolley at a snail's pace behind a harassed-looking woman who had five kids milling around her, all asking her over and over for something they wanted out of one of the shopping bags.

Nearing the exit Evie sensed someone was watching her, and looking back over her shoulder she instantly made eye contact with her neighbour once more. She smiled and gave him a small wave, then pushed on through the now open sliding doors.

When Dash looked up again she was walking towards the exit, slowly pushing a half-full trolley in front of her. His eyes were following her of their own accord and he was openly admiring her overall look when she turned her head and looked straight at him again. Lifting one hand from its hold on the trolley, she gave him a quick wave and another friendly smile, then he lost sight of her again as she went out through the supermarket doors.

'Hmm ... what an attractive-looking woman ... gorgeous smile and friendly ... I wouldn't mind seeing *her* again.'

The rumbling of more thunder brought him back to his present mission. Shaking his head slightly to clear the image of the woman from his mind, he was determined to get on with what he was there for so he could then get back home. He was hungry and was planning to cook up some bacon and eggs for a late breakfast.

Chapter Twenty-Two

Struggling to carry all five bags of groceries up the steps in one go, Evie still had a smile on her face when she arrived back at her flat. She was wondering if her new neighbour was going to be home by the time Liz got there, because she knew how much her friend was wanting to check him out for herself.

Thankful that the rain had now completely stopped, she sat the bags down and stood at the balcony railing. Looking across the bay she watched the storm heading towards Melbourne, still continuing to exhibit an electrifying demonstration of its power. As she listened to the deep, distant rumblings she breathed in deeply, smelling the freshness in the air that the rain had produced.

The sun had returned with a vengeance and even though it was cooler than before, it was now more humid. Noticing the ethereal wisps of steam rising from the drying roadway she became entranced for a moment, staring at the swirling vapour until, giving herself a mental shake, she finally took the groceries inside.

Five minutes later, when all the groceries were put away except for one bag of perishables, she heard a familiar voice.

'Hi Evie … ohhh … I feel terrible … why oh why did I drink so much last night? I think I need to lie down again.' Liz was slowly opening the door. With one hand holding the door frame she gingerly made her way into the lounge room. She was not looking her best.

Evie poked her head around the kitchen door.

'Hi Lizzy … oh … you look terrible too.'

'Gee, thanks,' Liz replied, gently lowering herself down into an armchair. 'Is that supposed to make me feel better?'

'Sorry Liz,' Evie laughed. 'But you do. You look like someone's just dragged you out of your bed backwards. What did you get up to last night?'

'Well … after we dropped you off, Jason decided he wanted to catch up with Gordy and Frank.'

'What time did you get home then?'

'About four o'clock,' she groaned tiredly.

Evie was trying to be sympathetic but found it hard not to smile as she put an assortment of salad vegetables into the crisper. 'How's Jason this morning?'

'Not the best. As soon as we arrived home he crashed

onto a couch.' Liz leant her head against the back of the chair, closed her eyes then continued on. 'I woke up on the other couch about an hour ago when Kaye phoned. She wanted to know if you, me and Jase wanted to come round for a barbie and a swim.'

'Oh yeah ... that sounds great,' Evie called out, her head still in the fridge. 'I love her pool.'

'Yeah, that's what I said.' Liz slowly stood up and, after steadying herself, made her way into the kitchen. 'Come on then, get whatever you need to take, Jase will be back in a minute, he just went to pick up Simon – they're back together again.' Then, gradually focusing on Evie's face properly, she said, 'What have you been up to? I haven't seen that look on your face for a while.'

'What look?' Evie asked with simulated innocence, her chores now completed.

'A look like you've just seen a gorgeous man,' Liz grinned. 'Come on, tell mama.'

Evie laughed and said, 'I'll tell you all about it later. Come on, I can hear Jason tooting his horn.'

'Why does that conjure up such a lewd image in my mind?' Liz grinned.

They were both still laughing while Evie grabbed what she needed for a day by the pool and they headed out the door.

Chapter Twenty-Three

Having finished his breakfast and cleaned up most of the mess he'd made in the process, Dash decided to leave the dishes to soak in the sink for a while. It had taken him longer than expected to find all the grocery items he needed; even longer to get through the checkout process. Now he just wanted to take it easy for a while, so headed out to his balcony with a steaming cup of tea. Thoughts of the woman who'd smiled at him in the supermarket had stirred something up in him, and he now had a pensive expression on his face.

'I'm probably just feeling horny, it's been ages since I've had a root,' he thought to himself. But he knew it was more than that; he just couldn't put a finger on what it was yet. Not many women caught his attention, and he thought it was strange to feel the way he did about a woman he'd never even spoken to. Trying to work it out, her image invaded his thoughts again, and this time her smile unexpectedly triggered a memory of his ex-wife. It had been *her* smile that had first caught his attention all those years ago.

He'd been nineteen, two years younger than Trish when they'd married. Trish was over the moon at the prospect of having a baby in six months' time. Her parents had been quite well off and had bought most of the necessary nursery equipment for them, which had been just as well because neither of them had been earning much at the time.

Not long after their daughter's first birthday, Dash had come home from work one day to an eerily quiet house. Finding the letter that Trish had left for him explaining how she needed to fulfil her dream of living as a hippy in a commune, Dash had been stunned. She'd often talked about it but he'd never taken that much notice as she'd always been coming up with some crazy idea or another. Trish had insisted on calling their baby Marley, after Bob Marley, because reggae was her favourite music, and Dash had found out later, after finally tracking them down at a commune near Byron Bay, that she'd changed her own name to Summer Rain.

Marley had been nearly two years old by then – running around half naked with the other commune kids; coloured beads decorating her hair. He'd picked her out straight away. She had his thick, dark hair, stocky body and a very determined look on her face. Marley didn't remember him, which had hurt Dash more than he'd thought possible, but she was such a lively, friendly child it hadn't taken long for her to squeal in delight at his playful antics.

Trish was happily living with a bearded, long-haired guy going by the name of Mr. Wizard. Dash nearly choked trying not to laugh when they were first introduced. Realising how much Trish had morphed into her happy hippy identity he no longer felt the same attraction as before, which had surprised him. He'd been ready to smash anyone she'd been sleeping with before he arrived there.

Mr. Wizard, though, was a gentle, laid-back bloke, into carving beautiful sculptures out of fallen tree branches, which he then sold for good prices at the local markets. He and Dash had chatted for a while, then Dash took Trish aside and spoke to her alone and at length. They both honestly told each other how they felt, resulting in Dash leaving by himself.

Before he left though, he'd spent nearly two hours playing with the mini image of himself, knowing it would be a while before he'd be able to come back again. Seeing how carefree and happy the boisterous little toddler was living in the small, close community, he'd finally been freed from the anxiety he'd felt since Trish had wrenched her from his life.

Working fifty-six hours a week or more, and living in mining camps and pubs, he'd had no way of looking after

Marley himself so had decided it was best for her to stay where she was. After getting Trish's bank account details so he could deposit child support money, Dash drove off not knowing then that it would be nearly two years before he'd see his daughter again.

Soon after, he moved to Western Australia and got work at a gold mining site near Kalgoorlie. He tried his best to get on with his life. Trish had never had a phone and Dash had never been into writing letters, so when he showed up the following Christmas with presents for Marley he found out then that she, Trish and Mr. Wizard had all moved on. No one in the commune seemed to know exactly where they'd gone, just saying that they'd moved north somewhere.

It had taken him six months to find out where they were living, and that was only thanks to his mate Ron who worked at Centrelink. Ron had owed Dash a big favour from ten years back when Dash had stepped in and saved him from getting a solid biffing from the two McFadden brothers. Because of work commitments though, it'd been another six months before Dash had been able to travel to the hinterland of Cairns to see Marley again; but again, she didn't remember him. Dash emphasised to Trish that she had to let him know if she planned to move somewhere else in the future. She'd agreed, but the same thing happened eighteen months later then several more times after that. This resulted in Dash only seeing his daughter about six times by the time she'd turned sixteen, at which stage she'd taken off to Sydney with some wannabe rock singer. He'd only caught up with her once since then and that was for her eighteenth birthday.

She'd been living with an art professor in a small flat in Coolangatta, and Dash had been travelling north to the Gove Peninsula where he'd secured work at the bauxite mine. Luckily finding out where she'd been living from Trish's parents, who'd only occasionally shown an interest in Marley, Dash had then surprised her by showing up unannounced the day before her birthday. He'd had to fly out again later that night so they hadn't had as much time together as he would have liked.

Remembering the look on her face when he'd given her an opal he'd found in Coober Pedy as a birthday present, his face smiled slightly; but it was a smile tinged with sadness. 'Hard to believe she's nearly twenty-six now,' he thought as he finished off his now cold cuppa.

It had wounded Dash deeply that he'd not been able to be a proper father to Marley. When he was young he'd watched and remembered how some of his mates had lived with fun and laughter as well as guidance and discipline from their parents. Back then he'd confidently looked forward to one day having the same type of family, not knowing then that just ten years later he'd feel that he'd failed at marriage and fatherhood. He'd tried to bury that feeling of failure by making sure he succeeded at everything else that he chose to put his mind to.

Being able to operate a crane was one of the things he'd always wanted to master. He'd loved watching them as a kid whenever he saw them working on a construction site, and had promised himself that one day he'd be able to operate them too. Now he held his open ticket, allowing him to operate the real big buggers, and he loved it.

The thought of Marley wanting to contact him had thrown him a bit; he wasn't sure if he felt excited or apprehensive.

'Oh well. No point worrying about it,' he thought. 'She may not even ring.' Sighing, Dash stood up and wandered back inside; checking what time it was as he put his empty cup into the sink of sudsy water.

'Hmm ... quarter to twelve already, I'd better get my arse into gear.'

Quickly washing the dishes he was then ready to head off to Ocean Grove. Tommo had invited him and a few other blokes from work to come around for a barbeque and, because they all had a rostered day off tomorrow, he and a couple of others decided they'd stay overnight. That way they could have a few beers and not worry about having to drive home.

Chapter Twenty-Four

After waking late the next day with varying degrees of hangover symptoms, Dash and the others had another cook-up on the barbeque for breakfast, all feeling much better for it afterwards. Dash then left them to it, not wanting to spend the whole day drinking again, and drove back into the city looking for the bedding store that he'd recently seen advertised.

'Can it be delivered today?'

'Yeah, no worries,' the salesman replied 'Where do you live?'

After Dash gave the salesman his address, he was informed that it could go on the next truck.

'We can drop it off first ... we'll be there in about twenty minutes.'

'Yep, that sounds good,' Dash grinned, having one more look at the comfy queen size bed before handing over the cash.

Smiling in anticipation of a great night's sleep as he walked up the last couple of steps to his flat, Dash didn't notice that his next door neighbour was sitting out on her balcony ... until she spoke.

'G'day, you must be Dash.'

Dash stopped and turned, startled by the unexpected comment. The security door separating their balconies was still propped open so the first thing he saw was that gorgeous smile again. His mind went blank as he took in her sudden appearance; he actually just stood there for a couple of seconds before he managed to say, 'Oh ... yeah ... g'day ... and you must be Evie.'

'That's right, nice to meet you,' she replied, standing up and extending her hand for a handshake.

Chapter Twenty-Five

Marley was still in two minds, but she was here now so reasoned that she may as well see where it would lead. Sighing, she took her daughter's hand and looked for a taxi.

'Come on Bluey, we'll go and see the Scienceworks show next. That should be good, shouldn't it?'

'Yes,' a small, excited voice replied. 'And we're going to see the Plantatarium too, aren't we Mummy?'

'It's called a Plan-et-arium, Blue.' Marley sounded the tricky word out for her inquisitive offspring. 'And, yes, we'll go there as well.'

'How long will it take to get there? Are we going to get a taxi? I like it when we go in a taxi.'

'I'm not sure, yes, and me too.'

'Oh, Mummy, you're being silly.'

'Well, ask one question at a time.'

'Okay ... I'll try ... oh look Mummy,' Bluey said, excitedly pointing her finger. 'There's a taxi over there.'

'I'd better ring him, I suppose,' Marley decided, absentmindedly looking out the taxi's window. 'I can't just rock up later, unannounced.' Turning to look at Bluey, Marley smiled when she saw her daughter was completely transfixed by the sight of the tall skyscrapers. Taking a deep breath she nodded slightly, having decided she'd make the phone call as soon as they arrived at their next destination.

Chapter Twenty-Six

After Evie explained how she'd recognised him at the supermarket the previous day, Dash then understood why she'd smiled and waved at him. Although feeling slightly disappointed to realise that it hadn't been because she fancied him, he was smiling as he said, 'Thanks for lending me your CD player. I'll buy myself a new one when I have the time.'

'That's okay,' replied Evie. 'There's no rush. Umm, would you like a beer?'

'Yeah, that'd be great. Thanks.'

As Evie went inside to get a couple of coldies out of the fridge, Dash's phone rang. Hurrying inside to answer it, still a little bit stunned, he spoke cheerfully. 'Hello.'

'Hello ... Dad?'

Dash's mind went blank again for a second before he

realised who it was. 'Marley?'

'Yep, it's me. I got your phone number and address off Uncle Laurie the other day. I hope that's okay.'

'Of course. How are you ... *where* are you?'

'Well, I'm actually in Melbourne and I hate to put it on you like this, but I was wondering if I might be able to stay with you for a couple of days. I know it's really short notice and if you can't, well, that's okay,' Marley stopped for breath.

'Of course you can stay here, it'll be great to see you; it's been ages. When do you think you'll get here?'

'Thanks. I'll be there in a couple of hours.' She paused nervously then added, 'I have bit of a surprise for you too.'

'Oh yeah, and what's that?'

'Well, if I tell you now it won't be a surprise, will it?'

'Hmm ... alright then, I'll wait,' Dash said, puzzled but smiling.

'See you soon then.'

'Okay, see you soon.'

Dash hung up the phone, a bemused expression on his face as he wandered outside again just as Evie returned with two chilled stubbies; snug in their rubber holders.

Passing one over to him she said, 'Cheers', slightly raising her stubbie towards Dash.

'Cheers,' Dash echoed, doing the same. After demolishing a good part of the amber liquid, he took a deep breath and tried to relax. Consciously putting all thoughts of

Marley to the back of his mind, he once again turned his attention to Evie.

'You've got a great balcony here, much bigger than mine,' Dash said, running his eye over her assortment of furniture and plants.

'Yeah, it is great isn't it? I spend a lot of time out here; as much as possible actually.'

They were standing side by side against the railing, looking out across the tranquil bay, and Dash was experiencing a combination of schoolboy excitement and a feeling of being really comfortable with this interesting woman.

'So where are you from Dash? Anywhere around here?'

'No mate, I'm originally from Tassie, but I've pretty much been most places. First time in Geelong though.' Grinning at her he then said, 'If I'd known the place had such lovely attractions I would have been here sooner.'

Evie couldn't help but grin at his flirting, but before she could respond the distinctive sound of a large truck pulling up abruptly out the front of the flats caught their attention.

'Oh ... my new bed's here already,' Dash said surprised. 'Damn, look ... I'm going to have to see if they can deliver another one straight away. I've just found out my daughter's coming to stay for a while. How about I catch up with you later? We can have another beer then – my shout.'

'Okay,' smiled Evie. 'I'll see you later then.'

Chapter Twenty-Seven

'Hmm ...' Evie was still smiling slightly. 'He's got a nice voice too.' Frowning a little as she watched him talking to the delivery men, Evie was wondering what it was about this guy that had captured her interest so much. She'd met a plethora of men over the years, but this was the first time that she'd felt this strange, different sort of feeling inside, and it was a bit unsettling.

She all at once became aware that she must have been staring because Dash turned his head and looked back up towards her, smiling as he did so. Smiling back, she felt that weird feeling inside again. She wandered back into her flat and stopped just inside the front door.

'Hmm ... I'm not sure what's going on ... he's definitely nice looking...' Evie was pondering and grinning at the same time.

'Actually ... I reckon he's rather gorgeous ... I love his smile ... and that cheeky look he's got.' Head to one side, she sighed. 'Oh well ... no doubt he's already spoken for, knowing my luck.'

But a niggling thought of him continued to stalk her as she surveyed the contents of her fridge. Deciding that she'd better eat something, as she'd woken late and had only had a cup of tea so far, she was reaching for the eggs when the phone rang.

'Hello.'

'Hi Evie, just me,' Liz spoke in a rush. 'Do you want to go and see Thelma and Louise at the pictures? I haven't eaten yet and I am a bit hungry but we have about forty-five minutes before it starts. What do you think?'

'Hi Lizzy, well, we'll have to eat first whatever we do because I'm hungry too. I was just going to cook some eggs. What would you prefer; scrambled or poached?'

'Ooh ... scrambled please. I love your scrambled eggs. I'll be there in ten minutes then, okay?'

'Okay. Where are you now then?'

'I'm just about to leave Ingrid's place. I finally remembered that was where I'd left my sunglasses so I drove in to pick them up. She's been raving on about the movie for the last half an hour, saying how much she and Robyn and the others all loved it. So, as I've got the day off I thought we may as well check it out; you're not busy doing a chart, are you?'

'Well, I've got one started but I don't have to have it finished 'til Wednesday. So as long as I get back into it later tonight I'll be okay.'

'Good, that way we can see the movie and I can get an early night tonight – by God I need one. I'm definitely not as young as I used to be.'

'Okay, so hang up the phone before you get any older and get yourself around here. I'm going to start the eggs.'

Chapter Twenty-Eight

'Right … that's my bed done,' Dash exhaled. He stood there for a few seconds admiring his new purchase until Evie's smile materialised in his mind again. 'What is it with that woman?' he asked himself. 'I can't seem to get her out of my head.' Smiling, he had to admit that she *was* good looking, and in an interesting way too, not like the over-made up women that he often came across in his travels. 'Hmm … there's a very good chance that she's already spoken for though,' he sighed as he walked over and opened up the other bedroom door.

He'd rung the guy at the bedding shop who'd been only too happy to sell him another queen size bed; he'd even thrown in a couple of pillows and a doona set. Hearing footsteps coming up the stairs, Dash thought he'd better check and see if it was the delivery guy with the other bed already.

'One of the beauties of living so close to the city,' he was thinking as he stepped out onto his balcony, only to literally bump into an attractive-looking blond woman. 'Oh, sorry love, I thought it was my bed being delivered,' Dash said in surprise, stepping backwards to remove his chest from her ample breasts.

'Oh, is that right?' she grinned, her blue eyes looking Dash up and down appreciatively. 'I'll tell you what, I'm built for comfort, so if it doesn't show up let me know – I'll be next door.' With that she gave him a wink, turned around and walked in Evie's door.

Dash just stood there for a moment, a huge grin on his face. 'Cheeky bugger,' he thought as he turned and went back inside to the fridge. Still smiling, he twisted the lid off a beer then stretched out in one of the old armchairs, resting his feet on a small coffee table he'd found in his garage. His usually animated face looked preoccupied as he tried to make sense of his jumbled thoughts, ultimately causing a frown to appear on his forehead.

'I've got to stop thinking about Evie, that's the problem,' he sighed, unconsciously shaking his head as if to clear it. 'Marley will be here soon and I still don't know what to make of *that*.'

He'd just finished his beer when he heard the distinctive sound of the old delivery truck pulling up out the front again.

'Yep, that's about got it ... a bit more to the right...' Dash was helping the delivery guys to manoeuvre the large mattress through the front door when he heard Evie coming out of her flat. His head turned in her direction without warning, and he was immediately hit with that smile again.

'Dash ... I'd like you to meet a good friend of mine, Liz ... Liz, this is Dash.'

Dash extended his hand, grinned and replied, 'Yeah ... we bumped into each other before ... g'day Liz.'

'G'day yourself, I see the bed arrived ... so ... I may as well get going,' she smiled back.

'Liz, you're a shocker,' Evie said shaking her head. 'Come on or we'll miss the start of the movie. I'll see you later,' she smiled at Dash as she ushered Liz down the stairs.

'Okay.'

'Bye Dash.'

'Bye Liz.' He'd been a little disappointed to see Evie go. 'Oh well, not to worry. At least I know where she lives now,' he grinned.

Marley's bed was now all set up. Dash pushed the second pillow into its tight case and sat it next to its twin at the head of the bed. Happy with how it all looked he turned and headed for the kitchen. Checking the time, he then wandered out to the balcony and leant against the rail for a while. Thinking that it was a view that you wouldn't get sick of in a hurry, he was trying, unsuccessfully, to take his mind off the imminent arrival of the daughter he hardly knew.

176

Chapter Twenty-Nine

'Are we nearly there, Mummy? You said it wouldn't be very long a *long* time ago so we must be nearly there by *now*.'

'Yes Bluey, we're nearly there.'

The drive from Melbourne to Geelong had been a bit boring. Once they'd left the built-up area the scenery had mainly consisted of paddocks full of dried-out grass. Bluey had been reading a book on solar systems that Marley had bought at the Planetarium when she'd suddenly spotted some mountains in the distance, through the trees lining the highway.

'Look at the little mountains, Mummy. Is that where Poppy lives?'

'No Bluey, Poppy lives in a city.'

'Oh ... does anybody live on the mountains?'

'I don't know.'

It was then that the amused taxi driver explained that the mountain range was called the You Yangs, and that nobody lived there.

'It's a great place for a day out and a barbeque though,' he'd said. 'And you can walk right up to the top if you want. You might even see some koalas and kangaroos.'

That, of course, had set off another barrage of questions from her quizzical daughter. Luckily for Marley the taxi driver had been happy to answer Bluey's never-ending queries, allowing her some time to mull over her decision to track down her father.

Unconsciously playing with a beautiful, iridescent opal hanging on a chain around her neck, she became aware of her reflection in the car's window. Smiling, she remembered the day that her dad had surprised her with a visit on one of her birthdays, giving her the opal as a present. She sighed then as she realised that it was the last time she'd seen him. It was partly her own fault, she knew, as she'd been so caught up in her own life for the past several years; but mainly she blamed her mother.

The constant moving from one part of the country to another had been fun when she'd been young, but as a teenager she'd rapidly become sick of it. She shook her head as she remembered the night, nearly ten years ago now, that she ran off to Sydney with Angus – her one and only bag stashed under his guitar in the back of his Kombi. They'd only been together for a few months when he'd left for a gig in Perth, leaving her heartbroken, and the use of his grungy little flat.

After she'd moved to Brisbane with a couple of girlfriends she'd enjoyed having several boyfriends, none of which had lasted very long though. But when she'd met Mitch at an art exhibition she'd thought she'd found true love at last. He was a very charismatic art professor, twice her age, and she'd lived with him for twelve months before the age difference proved to be their downfall.

It had been her on-again off-again relationship with Declan though, plus her unplanned pregnancy, then his obvious indifference towards their daughter, which had initially caused Marley to re-evaluate her life. Then a few years after that, Declan's callous rejection after her surgery had been the incentive she'd needed to leave him for good and to find her father. She hadn't realised how much she'd been craving to be part of a family until then. As Bluey's laughter broke into her thoughts she smiled again, knowing that the only good thing to have come out of that turbulent time had been her precious and precocious little daughter.

'I hope it works out with Dad,' she said softly to herself. 'I want to finally get to know him, and I'd love for Blue to have a grandfather in her life.'

They'd entered the outskirts of Geelong about fifteen minutes ago and were now driving over an overpass, Corio

Bay visible on their left.

'Look over that way Bluey,' Marley said, pointing out the window. 'You can see the sea.'

'Ooh, yes. Can we go to the beach later?'

'Not today, but yes, we'll go the beach while we're here.'

'Can we …'

'Shush for a minute Blue. Look at that street sign.' Marley pointed to the right. 'That says Skene Street, where Poppy lives.'

The taxi did a U-turn at the next set of lights, then shortly after turned left, slowed down, and pulled up opposite number 6, which was a two-storey block of flats. Marley paid her fare, and as she waited for her change she couldn't help glancing out the window to admire the colourful gardens.

After helping the youngster out of her seat belt and onto the footpath, Marley retrieved the couple of bags she'd put in the taxi's boot. Then, looking up towards the flats, she immediately saw her father. He was standing at a balcony on the first floor, looking down at where she and her daughter stood.

Chapter Thirty

'Is that Marley?' Dash thought, looking down towards the young woman. 'It is,' he realised. 'But she looks so different. I've never seen her with such short hair ... and who's that little kid I wonder?'

He walked down the stairs to greet her and was then nearly knocked off his feet when the little girl ran straight at him and grabbed him around his legs.

'Hello Poppy' she giggled. 'You don't know me, do you?' She looked up at him and said, 'My name's Bluey and we've come to stay with you for a while.'

Dash couldn't help smiling at the exuberance of the little girl, and also at her hair. It was a gorgeous, curly red but was chopped of in chunks and stood out at all angles ... then he realised that she'd just called him *Poppy.*

Marley saw the questioning expression on his face and

nodded, saying, 'Hi Dad ... yes ... Bluey's your granddaughter.'

Fifteen minutes later, after hugs and hellos, Dash and Marley were at the kitchen table having a coffee – Bluey quietly sitting in an armchair drinking a can of lemonade that Marley had brought along. There was a children's show on the TV and the little girl was happy to sit and watch it.

'Well ...' Dash started then stopped. 'Well, you did say you had a surprise for me, but I never thought it would be a grandchild.'

Marley smiled an apologetic look at him and said, 'Yeah, sorry Dad. I should have let you know a long time ago, but ... different things were happening at the time and ... it took a while to sort out.'

'That's okay, that's the way things go sometimes. Is everything alright now?'

'Well ... yes and no.'

'Hmm ... okay then, tell me the worst of it.'

Pausing slightly, she then replied, 'I've had breast cancer.'

There was an interminably long two seconds of silence, then Dash stood up and walked to where she sat, carefully pulled her up and gave her a huge, tight hug. 'Oh Marley,' he gently said. 'When did this happen?'

'January last year,' her voice sounded slightly muffled by Dash's shirt front. 'I've finished chemo now though ... thank goodness.'

'So that's what's happened to her long hair,' he thought as he slowly stroked the back of her head.

'I basically have to wait and see now,' she continued. 'I saw one specialist this morning and I'm booked in to see another one in Melbourne again next week.'

'What have the doctors had to say?' Dash asked, then held his breath.

'They're optimistic that they got it all.'

Exhaling, Dash felt his body relax a little. But unable to speak he just held her.

'Poppy, could I have another drink please?'

Dash gave Marley another tight hug. Then, looking her straight in her eyes whispered, 'Don't you worry about anything now, okay?' Raising his voice a little he said, 'Of course you can Bluey. What about you Marley, would you like another coffee, or a beer?'

'Oh ... I think I'll have a beer then. Are you having one?'

Grinning, he answered, 'Do bears shit in the woods?'

'Poppy, you're not supposed to say that word,' Bluey exclaimed from the lounge room.

'What, *bears*?' he said, grinning at her as she came into the kitchen.

Bluey's concerned expression immediately turned to giggles. 'No, not bears,' she laughed. 'You're being silly.'

'Blue...' Marley gave her daughter a look that said: don't

call your grandfather silly.

Dash picked up on it straight away. Laughing himself, he said, 'I was being silly, wasn't I? Come on, you can help me get the drinks.'

Later that night, after Bluey had fallen asleep on one side of Marley's new bed, father and daughter were finally able to sit and talk properly.

'You've got a lovely place here; great view.'

'Yeah, I was just lucky on the day.' After bit of a pause Dash then asked, 'I hope you know you can stay here as long as you like, both of you I mean, but I was just wondering what your plans were if you have any?'

'Thanks Dad, that means more to me than you know. Well, my main plan was to catch up with you. Mum's been hopeless as usual and Gran and Grandpa are too busy with their social life to worry much about me. They gave me ten thousand dollars and said to let them know if they could do anything, then they left for a three-month holiday in the Mediterranean. The money *has* come in handy though. Just being able to afford to get a taxi to here was a bonus, and Bluey loved it,' she smiled.

Dash's grin was followed by another questioning look. 'Is Bluey her real name or is it a nickname because of her red hair?'

This time it was Marley's turn to grin. 'No, it's her real name. When she was born and Mum saw her hair she wanted me to call her Ginger, Ruby or Scarlett, but me being me I did the opposite. I'd been so annoyed with Mum for so long that I just said, 'No, I'm going to call her Bluey.'

Dash smiled at the image in his mind and then at Marley, thinking how much he liked her. He still found it hard to believe that she was here, all grown up. 'Um ... I don't want to say the wrong thing ... but what's with Bluey's hair?'

Marley laughed for the first time that day. 'I know, it looks shocking doesn't it? She cut it herself this morning, wanting to look like I did when I'd lost my hair. I'll take her to the hairdresser tomorrow and get it fixed up.'

They both had a laugh at the things kids do sometimes, then Dash queried, 'Is her father still in the picture?'

'No, not anymore.'

'Do you want to talk about it?'

'There's not much to talk about.'

'He didn't hit you or anything like that, did he?' Dash quietly demanded.

'No, no, nothing like that.' Gazing straight ahead for a moment she then took a deep breath before replying. 'He left me because he couldn't handle looking at my operation scar.'

Fuming at the shallowness of the man, Dash scowled. '*Bastard*, what sort of a bloke does that?'

'Yeah ... I was a bit slow on the uptake to see what he was really like ... it only kicked in after I'd had Bluey. But ... I've learnt some big lessons from it ... one being that no matter how great a person might *look,* it can never compare to having a great character. If you haven't got that you haven't got anything.'

Chuckling, Dash agreed. 'Yeah ... I'd hate to have had to rely on *my* looks to get ahead in life.'

'Oh Dad, there's nothing wrong with your looks ... you've got that rugged, manly look that a lot of women love.'

'Oh yeah,' he grinned. 'I have to beat them away with a stick.'

They laughed, had another beer and sat and talked for another hour. Marley then decided to have a shower and hit the hay after her long day. Both had shared quite a few funny anecdotes, but neither had touched on the subject of their long estrangement. That could wait for another time, although it didn't seem important to either of them now.

Chapter Thirty-One

Standing opposite the kitchen window drinking his coffee, Dash was closely gauging the early morning sky, wondering if it was going to rain later or not. An unexpected ringing right next to him startled him back to the here and now. His hand quickly reached for the phone, hoping the shrill ringing wouldn't wake up Marley or Bluey. Wondering who'd be calling at this time he put the phone to his ear.

'Hello.'

'G'day mate, how're things going?'

'G'day Bob, you old degenerate. Yeah, I'm good mate, what about you?'

'Good mate, good. Hey, are you working yet?'

'Yeah mate. I got a start last Friday. I'm about to head off shortly.'

'Bugger, I need another good crane driver for this Port

Hedland job.' Pausing to have bit of a chuckle he went on, 'I couldn't get a good one so I thought I'd ring you … where are you anyway?'

Dash was grinning as he replied, 'Geelong mate.'

'*Geelong* … Nev said you were heading over *this* way.'

'Yeah, I had been thinking of doing that before I rang Enzo. '

'What's that blue-eyed bastard been up to this time?'

Dash then relayed the phone call he'd received from Enzo, as well as a brief rundown of his overnight stay.

'Bloody oath I know he can drink,' Bob was agreeing with Dash. 'I made the mistake of going shout-for-shout with him one night in the Rex Hotel in bloody Port Melbourne. I ended up flaking out while he went on and chatted up all the chicks. Anyway, what's this new job of yours about?'

'It's a big extension on a retirement village. I finished putting the air-conditioner in your room yesterday.'

'Ha, ha, very funny; who's got the contract anyway?'

'Condor Constructions; I ended up having to see a bloke called Tom Connors – didn't seem like a bad sort of a bloke.'

'Connie, yeah I know Connie. He's not a bad bloke. Hits the piss a bit though, or he used to.'

'Is that so?'

'Yeah, I worked with him years ago at Karratha. I mean, just about everybody hits the piss up there but he used to wipe himself out, either that or he'd end up in a blue with someone. He can fight, the little bastard, I'll give him that.'

'Well, I'd better not cross him then,' Dash grinned. 'Where are you anyway, still in Perth?'

'Yeah mate, still here. There's a bit of work happening so I'll be here for a while I'd say. Hey, guess what I've just bought?'

'I dunno. What?'

'One of those new mobile phones, they call it a 'brick' because of its shape. I'm on it now out in the ute … not bad, hey?'

'A brick … hmm … that's a coincidence.'

'A coincidence, why's that?'

Dash couldn't help chuckling before replying, 'Well it matches your IQ mate.'

'Oh, very funny, you're just full of it today, aren't ya? I don't know why I bloody bother with you sometimes. But I tell you what mate; it's a handy bloody thing. I reckon everybody will have one, one of these days. It'd be good if they could make 'em a bit smaller though … and before you say any more about my IQ, tell me how the new job's going?'

'It's been good so far mate. I've been doing a bit of rigging as well as operating the Franna, but today I'm on the 100 tonner again because All Bran's still crook.'

'All Bran?'

'Yeah, All Bran.'

'What, does he gives everybody the shits?'

Dash laughed, 'that's it mate.'

They both had a chuckle then Bob went on. 'Yeah, there's a young bloke over here they've nicknamed Jungle because he's thick, green and dense; it bloody suits him too. But listen, back to the Hedland job, are you interested or are you happy where you are? '

'Hmm ... I probably would've been except Marley's staying with me for a while.' He quickly filled his long-time mate in with the basic details of Marley's visit.

'Gee, mate, that's no good. Give her my love. I haven't seen her since that time we tracked Trish and her down in Cooktown.'

'Yeah, it was her tenth birthday. Hey, guess what? I'm a grandfather.'

'That's great mate.'

'I'll tell you what it was a bit of a surprise, but she's a great little kid. I'm not too sure yet how long they'll be staying though – not that it's a problem – but I want to spend as much time with them as I can.'

'No worries mate, I can understand that. Do you know anyone else who might be interested?'

'Well, you could give Enzo a call, he's in Tassie at the moment but knowing him he'll be ready to escape again by now.'

'Okay, I'll give him a bell.'

After a bit more chat Bob asked, 'So have you found

yourself a woman yet, or what?'

'Well ... no ... but there is someone I'm going to ask out, if she's not already spoken for that is.'

'Good, I hope it works out. It's about time you were as miserable as us married bastards.' Bob was laughing as he hung up his phone.

Chapter Thirty-Two

Evie had been busy working on the chart for Rita Richardson's house all morning. Basically finished now, all she had to do was write down her recommendations and she'd be ready to take it back tomorrow as arranged.

It had taken a lot of study and determination on her part to master the specifics of preparing a Flying Stars Feng Shui chart, but Evie had been fascinated by it all. The environmental features surrounding a house were of vital importance, as their size and location could either enhance or detract from the flow of energy which was all around. Tall buildings, trees or hills behind a house indicated support for the family; whereas if these features were directly in front of the house they could overshadow and restrict fresh energy from entering the property. She'd also been intrigued to learn how this rule was reversed under certain conditions.

Her extensive calculations had shown that the Richardson's decision to position their office at the rear of the house hadn't necessarily been the best one. The Stars in that area were completely unsuitable for that purpose – the energy being more conducive for sleep – so she was advising them to convert one of the unused front bedrooms into an office instead.

Among other things, she'd recommended they place a water feature, such as a fountain or a fishpond, in their front yard; she'd just finished highlighting the area where it should go. As water represents money in Feng Shui, a water feature positioned in the wrong place could stimulate negative energy, making financial matters worse. Opposite the diagram she wrote quickly, explaining that the water must always be kept clean and moving as stagnant water will produce an unfavourable energy; dulling their finances further.

Suddenly becoming aware that someone was watching her, she turned her head to the left to see through the lounge window, then laughed in surprise to see a little red-headed girl standing there with her face squished up against the glass. The cheeky face then pulled back a bit and grinned straight at her.

'Looks like someone's got visitors,' Evie thought, smiling back, 'I wonder if she's supposed to be off on her own though. Hmm ... I think I'd better go and see where she's come from.'

Opening her door she was immediately confronted with, 'Hello, my name's Bluey, what's yours?'

'Hello Bluey, my name's Evie. Where have you come from?'

'Well ... I came on a plane from Tasmania ... and ... before that I was visiting my great grandma and great grandpa – they live on the Gold Coast but there isn't any gold there ...' she stopped for breath. 'And before that ...'

'Whoa,' Evie said, still smiling. 'I was wondering who you're visiting today.'

'Poppy.'

'Oh ... Poppy, and where does Poppy live?'

'Well, right there silly,' she said, pointing to the adjoining flat. Then quickly covering her mouth she looked up at Evie. 'Sorry,' she said after removing her hand. 'Mummy says it's rude to call big people silly.'

Evie couldn't stop smiling at the little red-headed girl. 'Where is Mummy?'

'She's having a cup of tea; we just came back from the hairdressers. Do you like my hair? Mummy said it looked like a dog's breakfast before.'

Big brown eyes were looking up at her expectantly as Evie replied, 'Yes I do; it looks lovely.' She then had trouble trying not to laugh, watching as Blue's earnest expression quickly switched to one of wonder.

'Oh ... guess what I saw today?' the little girl questioned.

Just then a woman who could only be Dash's daughter appeared from the adjoining flat. 'Bluey, what are you doing? You're not annoying people, are you?'

'No Mummy, I'm just talking to Evie.'

Still grinning, Evie held out her hand. 'Hi, I'm Evie.'

Marley shook her hand warmly. 'Hi, I'm Marley. I see you've already met Bluey. I hope she hasn't been bothering you.'

'No not at all. So you're staying next door for a while are you?'

'Yes, with my Dad. I'm not sure how long we'll be here though.'

Evie's phone rang then so she excused herself to go and answer it.

'Come on Blue, you have to get your togs, hat and sunglasses on if we're going for a walk to the waterfront. You'll be able to have a swim and a play in the sand then.'

'Can we get a taxi?'

'No, we're going to walk. It's not too far. Maybe we'll get one when it's time to come back again.'

When Evie finished her phone call she went back outside in time to see Marley and Bluey walking down the stairs. 'Drop in sometime for a coffee if you like,' she called out.

'Okay,' piped up the cheeky youngster.

Both Evie and Marley laughed. 'Thanks,' replied Marley.

'That'd be great. We'll see you later then.'

Evie was smiling as she wandered back inside. Sitting back at her desk she was thinking about Dash having a daughter *and* a granddaughter – he hadn't mentioned that.

'That Bluey's a little character,' she chuckled. 'She must keep Marley on her toes.' Shaking off the images that sneakily tried to surface in her mind of what her own daughter might have looked like, Evie then put all her focus on completing the chart for delivery tomorrow morning.

Chapter Thirty-Three

Dash was still smiling when his dogman, Rick, gave him the whistle to boom up. He'd been watching the boys rigging the load and it looked good to him. Thinking how much easier and enjoyable life was, working with a good crew, his eyes watched the load while his hands operated the levers automatically. The crane's boom effortlessly lifted the massive air-conditioning unit up and up. After a couple of minutes he couldn't see the load anymore, so relying on instructions from Rick on the two-way he slewed smoothly to the left, and then down, ultimately placing it exactly in the right position.

'Good one Dash,' crackled Rick's voice over the two-way.

'Thanks Rick.' Dash was happy to be behind the controls of a crane again. Still smiling, he thought about his decision to ask Evie out for a meal; if she was already seeing someone he'd find out then. 'Nothing ventured, nothing gained,' he thought optimistically, waiting for the riggers to unshackle the lifting gear.

Taking his hard hat off as he entered the crib hut at smoko time, Dash was vaguely aware that some of the blokes were smiling and looking in his direction. But he was starving so most of his attention was on the salad roll that the Peggy had gotten from the shop for him. After he made himself a cup of coffee and sat down, he noticed several of the blokes around the table were trying to keep a straight face as well. Wondering what was going on as he took a bite of his salad roll, their grins soon had him asking, 'Okay, what's going on? What are you bastards laughing at?'

With that everyone cracked up. 'You must have been stressin' this morning mate,' laughed Tommo, 'you're sweatin' grease.'

'What ... oh ... you bastards.' Dash rubbed his forehead then couldn't help grinning. He realised that someone had put a smear of black grease inside the band of his hard hat before he'd put it on. Everyone had a good laugh at his expense but he didn't mind, knowing it was all just good fun. 'Yeah, righto ... but it's my turn next,' he said with a wicked grin before getting stuck into his roll again.

'Hey, Dash,' asked Big Dave. 'Where are you from anyway?'

'Tassie mate.'

'Tassie? Oh … so when did you have your second head removed?' he grinned.

'Just before you had your arse transplanted to your face,' Dash grinned back.

Everyone had a laugh at that – even Big Dave had a grin at Dash's quick comeback.

'Yep, gotta pay that one,' Slim chuckled. 'I thought you were growing a beard, Dave, but now I see it's just arse-crack hair.'

They were still laughing as Robbo started reading out the quiz questions in the Geelong Advertiser – something they did every morning.

'Okay, first question: who invented the telephone?'

'A woman,' called out someone from the back of the hut.

Rick nodded his head in agreement. 'Yeah … my bloody mother-in-law.'

'No, it had to be one of the Ringling brothers, didn't it?' said Big Dave before laughing at his own attempt at humour.

'I think it was Edison,' Kenny said as he got up to make himself another cup of coffee. 'Or was it Einstein?'

'I can see you're no bloody Einstein,' Robbo shook his head. 'No, it was Alexander Graham Bell. Okay, next one … what's the name of the ruthless dictator who's ruled Zimbabwe since 1980?'

'Now, that's definitely my mother-in-law,' sighed Rick, 'she commutes between there and my place all the time.'

Everyone was grinning at Rick's answer before Owen, his mouth half-full of some dubious-looking leftover pizza, mumbled, 'It was Mugabe.'

'Right, give the man a cigar,' Robbo grinned. 'Okay, next one ...'

When Dash arrived home that night he felt good about his day's work; in fact, he was feeling good all round. He was working again, and with a great bunch of blokes; he had his daughter and a granddaughter in his life again; and he was living next door to a gorgeous-looking woman. Smiling to himself as he dropped his old canvas workbag onto the floor just inside the front door, he was thinking about his decision to ask Evie if she'd like to go out for a meal sometime. He'd already noticed that she wasn't home yet so decided to have a cold beer first before jumping under the shower.

Stripping down to his shorts and shirt, he left the rest of his clothes and boots in a pile near the door. Then, putting his hand to his head, he felt a small bit of grease that was still clinging to his hair. Shaking his head and grinning at the same time, his thoughts lingering on the antics and nicknames of some of his crew, Dash walked back out to his small balcony.

Relaxing back in his old deck chair, he positioned his bare feet up on the cool metal of the balcony railing, then took a huge swig from his stubbie. 'Ahh ... yes ... that tastes good.' Smiling, he'd just begun thinking of some good paybacks for the blokes at work when his phone rang. Reluctantly lifting himself up from his comfortable position, he ambled inside with his beer, then removed the insistently ringing instrument from its wall mount.

'Hello.'

'G'day mate. Have you cracked on to that sheila next door yet?'

'G'day Enzo,' Dash grinned. 'Not yet mate, but I'm going to.'

'Yeah, I knew you would you lucky bastard. She's not bad, is she?'

'Yeah, she's not bad at all,' Dash smiled as he sat down again, this time on the nearest kitchen chair. 'So, do you want me to bail you out of jail or lend you a quid?'

'Neither mate,' Enzo chuckled. 'But hold that thought. I'm actually in Perth waiting for a flight to Hedland so I thought I'd ring and say thanks for putting Bob on to me; couldn't have come at a better time.'

'Why, what've you been up to now?' Dash asked, grinning.

'Well, remember that three grand I had?'

'Yeah.'

'It's gone mate. I've got two hundred bucks left and no car.'

'Gee mate, that's pretty good even for you,' chuckled Dash. 'What happened to your car?'

'Paula's got it. She said she was sick of driving the bloody shit heap that she had and wanted a new one. Then this job came up – fly in, fly out – so I said she may as well keep mine. Luckily she was happy with that because I'd already blown most of the money at the races and couldn't have bought another one if me life had depended on it.'

'You dopey bugger, so is it all sweet with the missus again, or what?'

'Yeah ... well ... more or less. I took her to the casino the day after I got back. We stayed there the night and had a ball. Cost me a thousand bucks, not that it worried me, but the next day it was a different story. She bloody got stuck into me for not being home enough to pull the kids into line. Mate, she's driving me nuts; I can't be everywhere and someone's gotta earn the money.'

'Yeah mate, you've got to go where the work is.' Dash could only too well empathise with his work situation. 'How's young Ricky? Did you manage to get him sorted out?'

'Ahh mate ... I dunno. He's bloody fifteen and he bloody thinks he knows bloody everything. He's such a little smartarse sometimes too. I threatened to take him out the back and teach him some manners; luckily he knew that I meant it and he pulled his head in a bit.'

'Oh yeah,' Dash couldn't help chuckling again. 'And I wonder who he inherited the smartarse mouth from? He sounds a bit like you were at fifteen.'

'Thanks mate, just the sort of moral support I need.' Enzo couldn't help laughing a bit himself. 'Yeah ... I was a bit of a bastard of a kid, but getting belted by the old man most nights whenever he was pissed wasn't much fun either. I left home at fifteen to get away from it, remember?' Without waiting for a response he sighed loudly and kept talking. 'And mate, it's not just Ricky ... Danielle's just turned fourteen and I swear it's like living with a banshee – if she doesn't get what she wants it's a nightmare. You should have *seen* what she wanted to wear last Saturday night. Her skirt was just covering her arse and the top she was wearing looked two sizes too small. When I said she wasn't going out dressed like that all hell broke loose. Then I had Paula saying that if I was *home* more the kids wouldn't *be* so unmanageable. I tell you what mate, when I got the phone call from Bob this morning I could have kissed him – I was on the next plane and out of there. Hang on a minute ... another pot thanks mate ... yeah, VB ... I tell you what mate, this beer's going down good, it's bloody hot over here. Hey, when are you going to ask your neighbour out? What was her name – Evie?'

'Yeah mate, Evie. I'm going to ask her tonight. She's not home yet. I'm just about to have a shower and spruce myself up a bit first.'

'Geez, mate, it'll take more than a shower to make you look presentable,' laughed Enzo.

'Yeah, righto, thanks mate.' Dash couldn't help grinning at his long-time friend though. They'd known each other since they were thirteen and had always kept in touch with each other. The most amazing thing was that they were both still alive and kicking after being in several car accidents, pub brawls and fights.

Enzo had rolled his first car when they'd both been pissed and hooning around, the week after he'd got it. Then a month later they'd gotten into an altercation with the Murdoch brothers in the Imperial Hotel, and after doing wheelies showing off in *his* car, Dash had lost control of it and crashed through a fence; narrowly missing a huge Huon pine.

Getting another beer, Dash told Enzo about Marley and Bluey staying with him, and why.

'What, you're a grandfather? You old bastard,' Enzo joked.

'Yeah, she's a great little kid, and Marley's a great mum. I'm really enjoying having them around.'

'Give her my love when you see her later. Are you sure she's okay now?'

'That's what the doctors said.'

'That's great then mate. So how's the job going?'

'Good mate. The money's not as much as they're paying over west, but it's not so bloody hot.' Chuckling a little he told Enzo about the grease in his hard hat that morning.

'I found out it was a bloke they call Show Bag who did it,' Dash grinned.

'Show Bag?'

'Yeah, he looks good on the outside but he's usually just full of shit.'

They both laughed at the funny but apt nickname, then continued to talk about work for another ten minutes or so.

'Okay mate, I'm going to go and have a piss before they call my flight. There's no way I'm going to miss it – I can't afford to.'

'No worries, Enzo. Let me know how the job goes.'

'Yeah mate, and you let me know how you go with Evie. I wouldn't mind chatting her up myself.'

'Too late mate, you had your chance. And I hate to say it but Paula might have something to say about that,' Dash grinned. 'Now why don't you go and have a piss and then piss off, you've got to leave some of the women for someone else you shifty bastard.'

Laughing, Enzo said his goodbyes then hung up. Finishing off his stubbie Dash wandered over and turned on the stereo. He thought it was way too quiet without 'his girls' there; Marley having taken Bluey to explore the zoo, catching a train up to Melbourne this morning. Knowing that they should be back soon, Dash smiled in anticipation of all the things his little granddaughter would have to relay to him. His thoughts then unconsciously returned to Evie. Checking the time on the old wall clock he then headed for the shower, surprised to realise he was feeling a little bit nervous. He was shaking his head as he turned the shower taps on.

'What is it about this woman?' he asked himself once more as he lathered the shampoo into his hair. Before he could try and answer himself he heard Marley and Bluey arrive home.

'Poppy, Poppy ... where are you, Poppy? You'll never guess what I saw today ...'

Chapter Thirty-Four

When Evie woke up in the morning she already had a smile on her face. She'd been dreaming about flying over the Great Barrier Reef then diving beneath the aquamarine surface; exploring all the wonders that were hidden from everyday view. Jumping straight out of bed she headed for the shower, all the time thinking about how Dash had asked her last night if she'd like to go out for a meal sometime. He'd actually seemed a little bit nervous until she smiled and said she'd love to.

After getting dressed and having a quick cup of tea she was in her car and driving to Rita Richardson's place, the completed Feng Shui chart beside her and the smile still on her face.

Forty minutes later she was back in the car and on her way home, pleased that Rita had been amenable to the changes she'd suggested. Deciding to then drop in and visit Hilda, she started happily singing along to the song on the car stereo: 'Baby I'm-a want you ... baby I'm-a need you ... you're the only one I care enough to hurt about ...'

'I'm at my wits end,' Hilda was saying in her soft German accent. 'I just don't know what to do with Willy. He's such a good boy but lately,' she shook her head. 'And now ...'

'What if I take him to the beach?' Evie interjected brightly, standing at the opened front door.

'Oh Evie, would you? You are an angel, he'd love that, I'm sure he would.' Clasping her hands together Hilda just stood there for a moment then sighed, 'But I don't know where he's gone. Oh, I'm being so rude, where are my manners? Come in, come in, sit down. Would you like a cup of tea or a cold drink? I have some cold ...'

'I'd love a cup of tea but I'll make it, and I'll make you one as well. Now you sit down while I put the kettle on,' Evie insisted.

Hilda slowly eased herself down into her favourite chair without complaining, the worn floral design comforting in its familiarity. Her normally smiling, cherubic face was saddened; lines appearing that weren't usually seen. Turning her head she looked at Evie with tears in her eyes.

'I am so worried about him. It's not his fault though, he didn't ask for any of this.'

'Why ... what's happened? What's wrong?'

'He has just found out ... his dad has died ... in that prison riot.'

'Oh no, that's *terrible*...when did you find out?'

'Just this morning ... someone ... from the prison rang ...I didn't know how to tell him ... he knew something was wrong ... when I started to cry ...' She blew her nose on a beautifully embroidered hanky she had clutched in her hand then went on. 'He knew it was something to do with his dad ... and then ... I had to tell him.'

'Oh no,' Evie sighed sympathetically. Sitting down in the matching armchair positioned next to Hilda's, she put her arm around the elderly woman's shoulders. Slowly shaking her head, Evie just sat there for a minute, holding her while she dried her eyes.

'Okay, the first thing for us to do is find William. Have you any idea where he might have gone?' Evie queried.

'No ... he's run off a couple of times now ... but he's never said where he's been.'

'How long has he been gone?'

The distraught woman squinted up at the ornate, Swiss chalet wall clock. 'It was about eight when the phone rang ... so he must have been gone nearly ... two-and-a-half hours. Oh, what are we ... *Willy* ... Oh Willy. I've been so *worried*,' Hilda suddenly exclaimed as the young boy opened the security door.

Thirty minutes later Evie was driving towards Torquay, William sitting silently beside her. He started pressing the buttons on the car stereo, going from one station to the next until he finally stopped on an AC/DC song. Staring out his side window as 'Jailbreak' rocked its way around the car, he then just sat there as if in a trance when it finished. Evie's attempts at conversation were met with a stony silence.

Slowing down as they hit the outskirts of Torquay, they then drove past the huge array of surf shops situated along the highway. Evie glanced at some of the names as they passed by – Quicksilver, Billabong, Roxy, Ripcurl – marvelling at the usual multitude of tourists, no doubt all looking for a bargain.

'Well, we're here,' Evie said a couple of minutes later as she cruised along the beach front. 'There's not too many people here either,' she said as she chose a car parking space in the shade of a large tree. After getting their towels and Evie's bag out of the car, they both instinctively turned towards the magnificent vista.

It was a great day for the beach – thirty degrees but with a slightly cooler breeze coming off the ocean. Two Jet Ski riders were racing each other behind the breaking waves, their machines bouncing and leaping as they powered on towards the rocky curve of the coastline. The first one suddenly swerved left sending a sparkling sheet of water spraying in a wide arc, immediately replicated by the second rider. Swinging back to the right they rounded the jutting outcrop of rocks and were then lost to view.

'Could you give me a hand to lift the esky?' Evie asked William as she opened the car's boot. 'Thanks. I think your oma must have packed enough food and drinks in here for six people.'

Holding the heavy cooler box in one hand each they wandered over the grass and down onto the beautiful sandy beach.

'This'll do ... what do you reckon?' Evie asked as she scanned the beach before dumping everything where they stood.

'Can I go for a swim now?' William abruptly asked.

'Yeah, sure, I'll just sit here for a bit.'

Watching him as he unhurriedly walked straight into the small waves that were leisurely rippling their way over the shoreline, Evie felt a strong protective pull towards him. Remembering how she'd felt after hearing that her dad was dead, she thought that William might want a bit of time to himself. So, opening the esky's lid she grabbed a bottle of orange juice before surveying her surroundings some more.

They had a great spot. A large Norfolk pine was providing some shade as she watched the wide expanse of sand being covered once more by the incoming tide. Sitting down after she'd spread out her towel, she wriggled her bottom from side to side a bit and, using her hand, smoothed out a lumpy bit of sand into a more comfortable shape.

Finally happy with her position, Evie sat slightly hunched over as she hugged her knees and sipped her drink, watching William as he dove through each and every glistening green wave … one after another …over and over … until Dash's smiling face inevitably materialised in her mind again. This automatically produced a smile on her own face as she continued to watch the young boy in his seemingly unstoppable assault on the waves.

Chapter Thirty-Five

William finally blanked out the jumble of thoughts that had been fighting for his attention. Conscious only of the numbing chill every time he dove into a glassy wall of water, then the jade green colour of each wave as he surfaced, he eventually felt the tension leave his body.

Then, turning over, he floated on his back over the small but powerful swells, keeping his eyes closed, feeling himself slowly *become* the wave. It was so peaceful. The rhythmic rolling motion combined with the oddly muffled sound of the ocean in his ears, was thankfully blocking any new thoughts from surfacing in his head.

'What ... arrh ... *shit* ... it's just a bloody piece of seaweed.' He'd instinctively yanked his legs towards him before standing upright again. Scowling at first at the fright he'd received, he then couldn't stop a small grin from creasing his face as he kicked away what had momentarily scared him. Glancing around he saw that he'd drifted down the beach a bit so turned and swam freestyle until he was nearly opposite where Evie was still sitting. Finally out of breath, he body-surfed the next wave up to the shoreline, then lay spread out on his stomach on the wet, sucking sand when the wave receded.

Looking to his left he saw there were quite a few rock pools a little further along the beach. So, after waiting where he was sprawled for the next wave to wash over him – rinsing off some of the sand – he then wandered over in that direction.

'Well, that's that then,' he said to himself. 'He's dead.'

He thought that if he heard the words coming out of his own mouth it might seem more real somehow, but no ... he still had trouble making sense of it.

'Where will I be shipped off to *this* time, I wonder?' he thought to himself, remembering how he'd begun living with his dad after his mum had died of a drug overdose.

She'd always been drugged out on something for as long as he could remember, and had never had him as a priority in her life. At the end of his first exciting day at school he'd run the short distance to the house they'd been sharing with her boyfriend, only to find her lying on the lounge room floor, vomit congealed on her mouth; quite dead.

The boyfriend was nowhere to be seen but a couple of

her druggy girlfriends were there, crying and carrying on. They'd decided in their distorted wisdom to leave his mum there for someone else to find, not wanting any involvement with the cops. Being only six, when they'd told him to pack some clothes into a bag and come and stay with them he'd done just that, living with them for a week before the police tracked him down. The police in turn then tracked down his father, who hadn't been overjoyed to see him but had taken him in and generally tolerated him living there.

Now sitting with his skinny legs dangling in a huge rock pool he sighed, thinking how nice it'd be to live in one place for a while. Staring blankly into the mesmerizing undersea world, he saw little silvery fish dart about like mad insects, taunting the fluttering fingers of the sea anemones, while a crab made hesitant sideways steps out from behind a rock.

A tear hit the surface of the pool causing small ripples to interrupt the stillness. Thoughts of his oma came into focus – she was the only one who cared about him and he knew it. When his dad had been sent to prison last year, Community Services had contacted her to see if she'd be able take him in until his dad got out. She'd agreed straight away, even though she didn't have much room or money.

'Who knows where I'll end up this time,' he said under his breath as he dropped a small, flat piece of rock into the pool, then watched as it rapidly zigzagged its way to the bottom. Hearing the sound of feet scrunching in the sand behind him he turned and saw Evie walking awkwardly towards him; two towels and her bag on one shoulder, the esky weighing her down on the other side.

'Are you hungry yet?' she asked, smiling.

'Yeah, a little bit.'

'Good, we may as well eat here then.'

She spread her towel out between them, then after removing the esky's lid, she retrieved a large plastic container and sat it down with a flourish. Taking the lid off, the selection of scrumptious looking sandwiches and cakes had her mouth watering.

'Your oma's a great cook – I know because she invited me for dinner on the night I moved into the flat upstairs. It was so thoughtful of her,' Evie grinned. 'I was starving by the time I'd unpacked all the main things; I was just going to phone for a pizza.'

The boy silently chose a sandwich then slowly proceeded to eat it. Evie sat with her legs dangling in the water beside him.

'Do you like living with your oma?'

'Yeah, it's alright.'

'I think she's a lovely lady,' Evie said. 'One of the nicest I know.'

They sat like that for a while, each with their own thoughts as they ate their way through the variety of yummy food.

'Do you know what's going to happen to me?' William abruptly asked, looking intently at Evie. 'Do you think my oma would want to keep me?'

'Well … I can't talk for your oma, but we could ask her later when we go back home.'

'Okay,' he replied, deceptively indifferent.

Evie looked straight at him, 'You know what? … I like you and I know you're going through a tough time. I hope you'll feel okay about coming up to my flat any time you want. I bought a new stereo about a month ago and I'm still not sure how to operate it properly. You might be able to check it out for me sometime.'

William had now finished eating and was repetitively dropping pebbles and pieces of broken shells into the shimmering water of the miniature lagoon. After a minute or so he broke the relative silence. 'What sort of stereo is it?'

'It's a Kenwood.'

'Hmm … they're supposed to be good.'

'Yeah well it *would* be good if I could work out what all the buttons and knobs do.'

'Hmm … I might be able to have a look at it sometime.'

'That would be great. Okay, come on then, let's pack this up,' Evie said, indicating the lunch debris. 'We can leave the esky a bit higher up on the sand then check out some more rock pools, they'll be under water again soon. We can always have another swim later if you want to. What do you reckon?'

'Okay.'

'Okay.'

Chapter Thirty-Six

'... then I explained how unused and broken items can accumulate a sluggish energy around them ...'

Dash couldn't help gazing at Evie – she was so animated and completely into the story she was relating to him. They were out on their first date, having taken a taxi to The Great Western, and he was thinking she had the type of face he'd be more than happy looking at for a long time.

'... so once they got rid of all their clutter they were surprised at how much the whole atmosphere of their home improved. Are you listening to me?' she suddenly asked.

'Yeah,' he smiled back; amused that she'd sprung him. 'You were saying something about the whole atmosphere of their home improving.'

'Yeah, it did.' Smiling back at him Evie knew he hadn't been fully listening, but seeing the look in his eyes fully compensated for it.

'Their house also had a reverse chart so they needed a water feature at the rear and a mountain feature at the front. The woman convinced her husband to landscape the front yard using some large boulders and trees, then they added a lovely circular fishpond with a little waterfall in their backyard. That, plus getting rid of all their junk made all the difference. She said she was going to tell all her friends about me.'

'That's good,' Dash said putting his pot of beer back on the table, 'word-of-mouth is always the best advertising.'

'I know; I had two messages on my answering machine this morning – one for a consultation in Highton tomorrow and another one in Portarlington next week. I rang them straight back to let them know what time I'd be there but had to leave a message both times. No doubt they'll get back to me if the times don't suit.'

Then, changing the subject, she asked Dash about his job, and he recounted the funny episodes he'd encountered so far, including the greased hat incident.

'They are a great bunch of blokes though,' he maintained as they laughed together.

They'd both drunk their first beer quite quickly – mainly because of an initial bout of nervousness – so after asking Evie if she'd like another, Dash made his way to the bar for refills. A few minutes later he was back, placing his and

Evie's fresh beers on the table before sitting down opposite her again.

'Cheers,' they said in unison, raising their glasses and smiling at each other. After enjoying a mouthful of the icy cold beverage, Dash asked Evie how William was going.

'Better, now he knows he can stay where he is, but he's still pretty low. I finally got him talking a bit yesterday when we drove back from the beach. It turns out he hates William for a name. Mainly because it's also his dad's name – and there's no love lost there – and also because people often call him Willy and he doesn't like it. He's also moved around so much he hasn't been able to keep in contact with a friend he had in Sydney, and now he'll miss a week of school with the funeral and everything.'

'Poor little bugger.'

'I know. It's hard enough fitting in when you first start high school without all he's had to deal with.'

'His first year ... I thought he'd be older than that?'

'No, he's not long turned twelve. He said it was a bummer having his birthday so close to Christmas.'

'Oh yeah, what date is it?'

'The seventeenth of December.'

'The seventeenth,' Dash was surprised. 'That's the same as mine.'

'Really,' Evie grinned. 'So you're a Sagittarian too?'

They sat and talked about the odd coincidence, Evie

saying 'there are no coincidences', setting them off on another tangent to discover more about each other. Often laughing out loud about something, they both felt completely at ease with each other.

'It's been different having Bluey around,' Dash's grin widened. 'I think I know what I was like now; I've been told I was an inquisitive kid.'

'Yeah,' Evie couldn't help laughing. 'She never stops, does she? But she's such a gorgeous little thing, and so bright. The things she comes out with sometimes are hilarious.'

Dash's eyes were again drawn to Evie's smiling face, and he was again aware of the feeling inside that he'd been unfamiliar with before meeting her. Wondering once more what it was about her that had him so interested, he decided to just go with the flow and see where it led.

'It's great that Marley's looking so well,' Evie said. 'She's been through a lot. Any chance she might settle in Geelong?'

'That I don't know. She hasn't really talked about her long-term plans. I think she just wants to get over this hurdle first.'

'Hmm ... yeah ... I can understand that.'

Their meals arrived just then and their conversation changed to other topics. By the end of the evening they both realised that there was a definite attraction to the other, and not just physically – on all levels. Neither of them had felt this happy and perfectly at ease with a member of the opposite sex before, and neither of them knew what to make of it.

'I'm not sure what's going on here,' Evie thought as she watched Dash's face as he related another funny story. 'What is this feeling?' She knew she loved his face; it looked different from different angles, partly because of a broken nose but mostly because of the character showing in it. Thinking what a great smile he had she was suddenly snapped out of her musings.

'Are you listening to me?' Dash was grinning at her.

'Yeah, you were saying something about driving from Broome to Perth.'

Dash's grin widened and Evie couldn't help laughing.

'Come on, let's get out of here,' Dash said. 'Do you feel like walking or getting a taxi back?'

'Let walk, it's a lovely night and it's not far.'

Chapter Thirty-Seven

Friday afternoon, after she'd finished her early shift at the travel agency, Liz dropped by to hear all the goss' about Evie's date with Dash. She couldn't remember the last time she'd seen Evie looking so alive, her whole being seemed to be lit by an inner glow.

'... then, when we got back, we sat out here on the balcony and talked for ages,' Evie was saying while smiling at her best friend.

'Did he kiss you?'

'Yeah.'

'Well ... what was it like?'

'Very nice ... more than very nice actually.'

'Hmm ... so when are you going out again?'

'Tomorrow.'

'Tomorrow ... hmm ... he must be keen then.'

'All I know is that we just sort of clicked and now I can't seem to get him out of my mind. I've never felt this way before though … it's quite strange.'

'Love can do strange things to people,' Liz smiled.

'*Love* … I think that's jumping the gun a bit,' Evie exclaimed, her dark eyebrows shooting upwards.

'We'll see. Was there any other hanky panky?'

'No, he was a perfect gentleman.'

'Bugger.'

Evie laughed along with her friend. 'You're impossible, you really are.'

Completely undaunted, Liz went on, 'I bet you thought about it though, you must think he's fuckable; I do.'

'Oh yeah, he's fuckable alright,' Evie grinned. 'But I'm definitely not rushing into anything this time.'

Liz just smiled.

'Don't smile at me like that, I mean it. I've learnt something from past experiences.'

'Okay, okay. What time is it? I've got to pick up Jason at four-thirty.'

'It's … ten to four,' Evie answered looking at her watch. 'Where is he anyway?'

'Just round at Simon's place; I promised him I'd drive him down to Lorne so he could have a few drinks with his dad. It'll be the first time they've gotten together since he came out. Simon wanted to go too, but Jase thought it'd be best to leave that for next time – if there is a next time.' Finishing her coffee she asked, 'What time does Dash get home from work?'

'I'm not sure, it depends on if they're doing overtime or not.'

'Do you want another coffee?' Liz asked standing up. 'I'm going to have one then I'll have to get going.'

'Yeah, okay, thanks.' Evie heard footsteps, and looking down from her position on the balcony saw Dash walking around the corner of the flats. He was looking up in her direction and they both smiled at the same time.

'Well, speak of the devil ...' Liz grinned, standing at the open door. By the time Dash had ascended the steps and was standing at his front door, Liz had casually positioned herself against the balcony rail to get the best view of him through the open security door.

'G'day Dash,' Liz said first, a dazzling smile on her face.

Dash couldn't help grinning. He liked Evie's friend, she was straight up and a bit cheeky.

'G'day Lizzy, how're you going?'

'I'm going great,' she replied. 'I'm glad the weather's a bit cooler though. I only like it hot if I can go to the beach or laze around a pool.' Smiling a winning smile she went on, 'I really don't know how you blokes can work in it day in and day out. I couldn't.'

'Well, I suppose it's good that you don't have to then,' he

smiled back. Shifting his attention to Evie, he said, 'G'day Evie, how's your day been?'

They chatted for a minute or so then Dash said he had to get his skates on as he had to meet Marley and Bluey in Melbourne.

'Marley had to go for one of her check-ups,' Dash was explaining. 'So I said rather than them getting the train back I'd pick them up and take them out for dinner.' He laughed then and went on, 'Blue said she didn't want to go *out* for dinner, she said she'd rather eat inside.'

They all chuckled at the little girl's take on things, then Dash unlocked the door of his flat. He turned and looked at Evie before going in, smiled and said, 'I'll see you tomorrow night then.'

'Yeah, see you then.'

'Hmmm ... I wish he'd moved in next to me,' Liz was smiling. 'He's nice. No wonder you like him.'

They were standing in the kitchen – Evie making coffee and Liz making appreciative noises.

'Hmm ... nice body too, I see what you mean about the sexy shoulders.'

Evie laughed, saying, 'Hey, down girl, down. You're getting drool on the floor.'

'Well, it's a while since I've met a manly man,' Liz laughed along with her friend. 'So you've obviously changed your mind about him not being your type then?'

'Yeah, I have. There's a lot more to him than I first thought,' she smiled, remembering the first time she'd seen him. Standing for a moment with her head slightly to one side and a thoughtful look on her face, she went on, 'I've just never had this feeling before ... it's thrown me a bit ... it's like my vibration's been enhanced ... I feel sort of tingly when I think about him.'

After another ten minutes or so of girl talk concerning Dash's looks, Liz checked her watch then sighed, 'Bugger, look at the time; I've got to go.' Reluctantly sitting her coffee cup in the sink and picking up her bag, she then asked Evie what she was doing later.

'Well, its Hilda's birthday today. Blackie will be here soon and we're going to make her a birthday cake.'

'Blackie?'

'Oh, yeah,' Evie grinned. 'William wants to be known as Blackie from now on, from his surname – Black.'

'Oh, when did that happen?'

'Just today, Dash thought a nickname might cheer him up so he started calling him Blackie when he saw him first thing this morning. William loves it – he came up and told me about it before he went to school.'

'You like having him around, don't you?' Liz asked on her way out the door.

'Yeah, he's a good kid; I don't mind at all.'

'Okay Evie, I'll call you tomorrow.' Liz waved and was

off. Passing William on the stairs as he was running up them two steps at a time, she said, 'G'day Blackie. How're things going?'

He stopped in his tracks, a big grin on his face. 'Great thanks Liz. I can't stop. Evie and me are going to make a cake for Oma's birthday. I'll see you later.' With that he turned and continued his race up the steps.

Wishing she had as much energy, Liz smilingly shook her head.

'Right, I'd better get going.' Turning round she carefully continued on to the bottom of the steps then hurriedly walked to her old car. Thinking that Jason would probably have kittens if she was late picking him up, she turned the key in the lock and opened her car door. Lowering herself into the bucket seat of her old Celica and shutting the door, she shut her eyes tightly and said a quick prayer.

'Please let it all go well. Jase really needs to have his dad in his life again ... thanks.' Liz's serious face then slipped away revealing her cheerful face once more. As she started the car she was thinking of her mother who'd died several years ago after being involved in a hit-and-run car accident. They'd been incredibly close and Liz still missed her every day.

'See what you can do Mum; maybe He will listen to you – you always were pretty persuasive.' Still smiling, Liz could feel her mum's presence next to her in the car as she put it into gear and drove off.

Chapter Thirty-Eight

'Look Poppy, there's Port Flip Bay over there.'

'No Blue,' cut in Marley grinning, 'It's Port *Phillip* Bay.'

Dash was driving them home and had chosen the left lane of the West Gate Bridge to give the youngster a better opportunity to see the panoramic view.

'Oh, okay ... oh ... look at all the twinkly lights ... aren't they pretty ... and look over there ...' Bluey continued to point out everything that she saw until they reached the other side of the massive expanse of bridgework then, finally exhausted from her big day out, dozed off in the back seat.

After having had a lovely meal at a flash restaurant to celebrate Marley's all clear they were now heading back to Geelong.

'You know what, I feel that my life's finally really beginning,' Marley stated. 'I know I've grown up a lot in the last twelve months or so, having had this to deal with, but I feel I've become a better person for it. Does that sound strange to you?'

'No, it doesn't sound strange to me,' Dash chuckled a little. 'Hardships are just opportunities for us to learn more about ourselves.'

'Oh yeah, and who told you that?'

'My nan ... your great grandmother.'

'Oh, is she still alive?'

'No, passed away several years ago unfortunately.'

They chatted about different family members until they pulled up outside Dash's garage. Bluey woke up then, wanting to know where they were.

'Where're home again sweetie,' Marley replied as she helped her sleepy daughter out of the car.

Sitting round the kitchen table after Bluey had been put to bed, Marley and Dash were enjoying a coffee.

'What's going on with you and Evie?' Marley smiled at her dad. 'How long have you two known each other anyway?'

Grinning, Dash replied, 'Not long at all. Last night was our first night out together.'

'Oh, I didn't realise that. How did it go?'

'Great.'

'Oh, so when are you going out again then?'

'Tomorrow night,' he continued, grinning.

'Hmm ... sounds like you're pretty keen, not that I'm

surprised. Evie's really lovely, no wonder you like her; I do.'

Half an hour later after retelling some of the funny jokes that Evie had told him, both Dash and Marley decided to call it a night.

Chapter Thirty-Nine

It had been a week since Evie had been out with Dash. They'd had another fun night which had ended with more canoodling on the now extended balcony; her security door was now permanently open, linking the two. Since then they'd only caught up for an hour or so each night, again on the balcony and again ending up in some lingering kisses. She'd been busy with her Feng Shui work – delivering a couple of completed charts in the evenings when all the family members had been home – and Dash had been working ten-hour days so had by necessity been having some early nights.

Now on her way to a Mrs. Ann Enright's house for a consultation, Evie was admiring the rolling green hills all around her and the glimpses of the sparkling bay in the distance. Having only been back in the Portarlington area a couple of times since leaving as a child, she was a little surprised to see that nothing much had changed.

'I wonder what the old shop looks like now,' she said to herself as she passed the 'Welcome to Portarlington' sign, 'and I wonder if I should go and have a look at it while I'm here.' She immediately felt a tight feeling in her stomach, which startled her a bit, so was not sure if she was ready to revisit her childhood home.

Deciding to leave it for another day, she took a left hand turn onto Point Richards Road, then a minute or so later turned left again onto Ramblers Road; pulling up at the address she'd been given.

Evie noted that it was a neat, brick and weatherboard two-storey house. There was a small patch of green lawn out the front and a magnificently hued, pink bougainvillea trailing over and down an old wooden carport. She sat and stared at the house for a moment as an odd feeling washed over her. Before she had a chance to analyse it the front door opened and an extremely well-groomed elderly lady walked towards her. Again Evie just sat there. She was still sitting in the car when the lady smiled at her through her open car window and softly said, 'Hello Evie dear.'

It had taken Evie another dazed few seconds before she realised it was Annie. Annie who'd given her back her dad's fishing hat so long ago. Annie; who'd been so kind to her when she'd cried her goodbyes to her dad. Having always remembered the green eyes and the gentle voice which had soothed her turmoil, Evie spoke.

'Annie?'

'Yes dear.' The woman's face held a smile tinged with sadness. 'You must be quite surprised to see me again ... but I'm being rude ... please, come in. Would you like a cup of tea?'

Evie's body operated automatically as she followed Annie indoors. Now sitting on a modern, cream leather couch she was relieved to note that her brain was starting to kick in again.

'Have you always lived here then?' she asked as Annie made herself busy in the adjoining kitchen.

'Oh no, this is a holiday house I bought years ago. I've been living overseas for some time now.'

Walking back into the spacious lounge room, Annie had a slightly odd expression on her face. She placed a wicker tray holding a lovely, silver tea service onto the coffee table, then looked directly at Evie.

'I'm afraid I've asked you here under false pretenses ...' she stopped for a moment then continued. 'While I get the cups you might like to have a look at some of the photos over there,' she said, nodding her head in the direction of a large, antique-looking sideboard. 'Then we can talk.'

Evie's head turned in the direction Annie had indicated, then almost of its own will her body slowly stood and walked towards the array of different size photographs. She was transfixed by what she saw; only her eyes were moving as they went from one photo to the next. There was one of Evie on her wedding day; another of the twins and their new husbands. A larger shot of Doug and his first wife caught her eye, then a couple more – one of Jo aged about eighteen, and one of Reen and Vince holding a baby. The rest became blurred as her mind screamed so many questions that she couldn't focus properly anymore.

'What ...?' she started saying, then shook her head, completely puzzled. Turning to look at Annie as she re-entered the lounge room, Evie's mouth opened but no words were immediately forthcoming.

'I know this is all going to be a huge shock to you,' Annie said. 'Please, come and sit down. I have a story to tell you.'

Evie finally found her voice. 'Why have you got these pictures of me and my family ... and who took them?' She was feeling a bit alarmed and slightly disoriented, but then felt the frown on her face relax a little as she took in the kind expression evident on Annie's face. Slightly shaking her head, she crossed the room and sat down on the edge of the couch.

'I'm afraid there's no other way to tell you but to tell you ...' Annie started, then stopped again. Sitting down next to Evie then taking a deep breath, she went on. 'Your father didn't drown all those years ago ... he faked his death so your mother could receive the insurance money and he could be with me.'

A deafening silence filled Evie's head for a moment, then the words she'd just heard seemed to parade themselves in front of her. '... didn't drown ... faked his death ...' She became aware that Annie had moved closer and had placed an arm around her shoulders, holding her the same way as she had done that day on the beach.

'You mean ... he isn't dead?' Evie slowly formed the question.

'I'm sorry dear, but yes, he is. He died about three months ago. That's why I can now tell you everything.'

'Everything, what's everything then?' She looked at Annie with puzzlement etched on her face.

'I think I'd better start at the beginning,' she said as she poured the tea. 'Would you like milk and sugar in your tea?'

Chapter Forty

When Dash arrived home from work he found Evie sitting out on her balcony, holding what looked like the green fishing hat that had once belonged to her father. She'd shown it to him after telling him the story of her dad's disappearance; after their first date. As soon as he saw her though, he knew something was wrong – her face held an odd, faraway look even when she smiled a greeting.

'G'day gorgeous, what's up? You look like you've just been told that the Earth's flat.' He sat down beside her on the old two-seater and waited for her to say something.

'I've just heard the most ... astonishing things ...' Evie said as she turned her head and looked directly at him. 'My dad ... he didn't drown ... he's been living in France all this time.'

'*What*? Who told you *that*?' Dash asked incredulously.

Evie relayed how she'd gone to Portarlington for a Feng Shui consultation and had then discovered that Annie had used that as an excuse to get her down there. She explained how Annie had organised for the Geelong newspapers to be regularly sent to them in France, and how her dad had read them religiously, looking for any mention of his children. That's how they'd known she was a Feng Shui consultant, from an advertisement she'd placed in the local paper after she'd moved back to Geelong. They'd also hired a private investigator to track down and photograph his kids when he'd read they were getting married, or had children, or special birthdays. When she got to the bit about her seeing all the photos, Dash could see how much it had affected her and gave her a hug. After taking a couple of deep breaths, Evie went on to relate how her dad and Annie had fallen in love, and how neither of them had intended to be adulterers, but that's what had ultimately happened; resulting in his plan to 'die' so her mum would receive enough insurance money to be able to look after all the kids properly.

Dash was speechless at first and actually shook his head as if to try and shake the words into some sort of sense. 'But how did he do it?' was all he could say.

'It's pretty incredible, I know.' Evie was also shaking her head as she stood and moved to the railing for a moment, then sat again, this time in the old armchair. 'It's like something out of a movie ... but Annie didn't know anything about it until he rang her that evening, and all he said was for her to leave her curtains open and lights on until he got there later.'

Speaking quietly and matter-of-factly she conveyed how he'd had it all planned out for quite a while beforehand.

'Apparently he could no longer stand not being able to see Annie like a "normal" couple, and the guilt he'd been feeling about the whole damn thing had just become too much. So, he put the plan he'd been hatching for more than a year into action – he'd already made sure that Mum would receive enough money so she wouldn't have to worry too much about the finances.' Evie stopped for a moment and looked up at Dash, astonishment plainly evident on his face, then went on.

'Annie said that his main concern had been for us kids – he didn't want us to suffer financially because of what he was doing ...' Her voice then lowered to a whisper as she stated, 'He knew he'd be hurting us but he just couldn't live with *his* hurt anymore.'

Dash leant over and gave her a hug but couldn't immediately find any words of comfort. Before he did, Evie straightened up again saying, 'It's alright, I'm okay, but I have to tell you the rest; you won't believe it.'

Sitting slightly forward in her chair, her hand grasping the armrests, Evie continued with the shocking revelations.

'Dad waited for a night with the right weather conditions

and made sure people had seen him as he set off from the boat ramp that evening. Later, when the squall had blown in that he'd been expecting, he'd motored in close enough to the shoreline to be able to slip overboard and swim the last bit, then watched as his small boat capsized in the breakers behind him.' Taking another deep breath she went on to say how he'd chosen a moonless night to reduce his risk of being seen, and how Annie had opened the curtains of her beach house so the light shining through would be his beacon in the darkness.

'… and after that he'd basically laid low for a while with Annie, until she'd been able to organise a private plane to fly them out of the country. It's amazing what you can do if you've got enough money to pay for it,' she ended with a sigh.

Dash was staring at Evie's pale face. 'Are you okay?' he asked her as he pulled her closer.

'I think so. I'm still a bit gob-smacked though.'

'Well, that would have to be an understatement. I've never heard anything like it before.'

'I know … it's quite astounding, isn't it?'

'So what happened when they got to France? And why France … where did they live?'

'Well, Annie had bought a house in the countryside of France the year before; something that Dad had encouraged her to do. She'd thought it a bit strange at the time, but he'd said it would be a good investment for her. And anyway, she had a couple of good friends living there so ended up thinking it was a good idea too. So they eventually made their way there and just quietly settled in. Dad grew a beard and moustache while they'd waited to leave Australia, and when she later told her friends that she'd re-married to a widower with no children, they just accepted him the way he was.

Annie said his one and only regret had been abandoning us kids; she said the guilt had sometimes brought him to tears. But you know what? She showed me some photos of herself and Dad ... I've never seen him looking so completely happy and relaxed. I was actually struck by the absolute joy showing in his face.'

Evie then stood and moved to where Dash was sitting on the two-seater then snuggled up and rested her head on his shoulder. Even though she still had trouble wrapping her head around what she'd been told, a wonderful peace seeped through her body. She felt happy finally knowing exactly what had happened that night, and more so knowing that her dad hadn't died a cold, lonely death after all. Looking down, she saw the hat sitting on her lap and immediately smiled, saying, 'Remember when I showed you this hat and said how a woman called Annie had given it to me all those years ago?'

'Yeah.'

'Well, she didn't find it like she said. Dad had it all along. When she'd heard from a neighbour that our family was moving, Dad asked her to go to the beach on the day of the move and wait 'til she saw me to give it to me. He knew I'd go there before we moved and he wanted me to have something to connect me with him. And you know what?' she smiled. 'That's exactly what it did.'

Dash was still stunned by the incredible tale and they both just sat there for a minute or so.

'Are you going to tell your mother that he's still alive?' he then asked.

'He's not. Oh, you've only heard the half of it yet,' Evie said, shaking her head again. 'You're really not going to believe the rest.'

Dash wasn't sure if he wanted to know or not, going by the weird expression on Evie's face, but before he had a chance to say anything Evie went on.

'Annie had felt a lot of guilt as well, especially regarding us kids no longer having a father, so she insisted that she and Dad invest a large part of *her* money into different shares for us. They then made provisions for the money to be directed to us after he died – he'd felt it was the only safe way to leave us something without getting caught out for faking his own death,' Evie explained. 'Annie said he died about three months ago, quite peacefully in his sleep.' Then, taking a deep breath she continued.

'Over the years the shares have done extremely well ... Annie said they're now worth a tad over two-and-a-half million dollars.'

Chapter Forty-One

The taxi pulled over then stopped under one of the massive old elms lining Eastern Beach Road. Evie insisted on paying, then after they'd both extricated themselves from the back seat they stood and surveyed their magnificent surroundings. To the left was a large marina full of gently bobbing boats of all types and sizes. The marina's many timber walkways were a hive of activity, and in the distance across the bay they could just make out the hazy outline of some of Melbourne's tallest buildings.

'I wouldn't get sick of looking at this in a hurry,' Dash said as he leant against the white balustrade at the upper entrance.

'Me either,' Evie agreed. 'It's always been my favourite place in Geelong.' Pointing down towards a circular shaped children's swimming pool, she went on. 'I used to come here for swimming lessons in primary school. I still remember how proud I was when I received my Herald Certificate.' she smiled.

Dash held Evie's hand as they started on the steep descent to the designated area for the family reunion. The panoramic view momentarily stalled Evie's racing thoughts and she breathed in deeply to savour one of her favourite scents.

'Mmm ... I love the smell of freshly cut grass,' she sighed.

The manicured lawns looked immaculate, resembling a brilliant green carpet covering the slopes on either side of where they stood. Majestic, old palm trees towered above as they descended the seemingly endless steps, before pausing for a moment to admire a fountain resplendent with sculptured bronze birds and turtles.

Their eyes were then drawn to the expansive view laid out in front of them. Beyond the children's swimming area was a huge, double-level wooden promenade, built in a half circle and enclosing a large area of the beach. A high-diving tower held several people and Dash and Evie stood and watched as a young man did a graceful swan-dive into the dark green sea.

'Oh ... that looks good,' said Dash with surprise in his voice. 'We'll have to go for a walk around there later.'

'Yeah, it's a pretty popular place here ... especially in the summer.'

'Hey,' Dash said softly to Evie. 'Don't worry … everything will work out the way it's supposed to.' He'd noticed her frown and knew she was feeling anxious about how her brother and sisters were going to react to her unbelievable news, so, enfolding her in his arms he gave her a light kiss on the side of her face.

'Come on gorgeous, the only way to do it is to do it.'

'I know … I'm just worried about how Mum's going to take it … I'm still not sure whether I should tell her or not.'

'Wait and see what the others think then take it from there,' Dash advised.

Taking a deep breath she then exhaled and said, 'Okay, let's do it.'

Holding Dash's hand in hers, they proceeded to descend the last of the steps.

The first person Evie saw was Aunty Ivy, dear old thing that she was, greeting everyone with a warm smile and a comment on how glad she was that they'd come. She was obviously reveling in the special event that she'd organised. Standing at the bottom of the steps, Evie pointed to a chubby woman with a mass of curly brown hair. She was dressed slightly eccentrically in a long, green and blue printed skirt and two tops – one pink and the outer one a white, flowing creation.

'There's Jo, you'll like her; she's really down to earth.' Evie smiled just as her youngest sister turned and saw her standing there. Using a bit of hand pointing indicating 'we'll say hello to Aunty Ivy first then catch up with you', they smiled at each other, then Jo's attention was taken by an elderly man wearing an old-fashioned pork-pie hat. He'd tapped her on the shoulder and soon had her deep in conversation about something.

Looking past Jo, Evie noticed Doug wandering towards the throng of people now congregating out the front of the Beach House Restaurant. He was holding hands with Erica and Evie noticed straight away that she was pregnant. Erica was Balinese and beautiful, having an extremely sweet smile and nature, and had so far been the longest serving of his matrimonial conquests.

'Evie my dear, how are you ... and what have you done with your hair?' Aunty Ivy asked as she admired Evie's shaven locks. 'I must say it suits you, how brave of you to try it.'

'Thanks Aunty Ivy. It has been one of my better ideas. I've had it this way for a couple of years now. I love it.'

'Hmm ...'she smiled, then turned her attention to Dash. 'And who might this handsome gentleman be?'

'Oh, sorry Aunty Ivy, I'd like you to meet Dash ... Dash, I'd like you to meet my Aunty Ivy.'

'G'day Aunty Ivy,' Dash said cheekily. 'I've heard a lot about you.'

'Have you indeed young man,' she smiled back. 'Well, I

hope to hear more about you, starting with how long you've been courting my niece.'

Evie smiled a look at Dash saying, 'and so it begins ...' which Dash acknowledged with a sparkle in his eyes, but before he could reply Evie spoke.

'Now, Aunty Ivy, you're not trying to garner a bit of gossip are you?'

'Too right I am. This reunion is going to keep me in conversation for years,' she chuckled.

All three laughed, then Evie tried to change the subject by enquiring as to her mother's whereabouts.

'Oh dear, didn't you know? Your mother twisted her ankle a couple of days ago, quite badly by all accounts. Apparently she'd been walking back from her next door neighbour's place, after arranging for her mail to be collected while she was away, when she tripped over that little dog of hers. She rang and told me about it as soon as she got home from seeing her doctor. He told her she's *definitely* not to fly anywhere while it's so swollen and bruised. She sounded *so* disappointed on the phone – she'd been looking forward to this reunion for *ages*.'

Evie felt part of the tension lifting from her body as she tried to sound disappointed at hearing this news.

'Oh no, I didn't know ... what a shame.'

'Yes.' Aunty Ivy's attention was suddenly side-tracked by the sound of a screaming infant. 'Evie dear, I'd better keep moving. I want to see if everyone's here before we eat, but I would like to catch up with you and Dash again before the day's over.'

Promising to catch up later, Evie and Dash left her to her task. Looking about, Evie then located Jo who was still talking to the same man as before.

'How are you going so far?' she asked Dash as they strolled towards her youngest sister.

'Great,' he grinned. 'I can see it's going to be a very interesting day.'

Reen had been hanging back a little, not over keen to see her mother again. Thirty years had passed since she'd stormed out of the house she'd called home, affirming loudly that she'd never be back. She'd held true to her word and had only seen her mother six times in the intervening years – and that was at her siblings' weddings. After scanning the crowd, Vince beside her and their two daughters off to one side trying to guess who was who, she sighed and said, 'Oh well, we're here now, we may as well go and mingle. At least I can't see Mum anywhere yet. Andrea ... Becky ... see that woman over there talking to your Aunty Evie and that man ... that's your Great Aunty Ivy; do you remember her? She's lovely ... it would be years since you last saw her ...'

A sudden confusion of sound and colour stopped Reen in her tracks as Pam and Bev arrived - together of course, followed by several of their now adult progeny, one of whom was carrying a baby.

'Oh my God, when are they ever going to get even half a brain between them?' Reen asked Vince as she took in her sisters' appearances.

They'd come dressed identically in lime green, silk t-shirts and short, white skirts. Snakeskin, high heel shoes were enhancing their tanned and toned legs with maximum effect. Matching blond hair looking casually tousled completed the facade.

'It looks like neither of them wanted the other one to look better so they decided to dress the same,' Vince couldn't help laughing.

'Yep, that's exactly what they've always been like – completely infatuated with themselves. It's no wonder Lenny and Craig both eventually chucked the towel in; I'm surprised they managed to stay married to them for as long as they did. They're both as bad as each other though ... although they'd both disagree.'

'Look Pam ... there's Aunty Ivy over there. She hasn't changed a bit has she?' Bev declared, then smiled a little, advancing in that direction.

'Well ... she does look like she's shrunk a bit, or was she always that small?' Pam queried, trying to get ahead of her sister.

'Well, she is nearly eighty, people do shrink a bit as they

get old you know.' Turning around but not slowing, Bev spoke over her shoulder. 'Melissa, would you like me to carry Megan for you?

'No Mum, I can manage.'

Pam took advantage of her twins' distraction by getting in first with her ingratiating greeting. 'Aunty Ivy ... how *are* you? I haven't seen you for *ages*.' Clasping the elderly woman's hands she stooped and placed an air kiss near her cheek and then went straight on. 'You're looking so *well*; did you know you've *always* been my favourite aunty?'

'Oh, hello dear, yes, it's so nice to see you again; both of you,' she replied a little hesitantly, looking from one to the other. 'But I'm afraid I'm no better at telling you two apart now than I was when you were born. Now, who's who?'

'I'm Pam, the pretty one; that's Bev ...' Pam nodded slightly in Bev's direction, then turning the other way beckoned her daughters over closer. 'And these are my three girls – Kimberly, Amy and that's Melissa holding Megan, my first grandchild. Isn't she *gorgeous*?'

Bev rolled her eyes listening to Pam going on about her granddaughter. Pushing herself forward, Bev smiled brightly at the bemused woman now in front of her, then bent over to kiss her powdery cheek. 'Hello Aunty Ivy, it's *so* good to see you again.' Leaving no time for Pam to butt in, Bev was already explaining why her son Richie and his wife Tammy couldn't attend the reunion.

'... and with Tammy already two days overdue they decided it would be best to stay home. They were both *so* disappointed they couldn't come,' she stressed. 'But my other two boys are here ... Chris, Mark ... come and meet your Great Aunty Ivy.'

When Reen eventually found out her mother was no longer attending the family get-together, after waiting for the twins to finish their noisy assault on their aunty, she was unable to hide her relief.

'Hallelujah ... there is a God,' she grinned at Vince as they moved on after saying their hellos.

Vince was as happy as she was – he'd never been able to form any sort of an amicable relationship with his wife's intractable mother, not that he'd tried much after that first time. He could laugh about it now, but at the time he'd been so angry. The way the old cow had completely ignored both himself and Reenie at the twins' wedding had been so childish, but he knew it'd hurt Reen, and that's what had pissed him off the most.

She was the absolute love of his life, and he knew he was lucky to still have her after his stupid fling with that woman in his office years ago. Reenie had been on the verge of leaving after she'd found out about it from a mutual friend. It was only later that she'd told him the only reason she'd stayed was that she wouldn't give her mother the satisfaction of saying, 'I knew it wouldn't last'. It had taken nearly two years for them to get back onto an even keel again.

'Come on Vince,' Reen said as she started to walk off. 'There's Evie over by the swimming pool ... and it looks like she's brought a man with her ... I wonder how long that's been going on?'

Doug had been surreptitiously keeping track of his sisters after he'd first spotted them amongst the hungry-looking hordes of old folk.

'I didn't know I had so many old relatives,' he commented to his wife. 'They've probably all come for the free feed.'

'They're lovely though; look at the character in their faces,' Erica replied. 'I hope I age as gracefully.'

She had her usual serene expression on her face, and when Doug glanced sideways at her he was again taken by the beauty which radiated from her.

'You'll always be beautiful,' he heard himself saying, Erica smiling back up at him.

His outwardly controlled demeanour was holding at bay a myriad of terrors and insecurities, the worst being the thought that Erica would leave him. He'd loved all his previous wives in the beginning – they'd always been laughing together about some silly thing or another, even when they'd had sex it had always been fun. Then after each of his children had been born, none of his wives had treated him the same again. They'd always been too busy or too tired to see to his needs the way he'd expected. After one blazing row he'd had with his first wife about her failure to fulfil her duties in bed, she'd screamed back that if he'd help with the never-ending housework she might have more time for him.

'Huh, fat chance,' he'd yelled back. 'Housework's women's work; don't expect me to work all day then come home to housework. You've had all day to get stuff done. Get your act together,' he'd shouted as he'd slammed the front door; heading straight to the pub to cool off.

So nothing changed, only the intensity of each successive argument. In due course each wife left him, taking each of his three sons with them. His rationale had always been that they hadn't loved him enough, even after he'd provided everything imaginable to give them a great lifestyle.

On the many lonely nights he'd had in-between relationships, when he'd either stayed home and read a book or pretended to have a good time out with friends, he'd held on to one thought: 'When I find the right woman, everything will be alright.'

But he was sure he'd now found the right woman, so why didn't he feel alright? He didn't realise he was scared; shit scared in fact. Every waking moment and even in his dreams he lived with fear – fear of not being good enough, of not providing enough, of not being smart enough; fear of failure, fear of loss and fear of fear itself. That insidious trembling that regularly clutched at his innards, squeezing the anger into surfacing through every pore of his prickling skin. The only way he knew how to keep it in check was to be in control at all times. As long as he felt on top of things he was fine, but if he felt his position was being threatened in any way he'd feel the blood start pumping through his veins, pulling the rage up with it.

After strolling around the perimeter of the gathering, Doug noticed that Erica was slowing down a little so asked her if she'd like to sit somewhere in the shade.

'No, not yet darling, we still have to offer our respects to your Aunty Ivy – she's such a lovely lady. Who is that with Evie?' she then queried, looking in Dash's direction.

'Don't know,' replied Doug, 'never seen him before. Come on then, we'd better do the right thing and say hello to everyone I suppose.'

Chapter Forty-Two

'Mmm ... pass me another one of those salmon puff things, would you?' Bev asked as she wiped a small flake of pastry off her lips. 'They're delicious.'

'I wouldn't have thought you'd be game to eat pastry with your hips the size they are,' Pam answered gleefully as she sipped her soda water.

'Oh would you two shut up for a while,' Reen demanded. 'I'm sick of your bickering already. How I ever managed to live in the same house with you two for as long as I did is a mystery.'

'Now now children,' Doug spoke sarcastically, 'try and behave like civilised human beings for once; you *are* out in public.'

'Ahh ... isn't it nice to be all together again,' Jo smiled at Evie.

'Oh yeah, it's a real joy,' Evie grinned back. 'Hmm ... these pastry things *are* delicious. Aunty Ivy's granddaughter's done a great job with the catering; she's running her own business now, did you know?'

'Yes, I was talking to her earlier,' Jo said, finishing off her selection of tasty finger foods. 'So, what is it you wanted to talk to me about anyway?' she then asked Evie. 'I'm a little bit intrigued.'

Dash was standing next to Evie and saw her hand pause for a second before she ate the last of her lunch. He knew the time was close when she'd have to inform her siblings of their father's deception. Reaching over, he held her hand then gave it a firm squeeze. She smiled back at him then turned towards her sister.

'Are you okay Evie? You've got a funny look on your face,' Jo asked, concerned.

'Yeah,' she giggled nervously. 'Um ... look, when the six of us have finished eating I'll tell you all at the same time. Okay?'

'Okay then,' Jo slowly replied, now really concerned. She knew Evie often giggled when she was under a lot of stress. 'What the hell's going on?' she thought to herself, her mind automatically scanning through a range of scenarios the way a computer scans for a fingerprint match. 'Why would she want the six of us together to tell us something?'

Rather than worry about it, Jo decided to wait and see.

There wasn't a lot that she did worry about, preferring to go with the flow of life. She'd come to the reunion by herself knowing she'd be grilled as to where Tony was.

'He's overseas with a couple of mates, trekking through the Himalayas,' she'd informed everyone who'd asked, not bothering to add that they'd split up.

She'd loved so much about Tony – they'd met when they were both exploring the beaches of Bali three years ago. It had been the night of her birthday, her thirty-second, and she'd been partying with a group of her girlfriends. Aussies attract other Aussies overseas so it wasn't long before Tony and his mates had joined them in celebrating her birthday and life in general.

Unfortunately the relationship had now run its race and it wasn't a winner. Tony was four years younger than Jo and still had an insatiable drive to explore the planet, while she felt she was ready to establish herself somewhere. Making the painful decision to go their separate ways, they'd both endured an emotional last night together before they'd parted. She'd then later scraped up enough money for the deposit on a small coffee shop in a little sea-side town called St. Leonards, about half an hour's drive from Geelong.

Now noticing that Evie had just spoken to Doug, leaving him with a puzzled expression on his face, and was now talking softly to Reen and Vince, Jo's interest intensified. Focusing her attention on Reen's face, she saw the same puzzled expression appear, as Evie then moved off in the direction of the twins.

Most of the older relatives had now gone, leaving a mixed group of children and their parents. As if on cue, her siblings detached themselves and followed Evie towards a large, shady tree; situated about ten metres away. There were a couple of bench seats concreted in place either side of a table and Evie sat at the first one, Dash standing beside her.

'I bet she's pregnant,' Bev ginned.

'No, she could have told us that anytime,' Pam countered as they both tried to be the first to reach Evie.

Waiting silently until her sisters and Erica had sat down, Doug opting to stand; Evie spoke.

'I'm still not sure how to tell you what I have to ...' she started then stopped, now fully understanding exactly how Annie had felt. 'So I'll just start. Yesterday I went to Portarlington to do a Feng Shui consultation. When I got there I realised I knew the woman from thirty years ago. It was Annie – I'd spoken to her when I went to the beach to say my goodbyes to Dad; the day we moved to Geelong.' Taking a deep breath, Evie ploughed on, 'The story she told me ... I'll now tell you.'

Evie could feel the intensity of their stares as she opened her mouth to speak.

'Dad ... didn't drown that night he went out fishing ... he faked his own death so he could be with Annie.'

Seagulls screeched noisily at each other, fighting over a discarded morsel of food, and children could be heard laughing and screaming as they frolicked in the crowded swimming pool. But it all seemed to be happening in another dimension for the people gathered around Evie – she could see it in the momentarily blank expressions on their faces.

'What the *hell* are you saying?' Doug then exploded. 'Are you *insane?* You really believe some demented old woman with a story like *that?* You're *crazy,*' he finished, his face now flushed with sweat.

The twins just sat there, eyes wide and mouths open. They turned and looked at each other simultaneously, then spontaneously reached for the other's hand. Before they were able to find the capacity to speak, Reen stood and leant forward across the table to be closer to Evie.

'What do you mean he faked his death? What are you talking about?' Her voice held a trace of desperation as her eyes bored into Evie.

Jo just sat. She didn't remember her father but she, too, was gob-smacked.

'I know this all sounds like something out of a cheap novel,' Evie went on. 'But let me finish ... *please.*'

Doug went to say something but Erica motioned for him to wait.

'Annie showed me heaps of photos of all of us taken at different times of our lives – photos of us on our wedding days, photos of your kids and some of you, Jo, when you first started going to uni. Then she told me the story of how she and Dad had met one day and how it had turned their worlds upside down. There'd been an instant connection between them she told me,' Evie went on in a deceptively calm voice, 'but neither of them recognised what it was at first, each thinking the other was just a friendly companion to fish with. By the time they both realised how they felt about each other it was too late. Neither of them had felt so completely at ease with another person, nor felt such a powerful need to love and cherish someone.'

Evie went on to describe how their dad had swum ashore and made his way to Annie's holiday house, not venturing outside again until the night Annie drove them to a small airport in South Australia, then how an ex-business partner and good friend of her late husband had flown them first to Darwin, then on to Indonesia in his own plane, no questions asked.

'... from there she'd arranged through friends other means of transport. They eventually arrived in France about three weeks later.'

'France; you mean Dad's been living in *France* all this time?' Bev asked.

'Yes.'

'But ...'

'For heaven's sake Bev, let Evie finish,' Pam cut in.

'Yes, go on Evie,' Reen softly prompted.

'Well ... the reason why Annie is now able to let us know the truth is ... because Dad actually did die about three months ago.'

A sob erupted from Reen and she immediately covered her mouth with her hand, trying to quell her rising hysteria. Vince squatted down beside her, trying his best to comfort her but feeling way out of his depth. He was blown away by the incredible story himself. Noticing Doug's face turn pale, Erica immediately stood up to allow him room to sit down. He stumbled slightly as he did so, his face frozen in a look of shock, then sat without uttering a word.

Evie knew she had to finish the story so pressed on.

'Apparently Dad's one and only regret was leaving us behind - Annie said he'd become depressed for days sometimes thinking about it. He decided he had to do something to show us all that we were always in his thoughts, and Annie felt the same way. It was her idea to put her money into a shares portfolio for our future, to be split equally between the six of us after Dad died.'

'Shares?' Bev queried, 'I don't know anything about *shares.*'

'Oh for God's sake Bev, you don't have to know anything about them,' Pam interjected, 'you pay someone else to do that.' Turning towards Evie she then asked, 'So, did this Annie person tell you how much they're worth?'

'Yes, she did.'

'Well ... how much?'

Evie hesitated for just a second before saying, 'A little over two-and-a-half million dollars.'

No one moved. It seemed as if glass shutters had been dropped down around them, sealing them off from their normal reality and comprehension. A couple of seconds passed in silence then everyone started talking at once.

'Two-and-a-half million ...'

'I don't believe it ...'

'Oh my God ...'

 'Are you sure ...'

'How much is that for each of us?'

'Over four hundred thousand dollars,' Evie answered.

'*Four hundred thousand dollars each; oh my God,*' Bev shrieked.

Chapter Forty-Three

It had been two weeks since the reunion. Dash was drinking another coffee while watching a documentary about the Amazon rainforest. There wasn't much else on and he was feeling restless. Bluey was visiting Hilda downstairs, and Marley was studying her notes from yesterday's lecture, having enrolled at the Gordon TAFE College to obtain the necessary qualifications to work in the welfare field.

He'd already tried and failed to get into the novel that Marley had lent him; his concentration seemed to have evaporated. A steady, autumnal rain was drumming on the tin roof above, its melodious percussion slightly alleviating Dash's tense mood. It was also the reason he was home on a Saturday. By eleven o'clock when it had become obvious that the rain had set in, the site had closed and they were off for the rest of the day.

Some of the boys had headed straight for the pub, but Dash was in a strange mood and decided to head on home. He knew he was missing Evie and it troubled him. He'd never missed a woman before, usually enjoying being a free agent. She'd left this morning for a girls' weekend away. There were eight of them in all and they'd gone to a health spa in Bellbrae, to indulge in some pampering, but because of him leaving so early for work he hadn't even had a chance to see her before she left.

Standing up to turn off the intrusive TV, thoughts of last night's encounter with Evie danced around his mind. With the cessation of the distracting noise, his jumble of images swiftly and smoothly formed into a full picture. He stopped and smiled, remembering how they'd snuggled up together on her couch on the balcony – talking and kissing, then kissing some more. Realising he was getting a hard on thinking about it he grinned some more, shaking his head as he did so.

'That woman … she's done something to me that's for sure,' he thought, grinning. He was rinsing out his cup when his phone rang.

'Hello.'

'G'day you old bastard, have you got it on with Evie yet?'

Dash chuckled then replied, 'G'day Enzo.'

'Well … have ya?'

'Fuck off mate,' Dash laughed. 'Is nothing sacred?'

'No, tell me all.'

'Listen mate, I really like Evie, and I don't want to rush anything.'

'I'll take that as a "no" then.'

'You can. So … what shit have you got yourself into this time, or is this simply one of your stimulating social calls?'

'Well mate … you're not going to believe this.'

'No, probably not, but go on.'

Enzo couldn't help chuckling at that then said, 'No mate, this is ridgey didge, I swear.'

'All right then,' Dash smiled. 'What is it?'

'I think I've found your brother.'

'*What*?'

'I know mate, it's spun me out a bit too I can tell you.'

'Oh yeah, and how do you know he's my brother?' Dash was waiting for the punch line of the expected joke.

'Mate, he looks just like you with a full beard. In fact, I thought it was you. I walked up behind him and slapped him on the back and said, "What the hell are you doing here, you old bastard?" He just turned slowly around, looked me up and down and said, "Do I know you?" I couldn't believe it … *he* wasn't *you*. His voice was a bit different but, mate, he's the same build, his hair's the same colour, and he's even got a broken nose like yours … mate, he looks just like you, and I never thought I'd see *your* ugly mug on anyone else.' Dash didn't say anything for several seconds. He knew Enzo well enough to know he wouldn't make up something like this.

'What's his name?'

'Bushy, that's all he said when I asked him.'

'Bushy,' Dash repeated softly.

'Anyway, I ended up sitting and talking to him for a while; I mean I had to explain who I *thought* he was. And he reckoned he couldn't have a brother because he was his dad's first child, and his dad had been with his mum up until they were both killed in a plane crash years ago.'

'Okay … so why are you still telling me you think he's my brother,' Dash asked, now a bit annoyed.

'Well, when I asked him where he was from he said he'd been born in Darwin but had grown up most his life in Broome, so then I just said what about his dad – where was he from. Mate … when he said his dad had been born in Tasmania and had then moved to the mainland as a young man … I felt the hairs on the back of my neck stand up. The thing is he's about ready to move on. Apparently he's got a job to go to on some big property in the Territory so I reckon you ought to get yourself on a plane and get over here. You've got an RDO on Monday, haven't you?'

'Yeah, I have,' Dash replied automatically.

'Okay, so … what do you reckon mate. I'm in Perth for my week off; you can stay here with me.'

Dash was completely thrown off balance by what Enzo had just told him. For years when he'd been younger he'd imagined what it'd be like when his real dad came back, finally wanting to have Dash as his son. Later that had changed to the occasional thought of possibly having unknown brothers or sisters somewhere. It had never been something he'd allowed himself to dwell on though.

'Come on mate, drag yourself away from your little lady for a couple of days and see for yourself,' Enzo prodded.

Curiosity and a sudden urge to get away for a while kicked Dash into action.

'Okay mate, I will. I'll get on to it now and see when I can get a flight. Marley can drop me at the airport and use the car while I'm away.'

Chuckling gleefully, Enzo responded with, 'I can't wait to see your face when you see this guy. I just don't know how I'll manage to put up with two of you; mate, that is pushing the friendship a bit far.' Before Dash had a chance to tell him to fuck off, Enzo laughed and went on, 'Let me know what time you land and I'll try and pick you up. See ya mate.'

Dash ginned and shook his head as he hung up the phone. He'd been mates with Enzo for so long now it was hard to remember what things were like before they were friends.

'What's he got me into this time?' Dash pondered for a moment. 'A brother ... I wonder ... no, I'll wait and see. The silly bastard was probably pissed to the gills and this bloke won't look anything like me. Doesn't matter though, I feel like getting away to new horizons for a bit.'

He was lucky when he rang for a booking – there were still a couple of seats available on the one-thirty flight. So after throwing a few things into his canvas overnight bag he rang Enzo to give him his arrival time, then he and Marley made a dash for the airport, making it with just minutes to spare. Hilda was more than happy to look after Bluey, and he smiled as he imagined her feasting on the array of goodies that Hilda would enjoy making for the little chatterbox.

Now looking through the small window to his left, he focused on the slowly receding view below until only glimpses were visible between the clouds. He wasn't sure how long he'd been staring out into the overcast sky when he was abruptly brought back to his present surroundings.

'Oh, I'm sorry sir. I didn't mean to startle you,' an extremely attractive air hostess was saying, a concerned look on her face. 'I was just asking if you'd like a drink of some kind.'

'Oh ... yeah ... that sounds like a good idea. I'll have a can of Melbourne thanks.'

Dash's eyes involuntarily followed her shapely behind until she turned back to hand him his cold beer. Smiling as he thanked her, Dash thought of how it was basically impossible for a bloke *not* to look at an attractive woman; it seemed to be hard-wired *in*. It didn't diminish or affect the feelings he now had for Evie though – she was the one he wanted to keep *on* looking at.

An image of her face appeared in his mind, and as his head turned to once more gaze at the cotton wool clouds far below, his thoughts turned to how well Evie had handled the whole bizarre final episode of her father's life. The way she'd accepted the story of her dad's duplicity had surprised him a bit, she'd actually been happy to know that he hadn't drowned and died all alone. The money factor hadn't seemed to faze her too much either.

His contemplations then turned to the reasons why they hadn't been able to spend much time together lately, as it seemed to Dash that events had conspired to severely curtail their time alone.

'Well,' he was thinking as he sipped his beer, 'Evie *has* been busy with her consultations, and what with Marley and Bluey living with me now, plus with me working overtime every day, it's no wonder we've been like ships in the night.'

The couple of times they had managed a rendezvous on the balcony had always left him wanting more. From the first 'hello' kiss to the last 'goodnight' hug, they always crammed in fun and laughter, talking and joking, kissing and cuddling. He was smiling at the recollections as he relaxed back in his seat, allowing his thoughts full rein to graze on his stored memories.

Meeting her family the day of the reunion had been fun. The twins, as they were invariably called, had been a bit hard to take and quite fascinating all at the same time; but then identical twins had always fascinated Dash. He'd never been able to imagine having another 'him' around, much preferring to be his own unique self. He'd agreed with Evie that Pam and Bev had taken the whole thing to a ridiculous extreme. They were forty-six now and Dash doubted whether either of them would know who they really were. In their distorted view, as long as they were 'better' than their twin they were 'winning'.

Reen he liked. He'd seen a steely determination in her which he could bet had got her into as much trouble as good. He'd also seen at once how striking she must have been as a teenager. Long dark hair hung simply down her back and her brilliant green eyes shone from a lightly suntanned face. Evie had mentioned that Reenie had piled on the weight after she'd had kids, and Dash had guessed she was about forty kilos overweight.

He'd taken a shine to Jo as well, finding her to be different again to the others – a lot quieter for one thing. She'd eventually confided in him that she'd just split up with her boyfriend and was feeling a little low. That had been Dash's cue to tell her a variety of funny jokes and anecdotes until she'd had tears from laughter running down her face.

It'd been after that when he'd been introduced to Evie's only brother, Doug, and his Balinese wife, Erica. Dash's first thought had been that if ever there was a bloke heading for a heart attack he was looking at him now. Doug had at first appeared relaxed and confident in his casual designer gear, but then Dash had noticed the vein pumping furiously on the side of Doug's forehead and the unhealthy flush suffusing his face. As Dash had been introduced to Erica, he'd noticed Doug clenching his fists over and over in his pockets.

'This bloke's got problems,' he'd thought as Doug made some comment about the impending birth of their baby. Dash could see the poor guy was besotted with his wife – and why wouldn't he be, she was gorgeous as well as sweet – but it had seemed that Doug had long ago adopted the habit of keeping himself bottled up and controlled. Even if he'd known what his real feelings were, he didn't know how to express them.

Surprisingly, Doug hadn't exploded when Evie finished re-telling the incredible story that Annie had told her. Instead, after an initial short burst of anger, Doug had then literally crumpled like a slowly disintegrating house of cards. Dash had been genuinely concerned for him, fearing that Doug's new-found knowledge of his father's deception might tip him over the edge.

'Excuse me sir. Would you like another drink?'

Dash was again brought out of his reverie by the cute air hostess, and realising his can was now empty, was happy enough to watch her rear end again while she got him another beer.

The instruction to fasten seatbelts roused Dash out of an extremely uncomfortable sleep. He'd been lucky enough to have a vacant seat beside him but still hadn't had enough room to stretch out properly. He was busting for a piss too, but he'd have to wait now 'til they landed.

Twenty minutes later, bladder relieved and overnight bag in hand, Dash was walking towards a taxi rank when he heard Enzo's unmistakable voice.

'Hey, over this way you old dero,' he'd yelled across the road, indicating towards the car he was leaning against.

Dash changed direction and, after waiting for a couple of cars to pass, walked over towards his smiling mate. Five minutes later they were driving out of the airport and towards the pub. With the time difference between the eastern and western states it was now just after three-thirty.

'We'll go to the Grosvenor, that's where I saw him last time,' Enzo was saying as he deftly manoeuvred between the traffic. 'I never actually told him I was going to ring you though, didn't want to scare him off.'

Dash grinned. It sounded as though they were on a hunting expedition or something. They talked about work for the rest of the drive, Dash wanting to keep his mind off the real reason for his visit.

They were nearly finished their first pot when Dash saw his brother walk through the pub door. He knew it was him – the resemblance was unmistakable, especially since the full beard Enzo had mentioned had obviously been shaved off. Fascinated, his eyes focused on the man as he paused for a moment just inside the front door. He seemed to be scanning the room, and the moment his eyes locked onto Dash's he stopped.

The noise in the pub sounded muffled to Dash as he stared across the room, completely unable to shift his gaze from the face that was staring back at him. As he got up from where he'd been sitting at the bar, Dash watched as his double began making his way through the crowd towards him.

'G'day mate,' Bushy said, grinning and holding out his hand. 'I didn't really believe your crazy mate here,' he nodded in Enzo's direction, 'but I think Blind Freddy could see that we're related.'

'G'day mate,' Dash said as he clasped hold of the proffered hand and grinned back. 'Yeah, I thought he was just talking shit again myself, but not now.'

Enzo was stoked to see he'd been right and, ignoring the insults, got up to buy the next round.

'What'll you have, Bushy – a pot?'

'Yeah, a pot of VB thanks mate.'

'No worries,' Enzo replied as he took the empties with him.

The two men then sat on a couple of vacant barstools, facing each other over a small round table. Staring at each other again, it was Dash who spoke next.

'So, what's your real name?'

'Aaron Dashiell. What's yours?'

'Dash McCallum.'

'Hmm … Dash and Dashiell … there's a coincidence.'

'There are no coincidences,' Dash replied, still grinning, remembering Evie once telling him that. 'How did you get the moniker of Bushy anyway?'

Before he could reply Enzo was back with the beers.

'Here you go mate, get that into ya,' Enzo said, passing Bushy his beer. 'And one for the ugly kid at the back,' he grinned as he gave Dash his.

'Thanks mate … now do you want to shut up or fuck off?'

'No worries mate, I'll leave you two to catch up. I'm just going to have a quick chat with that spunky little barmaid.' And Enzo was off.

After a couple of sips of his beer, Bushy began relating the story behind his name.

'Well … when I was little, about five or six, Dad started taking me out into the bush, teaching me how to survive out there and never get lost. I'd overheard him say to Mum one day that he was determined I become a good Bushy, so after the next camping trip I asked him if I was a good Bushy yet. He said not yet, but I was learning. I asked him that same question every time on our way back from a day out until, I think to shut me up, he said, "Yes mate, you're definitely a

Bushy now." When we got home that night the first thing I did was run in and tell Mum. But I was so excited, instead of saying "I'm a Bushy now", I said "I'm Bushy now". Everyone laughed and the name stuck.'

Dash chuckled at the story and drank some of his beer, then queried, 'How old are you anyway?'

'Thirty-eight; I'll be thirty-nine in August. What about you?'

'I was forty-two last December.'

They both stared at each other again, both with the same infectious grin.

It was Bushy who spoke first this time, asking Dash about his upbringing. Then after listening to Dash's story in silence, said, 'Geez, mate, you did it tough. I'm sorry to hear that. Must have been pretty hard not knowing who your dad was.'

Dash just nodded, then they both drank their beers in silence for a minute before Bushy continued. 'I can only say I had the best childhood I could imagine. We travelled a fair bit at times, all around the top end. Dad had a heap of different jobs from cattle mustering to oyster farming, but Mum always made it seem like home – wherever we were. We rode horses and camped under the stars, swam with dolphins and fished for barra' that we'd then cook up over a camp fire. Mum and Dad loved each other and us; there was a lot of laughter in our home.'

'Us?'

'Yeah,' Bushy answered softly, 'my sister Annabelle and me. She was my best friend growing up. Dad always used to call her Tinkerbelle.' He stopped and sipped more beer, a frown evident on his face. Then, almost to himself, he went on.

'I was supposed to be on the plane as well that day, the day of the crash. I'd been behaving like a little smart-arse for days though, as only a fifteen-year-old can, so Dad ended up saying that I had to stay home and mow the lawns. I was pretty pissed off I can tell you, even though I knew it was my own fault. The joy flight was part of Annabelle's thirteenth birthday present from Mum and Dad ...' He slowly shook his head, 'but they never came back.'

Dash could feel his brother's pain at the loss of his family, but found it hard to put it into words.

'Geez mate, that's no good,' he said, shaking his head. 'You've had your fair share of tough times as well.'

Looking at each other again, the realisation hit them at the same time. They had a bond – an actual, unmistakable blood connection. For Dash it was a first time feeling; both wonderful and strange. For Bushy it was a familiar feeling; both wonderful and strange.

'Oh yeah,' Bushy said as he reached into his shirt pocket. 'I brought these ... I thought if it turned out you were my brother you might want to see a photo of our father.'

There was now absolutely no doubt left in Dash's mind. The grinning face looking squarely back at Dash had the same dark, tousled hair and smiling eyes; even the way he was standing with his shoulders back and his head tilted slightly to one side was the same that Dash had seen in photos of himself. The craggy face was handsome in an interesting way and it exuded a love of life.

'What was his name?'

'Thaddeus Obadiah Dashiell.'

'*Thaddeus*?'

Bushy laughed. 'Yeah, imagine having that moniker. He told me he'd been adopted as a baby by an older couple who were apparently quite religious. He later called himself Tod – from his initials.'

His father had one arm around a pleasantly plump woman who had a fleece of golden hair. It rippled over her shoulders and gleamed in the sunshine. She was obviously in love. Frozen in time, she was gazing up at her man with an adoring expression on her lovely face. His father's other arm was wrapped around a young replica of his wife who could only have been Annabelle.

After silently looking at the half a dozen photos, Dash handed them back. But before he could speak, Bushy passed them back over and said, 'No mate, you can have these if you like, I've got some copies.'

'Oh, okay, thanks mate.'

Enzo came back just then with another round. Grinning from ear to ear and looking from one to the other he said, 'Well, fuck me ... two of you ... the world will never be the same again.'

Chapter Forty-Four

Tuesday morning Dash was back at work. He'd spent Saturday night and all day Sunday with Bushy, catching his flight back to Melbourne on Monday afternoon. He'd been thankful that he'd had time for a good sleep-in before he left; he certainly needed it after all the late nights.

Enzo had made himself scarce over the weekend, but Dash and Bushy hadn't missed him – once they'd started talking there'd been no stopping them. Finding out how much they had in common they'd both thought they would've been friends regardless of their connection.

He'd told some of the boys at smoko about his new found half-brother, and how he was coming over this way in a couple of weeks for a visit. They'd been amazed at the story. The same with Evie when he'd finally caught up with her last night.

'But that's amazing,' Evie had exclaimed. 'How fantastic … a brother you never knew you had. I can't even begin to imagine how you must feel …' she'd looked at him quizzically for a moment then added, 'Although you seem to be handling it pretty well.'

'I've had a bit of time to take it all in, that's all,' Dash had replied.

He was in fact still trying to make sense of his differing emotions. The joy of finding a brother was tempered with the knowledge that his father had obviously never tried to find him, and Bushy had then enjoyed the kind of childhood he himself had always dreamt of. He couldn't help but feel a pang of envy. This in turn was moderated by his knowledge of how unexpectedly Bushy had lost the lot – all brutally ripped out from underneath him, leaving him to flounder helplessly for quite some time. With no known family to help him out, the local community had pitched in and kept an eye on him.

Dash remembered reading a quote somewhere about it being better to have loved and lost than never to have loved at all. Thinking about it now he shook his head and said, 'Nope … I reckon it's shit whichever way you look at it.'

Just then someone tapped on the side window of his crane. It was Rick, his dogman.

'We're ready when you are Dash,' he yelled, then gave the signal to boom up.

Dash's hands were at home on the levers while his eyes were on the last of the massive air-conditioning units, now slowly lifting in front of him. The work here was starting to wind down and as yet he didn't know where he'd be working next. He knew he definitely wanted to stay in Geelong though, he wanted to get to know Evie more; a lot more he thought, grinning.

'Stop,' came over the two-way and Dash immediately stopped the crane's motion.

'Now, slew left nice and slow about one metre ... beautiful ... okay, stop ... now down about two metres ... a bit more ... nearly there ...stop.'

Dash sat back and relaxed again. That was the last lift before lunch time and he was starving. Thinking of food, he thought again about Evie, hoping she was still going to be able to have dinner with him later that night. He'd wanted to take the next step in their relationship since the day he'd met her, but she'd said some time ago that she wasn't rushing into anything. Respecting that, he'd actually thought the same thing himself.

He knew there was something special between them and wasn't about to do anything to stuff it up. He just wasn't sure how much longer he could last. It was all well and good having a wank every now and then, but being around Evie had him thinking about sex more than ever. She always smelt so nice and felt so good that he'd had trouble keeping his hands off her, not that she seemed to mind. Becoming aware of his expanding groin, Dash smiled and adjusted his position.

'That woman ... she's definitely got me by the short and curlies,' he thought. 'I think I'll see if she'd like to have a weekend away somewhere; in fact, I'll ask her tonight.'

Chapter Forty-Five

'No, I don't want to go with you ... no, it's got nothing to do with Pam ... I don't care if Doug is going with you ... Bev ... will you stop and draw breath for a minute ... thank you. Now, as I was trying to say, I'm going to visit Annie when I'm ready to, not just because you've all decided to rush over there together ... yes I'm sure ... no I'm not interested in getting a group booking ... I don't care how much I'll save ...Bev ... oh, for goodness sake will you shut up for a minute. I'm not going with you and that's that. Now I have to go ... yes I'm busy ... have a good trip, send me a postcard ... okay ... bye.'

Sighing and shaking her head, Evie finished the conversation and slumped down onto her couch.

'Family ... is it a good thing or not I wonder.' As she sat there in her underwear pondering the question, she realised how family issues had been dominating her and Dash's lives recently. Dash himself was never far from the forefront of her thoughts, and she was slowly becoming used to how much time she spent thinking about him. But there'd been so many changes to their lives of late it was a bit hard keeping up.

Deciding to put everything else out of her mind, Evie walked into her bedroom and opened a wardrobe door.

'Now, what will I wear?'

She wanted to look especially good tonight – it would be the first time she and Dash had been out together for a while. He'd said a quick hello and given her one of his yummy kisses when he'd arrived home after work.

'Are we still on for tonight?' he'd asked. 'I've booked a table for us at the Mecure.'

'Of course, I'm looking forward to it.'

'Okay ... I'll go and have a scrub up and be back. How does half an hour suit you?'

'Yeah, that's okay with me,' she'd smiled.

After another quick kiss he was off into his own flat.

Grinning, she remembered how she couldn't help but overhear Blue's enthusiastic welcome home for her poppy. Evie had pulled back a little after Marley and Bluey had moved in next door, thinking that Dash would want to spend as much time as possible with the daughter and granddaughter he hardly knew. But after spending the time that she'd had with Dash, her attraction to him was now undeniable and she was ready to do something about it.

Deciding to wear a figure-hugging dress she'd bought but never worn, Evie pulled the soft fabric over her head. Wriggling a little as it slid over her hips, she stood in front of the mirror to check out how it looked. Realising she needed shoes to get the best effect, she found them and put them on.

'Hmm … not bad.' The cotton knit dress clung in all the right places, the burgundy colour infusing her already flushed skin with an extra glow. Satisfied as to how it looked, she wandered into the bathroom to add some makeup, smiling as she did so.

She'd found she was usually smiling these days, ever since she'd met Dash. Thoughts of him had taken up residence deep in her mind, only to then shamelessly parade themselves, demanding attention at any time of the night or day.

True to his word, Dash was back thirty minutes later, looking and smelling extremely appealing. By the look in his eyes Evie knew he liked what he saw as well. He'd already rung for a taxi and it tooted as he stepped in her front door.

'Come on gorgeous, let's get out of here,' Dash grinned.

After a delicious meal and several drinks they were now enjoying a coffee in the cocktail lounge area, sitting side by side on one of the plush couches. Dash had one arm along the top of the couch, just touching Evie's shoulders, and was so conscious of her proximity he felt his body responding again.

'Would you like for us to have a couple of days away somewhere?' he heard himself say.

'Hmm ... I think that sounds like a great idea,' Evie replied, sitting her coffee cup down on the low table in front of them. 'When did you have in mind?'

'Well, I've got an RDO next Monday; we could leave Saturday afternoon and get back Monday sometime.'

'This weekend till Monday afternoon ... yeah, that suits me. Okay then.'

Neither of them could now get the smiles off their faces.

Chapter Forty-Six

The rest of the week went by in a bit of a blur for both Evie and Dash. They managed to see each other for an hour or so most nights, but that had just added more fuel to their simmering feelings. By the time the weekend arrived they were equally excited about their planned rendezvous.

Dash had booked a place which was nestled in the bush and overlooked the ocean, and as they reached their destination both commented on the fabulous view. Parking out the front of their cabin and turning off the motor, they could hear the crash of the waves on the rocks below.

'How about I unload our gear and then we can check out that view some more,' Dash suggested.

'Okay, sounds good to me.'

They both grinned at each other before getting out of the car.

'Mmmm ... I love the smell of the ocean,' Evie sighed, leaning back against the warm car.

'I love the smell of you,' Dash grinned over his shoulder as he unlocked the cabin door. 'Hey, this looks like a bit of alright; nice and roomy, and the spa's as big as they'd promised ... beautiful.'

Leaving the bathroom he found Evie checking out the bed. It was king size and covered in a fluffy faux fur bedspread. She was running the palm of her hand back and forth over the fur, smiling at the ticklish sensation. He knew he loved her, everything about her in fact, but hadn't yet said the words. He knew tonight would be the night.

'What do you reckon?' he asked. 'It's nearly five now; I thought after we have a look around we could wander over to the restaurant and have a meal, then after that we could come back here. I'll light the fire and we can test out the spa.'

Evie walked over to him and wrapped her arms around him.

'That sounds perfect,' she smiled. 'You're not just a pretty face, are you?'

Dash had to laugh at that.

'That's the first time anyone's said that I've got a pretty face; I didn't realise you had bad eyesight.'

'Not at all, I've got good eyesight. But you're right, you're not pretty, you're gorgeous.' Evie's hand went to the side of his face as she continued, 'I love your face; it's got so much character in it I don't think I'd ever get tired of looking at it.'

Dash then held her face gently between his hands and kissed her softly on her lips. For once he hadn't had a comeback; his mind had been filled instead by an overwhelming feeling of love. He knew he was a goner for her and had never felt so happy in his life.

Chapter Fort-Seven

They'd only been back in the cabin for ten minutes before they'd had their clothes in a heap on the floor. Their bodies had found their own way onto the bed, then their hands and lips had taken over. Finally being able to touch and explore each other's bodies had been bliss, and all too soon neither of them had been able to hold back a mind-blowing climax.

Dash had just opened the bottle of Moet that he'd brought along. After pouring out two glasses he stepped back into the churning, steamy water and sat down. Carefully handing one across to Evie, he raised his glass and said, 'Here's to us.'

'To us,' Evie repeated, adjusting her position in the spa before having a sip. 'Hmmm ... yummy.'

They sat and smiled across at each other, surrounded by an ever increasing amount of foamy bubbles.

'Well …' said Dash. 'That was worth waiting for.'

'Yes … it was,' agreed Evie, contentment oozing through her body.

'I do love you, you know,' Dash looked straight at her. 'I haven't been able to think of anything else but you since the first time we met, and that's never happened to me before.'

'I know; I've been the same with you. I have to say it threw me a bit at first. I didn't know what was going on.'

'And do you now?'

'Yes … I love you and you love me … I've never felt this happy in my entire life.'

Dash slid forward and gently pulled Evie towards him. They both wrapped their arms and legs around each other, sending a few clumps of foam to circle in the air before settling again. They kissed laughed and kissed some more before leaving the spa for the more comfortable bed, not bothering to dry off first.

Chapter Forty-Eight

Liz had every second Tuesday afternoon rostered off and usually used that time to catch up with Evie for coffee and a chat. As she hesitantly manoeuvred her car in a challenging exercise of parallel parking, a glowing expression never left her face. She was bursting with her news and as soon as she'd locked the car door was up the stairs to Evie's flat in record time.

'Hi Evie, it's just me ... you're not going to believe what I have to tell you.'

'Oh, hi Liz,' Evie said from the kitchen. 'What? You've won Tattslotto or met Mr. Right?'

Instead of the expected, 'Yeah I wish' answer that Evie had been expecting, Liz became silent for a moment. Evie poked her head around the door to see her friend just standing there with a look on her face that she hadn't seen before.

'Liz ... are you alright?'

Liz smiled and answered, 'I've never been so alright in all my life. It was simply what you just said ... about winning Tattslotto or meeting Mr. Right ... because I'm in love and it feels like I've hit the jackpot.'

'What ...? When did this happen ...? Who is it?' Evie had seen little of her best friend over the last few weeks. Liz had been driving Jason down to Lorne to see his dad quite a bit and she'd been busy with her Feng Shui.

'That's the bit you're not going to believe ... its Hugh ... Jason's father.'

'What ...? You're kidding ... no ... you're not kidding ... when did this happen?'

'Just over the last few weeks; I thought he was a bit of all right the first time I met him – remember when I drove Jase down there when he finally told his dad he was gay? Well, it turned out that he thought I was a bit of all right too.'

'But how old is he?'

'Fifty-eight, but he's so much fun and he has a real love for life. And guess what...? He loves my shape. He says I'm beautiful and gorgeous and the more there is of me the better; can you believe that?'

Evie was beaming at her friend's unabashed display of high spirits. She had to admit she'd never seen Liz this excited over a man before.

'That's fantastic Lizzie. At last, a man who loves you just the way you are.'

'I know; I feel fantastic too.'

'So, have you got down and dirty with him yet?'

'You bet ... it was great ... he was great ... well, he still is great ... God ... I'm babbling like a school girl aren't I?'

Evie laughed in delight at her friend's new found joy.

'Yes, you are, but I wouldn't worry about it. I think it's terrific, but what did Jason have to say about it?'

This triggered laughter in Liz who then replied, 'He thinks it's fabulous too. He's so happy for both of us he's been telling everyone.'

'So nobody felt any weirdness about it at all?' Evie quizzed.

'Yeah, of course, in the beginning; I'd only ever thought of Hugh as Jason's dad before, but that didn't last long once I got to know him. He's so charming and sweet, and he's got enough money to keep me in the style that I'd like to become accustomed too,' she ginned cheekily.

'Lizzie, you are impossible,' Evie laughed along with her mate. 'Listen, would you like a coffee or a beer? I've got something to tell you as well.'

'You've done it, haven't you? You and Dash ... I can see it in your face.'

'Yeah, we got back yesterday. We stayed at a great place at Eastern View, and before you ask, it was fantastic.'

The two friends sat at the kitchen table for ages just talking, laughing and imagining different futures for each other. When Evie relayed the news that Dash had a half-brother he'd not known about and who looked just like him, Liz jokingly groaned and said, 'Bugger, now I find out that he's got a brother. Damn, it never rains but it pours.'

'Yeah, and he'll actually be here on the weekend, staying with Dash for a few days.'

'Oh, it'll be a bit crowded with Marley and Bluey there, won't it?'

'Yeah, it will be a bit, but Dash doesn't care. He said Bushy could sleep in his swag on the lounge room floor. And anyway, the main reason for his visit is to meet Marley and Bluey – he didn't think he had any living relatives before. His other half-brother, Laurie, is coming over from Tassie as well so it will be a bit squashy in there.'

They both just sat for a moment then, sipping the last of their coffees.

'Hmm ... life's strange sometimes, isn't it,' Liz said softly.

'Yeah ... it sure is.' Putting her cup down Evie then stood up and said, 'Come on, let's go out and celebrate our new status; from singledom to coupledom.'

'Okay, what did you have in mind?' Liz stood as Evie picked up her bag and car keys.

'That new patisserie has finally opened in Pakington Street. I reckon we ought to buy ourselves the most delicious-looking cream cakes we can see.'

'Mmm ... yum ... great idea ... let's go ... um ... *coupledom* ... is that a word?' asked Liz as she followed her friend out the door.

Chapter Forty-Nine

The following weekend Marley was giving the flat a quick once over. She was extremely excited to be meeting her uncle, and one who looked so much like her dad had her quite intrigued. The photos her dad had shown her after his trip to Perth had rendered her speechless at first, especially the first one of her Uncle Aaron with his mum, dad and sister next to him.

'So, that's my Uncle ... and my grandfather ... oh my God ... you all look so much alike; it's amazing,' she remembered saying.

Looking at the clock above the sink she calculated her dad would be home in about twenty minutes, plenty of time to clean Bluey's hands before she smeared them all over her granddad's work pants. It thrilled Marley that her dad and her daughter were as close as they were – she'd missed out on that special bond you often saw between kids and their grandparents.

Walking out onto the balcony where she'd set up a small easel for Bluey to do her painting, she stood for a moment and watched her daughter. The concentration was evident on her serious little face; the tip of her tongue was poking in and out with each brush stroke.

'Come on Blue, time to clean up. Poppy will be home soon.'

'Okay Mummy. Do you think Poppy will like my painting? I did it 'specially for him.'

'Yes I'm sure he will; it's beautiful. I like the way you did the smiles on everyone's faces.'

'Yes, it's a very happy picture, isn't it? See, that's me, and Poppy, and you, and Poppy's new brother,' she pointed with her sticky, multi-coloured finger.

'Yep, it looks great; we'll leave it out here to dry then, okay?'

'Okay. How long before Uncle Aaron gets here? I've been waiting all day.'

'I told you before that I didn't know, just that it would be sometime today. Now, into the bathroom and wash those hands; pronto!'

Marley was giving Blue's hair a brush when they both heard footsteps coming up the stairs.

'Poppy's home,' the little girl squealed as she expertly

wriggled away and ran to the front door.

'Hi Poppy ...' Bluey stopped and put her head to one side. 'Poppy? You're not Poppy ... you must be Poppy's new brother. *Mummy ... Uncle Aaron's here.*'

Marley was unexpectedly nervous for some reason but didn't stop to think about it. Walking straight to the front door she opened it wide and said, 'Hi Uncle Aaron. I'm Marley, and I see you've already met Bluey.'

'G'day Marley' he stuck out his hand for a handshake, 'I'm really pleased to meet you.' He smiled then said, 'But you can call me Bushy if you like, most people do.'

As they shook hands they heard, 'what about me; are you pleased to meet me as well?' Bluey asked, gazing up at him.

'I certainly am, young lady,' Bushy smiled as he squatted down to her level. Putting out his hand she held it in her own as he gently shook it and said, 'G'day Bluey, I'm very pleased to meet you.'

'G'day Uncle Bushy, I'm very pleased to meet you too. You look just like my poppy but different.'

Bushy's eyes were twinkling as he grinned at the little redhead. Standing back up again, Marley had just started to invite him inside when he heard his brother's voice.

'G'day Bushy mate, you got here alright then I see?' Dash called out as he rounded the corner and saw him on the balcony.

'Yeah mate, just got here,' he grinned back.

After Bushy deposited his overnight bag in a corner of the lounge room, he and Dash took a beer out to the balcony. Bluey had said her hellos to her poppy and proudly showed him her painting, pointing out everyone in it again. Marley then distracted her daughter by asking her to help out in the kitchen, allowing her dad and uncle some respite from her constant chatter.

'Sit down mate, take a load off; you must be feeling a bit knackered by now.'

'Yeah, thanks mate; I am feeling a little weary.' They both relaxed back in the old deck chairs, then Bushy commented on the great view.

'Yeah, it's not bad is it?' Dash replied. 'There are a lot of nice places around Geelong.'

Before any more could be said, Evie appeared from Hilda's flat below. As she walked along the path towards the stairs to the upper level, Bushy grinned and asked, 'Who's that ... she looks like a bit of all right?'

Dash suddenly felt a cold clutch of fear constrict his insides but managed to keep his face looking neutral.

'That's Evie ... we've been going out together for a couple of weeks.'

They both turned towards her as she ascended the last step. Dash stood first, giving her a hug and a kiss before turning to introduce her to his brother.

'Aaron, this is Evie. Evie, meet my brother Aaron, also

known as Bushy.'

Even though she'd been prepared for the likeness between them, Evie was still thrown by their many similarities. After shaking hands with a smiling Aaron then chatting with them both for about ten minutes, Evie declined Dash's offer of a beer. Having decided it would be better to leave them to catch up as a family tonight, she soon left them to it and walked into her adjoining flat.

'Wow … unbelievable,' Evie thought as she shook her head. 'I can't believe how alike they look – it's uncanny.' She pressed the 'on' button on her kettle and went about the business of making a cup of tea, all the while remembering the story Dash had related concerning Aaron's parents and sister being killed.

'How tragic,' she thought, then remembered how Dash had also endured a terrible experience – his childhood.

Evie poured the now boiling water into her cup and jiggled the teabag up and down, sighing at the realisation of how a lot of people lived with their personal tragedies every day. Adding sugar and milk she then took her steaming cup and sat down at her desk.

It didn't take long, though, for her to realise that she was unable to concentrate on the chart she was compiling for a client. She was worried about Hilda. She'd just spent the last couple of hours talking with her in the neat little flat downstairs.

Apparently Hilda's older sister Ruth had asked Hilda to move into the lovely two-bedroom house she owned in Point Lonsdale. Ruth's husband had died last year and she'd been terribly lonely since, and now her health was suffering because of her depression. Sighing, Hilda had said she would have moved there with Will straight away except there was no bedroom where he could have his own privacy. She didn't know what to do. She couldn't leave Will to end up back in the system, but she felt compelled to help out her sister as well.

Evie suddenly smiled a little, remembering how Blackie had not long ago informed his oma that he didn't like the name Willy, and from then on he'd only answer to Will or Blackie. Not surprisingly, Hilda had chosen to call him Will from then on.

Neither she nor Dash had been able to spend much time with Blackie for a while now – something they both wanted to rectify. They'd both been in agreement that his start in life had been extremely crappy but he was still basically a good kid.

Evie always enjoyed it whenever he dropped in; often with a joke he'd heard at school to tell her. Sometimes she'd asked him to stay for tea, having previously let Hilda know, and he'd been happy to help her prepare their meal – even helping later with the dishes. Afterwards when they'd sit down to watch some TV, Blackie would invariably sprawl himself along the floor; his head resting on a cushion.

The thought that he could have moved in with her had to be dismissed as her flat only had the one bedroom. Dash's place was not an option either with Marley and Bluey staying there. She'd now finished her cuppa and was slowly stretching her arms out and around to try and ease the tightness she felt in her neck and shoulders.

'I think a nice hot shower might do the trick,' she thought to herself as she slowly lowered her arms down again.

'Poor Hilda,' Evie was still thinking as she adjusted the water's temperature. 'Blackie was just starting to settle down and now she's faced with this dilemma.' Shaking her head as she stepped into the cubicle, she positioned herself directly underneath the steaming torrent. Visibly relaxing as she stood there, Evie visualised clearing out all thoughts and worries, allowing them to be carried away with the warm wash of water.

Automatically giving her body a quick scrub, it wasn't long before she was reaching for a towel to dry off again. She had a thoughtful frown on her face though, as she zigzagged the towel across her shoulders and back, finally remembering the house she'd received as part of her property settlement ... years ago now.

Her father-in-law had been mortified when he heard that his son had left her, and just months after the miscarriage of his first grand-child. He'd then made contact with her lawyers to inform them she'd be receiving a house as part of her settlement, and also a hefty sum of money.

The house was in Terrigal, on the mid-coast of New South Wales, and she'd rented it out since becoming the owner. It was supposed to have gone to Phil. He'd often mentioned how his dad was going to leave him some terrific house one day; they'd always been going to check it out but had never done it.

Evie knew she could live and carry out her Feng Shui consultations anywhere, but now that she and Dash had gotten together she'd felt no desire to move. Now the thought of it being a perfect place for her and Blackie to live, solving Hilda's problems but creating one for herself along the way, had her in a quandary.

'Maybe I could just sell it and then buy a house in Geelong somewhere,' she considered as she pulled on jeans and a t-shirt. The sound of her phone suddenly ringing brought her out of her thoughts with a jolt. Dressed and staring at her reflection in the wardrobe mirror, she gave her head a quick shake then turned and walked towards the insistent ringing.

'Hello.'

'Hi Evie, it's me, Jo. I hope I haven't called at a bad time.'

'Oh, hi Jo, how're you going? No, you've actually called at a good time. How's the new business going?'

'Pretty good really; it'll be a lot easier once Dad's money comes through of course. Have you heard anything more about it?'

'No, the last I heard is that it could take a couple of months before we have the money at our disposal.'

'Hmm … well, that would make it about a month from now then, by my calculations.'

'Hmm … yeah, 'Evie agreed. 'That sounds about right. You could always ring Pam or Bev – no doubt they're onto the lawyers nearly every day.'

Jo laughed a little then said, 'Yeah, I can just picture them now, each wanting to be the first with the inside knowledge. But they left for France this morning, along with Reen and Doug.'

'Oh, I didn't know Reenie was going too; unbelievable. That's going to be an interesting trip – the four of them together again *and* in a foreign country.'

Neither could suppress some giggles at their own images of their brother and sisters co-existing again. It hadn't been good the first time and neither expected it to be any better this time.

'I wonder what Annie will make of them,' mused Jo, 'having them descending on her en-masse.'

Evie thought for a moment then smiled. 'I think she'll be fine, a bit exhausted maybe,' she chuckled, 'but fine. She's such a lovely person; I'm looking forward to spending more time with her myself.'

'When are you planning to go then?' queried Jo

'Oh, I've got no immediate plans, maybe next year sometime.'

'Hmmm ... what are you going to do with your share of the money, any idea yet?'

Evie was silent for a moment then said, 'I've just been thinking about the possibility of relocating; the money would come in handy for that, I'm sure.'

'Yeah, I'd reckon. I suppose you'll buy yourself a house now, but would you move away from Geelong? It's not long since you were saying how much you loved it there.'

'I know ... it's a long story ... do you have time to listen?'

'Of course I do.'

Just then Evie heard Dash's excited voice call out, 'G'day Laurie mate, I was just wondering what time you'd get here. Come in and meet Bushy ...'

Chapter Fifty

Early the next day Evie was outside relaxing on her comfortable old couch. It was a perfect autumn morning – crisp, calm and sunny. As she finished off the delicious banana smoothie she'd blended up, she watched a couple of magpies noisily intent on removing a trespasser from their neighbourhood; diving and swooping at the unfortunate interloper.

Their glorious warbling was one of Evie's favourites, and as they resumed their positions amongst the yellowing foliage they gave another magical recital. Closing her eyes she leant back against the soft, faded fabric, soaking up the morning's tranquil energy and the warmth of the sun's rays at the same time.

'Um ... are you asleep?'

Evie opened her eyes and was immediately confronted

with Bluey's face so close to her own that she nearly went cross-eyed trying to focus on it.

'Oh ... Bluey ... you startled me. What are you doing out here?'

'Mummy said I could come out here and play so I wouldn't wake up Poppy or Uncle Bushy or Uncle Laurie, but she said I wasn't to annoy you ... am I annoying you Evie?'

As usual, Evie couldn't help but smile at the earnest little face.

'No, of course you're not annoying me. Have you had your brekky yet?'

'No not yet. But Mummy gave me a drink of Milo before I came outside. She said she was going to cook some bacon and eggs soon, when the men are out of bed.'

Evie smiled as she listened to the little girl talking – she was so sweet and innocent – when an unexpected feeling swept over her body, catching her completely off guard. Her long-suppressed maternal urge had kicked in with a vengeance, leaving her feeling vulnerable and a little emotional. Reaching out she gave the child a quick hug then abruptly stood up.

'Come on then Bluey ... would you like some toast while you're waiting for your bacon and eggs?'

'Ooh yes please, can I have peanut butter on it?'

Ten minutes later they were both sitting outside again. Bluey was finally silent, eating her toast while studying a willy-wagtail sashaying its way closer to where she was sitting. Dropping a tiny piece of crust, Bluey's face lit up with delight when the bird picked it up and flew away.

'Did you see that Evie? I gave the little bird his breakfast.'

Just then the front door screen of Dash's flat opened.

'Good morning ladies,' Bushy grinned as he stepped out onto the adjoining balcony. 'Ahhh, what a lovely morning … sunny and crisp … beautiful.'

'Good morning Uncle Bushy. Would you like some toast and peanut butter?' Bluey asked. 'Or if you want to wait, Mummy's going to cook some bacon and eggs.'

Chuckling a little, Bushy replied, 'Hmmm … it all sound pretty good, but I think I'll wait for the bacon and eggs.'

Evie smiled at him and asked if he'd like a cup of tea or coffee.

'Yeah, a coffee would be great, thanks.'

Bluey chattered on to Bushy while Evie made the coffee, then just as she reappeared carrying two cups of the aromatic brew, Marley came looking for her daughter.

'Oh, good morning everyone,' she said brightly surprised, 'you're up nice and early. Come on Blue, time for you to get out of your pyjamas and get dressed.'

When Dash finally woke up and made his way into the kitchen he looked outside to see what sort of a day it was, but his eyes focused on Evie and his brother laughing about something that had obviously amused them. A sick feeling settled in his stomach as he watched them for a moment, until he was brought out of his ominous thoughts by Marley asking if he was ready for coffee then bacon and eggs.

'Too right I am ... by God I drank enough last night. Is Laurie up yet?'

'No, not yet, but I'm going to start breakfast now; the aroma will probably wake him up.'

'... yeah, that concept of living in balance with nature is also found in the Dreamtime stories I heard when I was a kid ...' Bushy paused as Dash made a casual appearance with his coffee.

'Morning Dash,' Bushy grinned. 'Feeling a bit average, are we?'

'Morning Bushy,' Dash replied. 'Yeah, I have felt better.' Turning his focus on Evie, he smiled and said, 'Good morning gorgeous, did you sleep well?'

'No, not really, I've been up for ages; what about you?'

'Well, I don't actually remember going to bed, but I think I must have died when my head hit the pillow.' Grinning, he went on, 'that bloody Bushy and Laurie – they're definitely a bad influence on me.'

After giving him a smile and a cheeky comment about 'birds of a feather', Evie then said she must go and have a shower because she had a Feng Shui consultation scheduled at Point Roadknight.

'It's for one of Hugh's friends. Sunday's the only day that he's down there; he lives in Melbourne during the week,' she explained. 'Liz teed it up for me. She also said I may as well keep on driving down to Lorne so I could finally meet Hugh. Actually, knowing Liz, she's probably expecting me to stay the night so I'm not sure when I'll be back.'

Dash only had time to say 'Oh ...' before Evie's phone started ringing.

'Sorry ... I'll have to get moving,' Evie apologised as she headed for her door. 'That's probably Liz wanting me to pick up some exotic ingredient for lunch or something so ... I'll see you later then.'

'Yeah, see you later,' he replied flatly.

Dash definitely felt deflated after Evie drove off. He'd waited for her to finish her phone call and had then walked her to her car, listening as she laughed about having to stop somewhere to buy some gooseberries for Hugh. She'd given him a quick kiss, had jumped in her car and was gone before he'd had a chance to ... well, he wasn't sure what he wanted to do ... but now that she'd gone he felt a bit empty, and he didn't like it.

As he walked back through the garden and up the stairs he was thinking of how his plans for the day had been quashed. He'd been hoping to spend some time with her today, perhaps going for a drive before later taking her for a nice meal somewhere.

He had to admit to himself that he didn't want to lose her, and he was uncomfortably aware that he'd seen some sort of an attraction between her and his brother. A gloomy feeling enveloped Dash as he thought his life was destined to continue its previous pattern – missing out on the love that should have been his.

Bluey came running out then shouting, 'Poppy ... I didn't know you were up ... guess what? Mummy's cooking bacon and eggs and I've been helping her.'

'That's great sweetie. Come here and give your old pop a hug.' Dash rapidly realised that he *did* have love in his life. Bluey and Marley had been like a godsend to him; he hadn't realised what he'd been missing before they'd moved in. He grinned as he thought of how Blue was usually straight on to him when he got home with ... 'Guess what Poppy ..', or 'Poppy, you'll never guess what I saw today ...' Sometimes she'd just hug him tightly around one of his legs, then look up at him with such love in her gorgeous hazel eyes, it had gripped Dash's insides with such a protective pull it'd scared him.

Bushy stood by the railing silently for a bit then said, 'You're a lucky man Dash. You've got a great family here.'

'*We've* got a great family here,' Dash stressed. 'You're part and parcel of this family now mate. Marley's your niece, and this little muppet here is your great niece.'

Before Bushy had a chance to respond, Bluey piped up,

'Am I a great niece?' Putting her head to one side she continued, 'Wow ... but how come I'm great all of a sudden? Mummy said I was naughty because I cracked open all the eggs, but I just liked cracking them and watching them plop into the bowl and forgot to count them 'til there was none left.'

Both Dash and Bushy were finding it difficult not to laugh at the seriousness of her question. Thankfully they were saved by Marley saying that Laurie was up and she was about to serve breakfast.

Chapter Fifty-One

After being talked into staying the night, Evie then enjoyed a delicious brunch the next day with Liz and Hugh on his expansive balcony. The sweet smell of lemon-scented gums wafted on the breeze, while a colourful variety of native birds fought noisily over positions on the bird-feeders; scattering bits of seed and fruit everywhere.

Admiring the magnificent view as they leisurely ate their way through smoked salmon and scrambled eggs, they still had something to say about the unexpected guests that had arrived yesterday, not long after Evie.

'All I said was they could have rung first, seeming as though we already knew that Evie was coming here for her first visit. Anyone for more coffee?' Hugh was standing near the espresso machine, a smile on his face and eyebrows raised in query.

'Yes please darling.'

'Oh yes ... I'll have some more too please.' Evie stood up and took the empty cups over to be refilled.

'I don't mind the "drop-in" visit,' Liz continued, 'I love the unexpected, and they've been to so many interesting places; they're both very entertaining guests. Isobel's such a lovely person too ... I can't believe she's sixty though – she looks fantastic.'

'I know ... it's unbelievable isn't it?' Evie shook her head. 'And she puts it all down to yoga, and eating everything she likes in moderation.'

'Hmm ... yeah ... well, she and Mike both look terrific and they *are* very interesting people, but I've been wanting to know more about the house in Terrigal that you started talking about just before they got here. You know I vaguely remember you telling me about it once ... seems like eons ago now though.'

Deciding to take their coffees downstairs and sit around the pool while Hugh made a few business calls, Evie finally talked to her friend about her dilemma, hoping that Liz could help her sort out her conflicting thoughts. Liz sat and listened until Evie had finished explaining how she couldn't help but be concerned for Blackie's welfare, '... especially since I know what it's like to lose a dad ...' she was saying.

Liz knew of Evie's long-held but fruitless desire to have her own child, and could understand her friend's urge to want to protect and mother young Blackie, so half an hour later they came up with a plan of action. Evie would drive up to Terrigal and check out the house first; after all, it mightn't be somewhere that she'd want to live. If that was the case, that would make her decision easy – she'd sell it and use the money to buy something closer to Geelong.

If, on the other hand, she did like it ... well ... she was still thinking of selling it. Even apart from her developing relationship with Dash, she didn't like the thought of moving away from Liz again. They were both really enjoying their lives now and having so much silly fun together; they both thought they'd miss each other too much.

Putting that aspect out of her mind for now, Evie asked Liz if she'd like to drive to Terrigal with her.

'I'm going to go tomorrow. Now that I have it in my head I want to get it sorted out, one way or another.'

'Oh, bugger. I would have Evie, but Hugh's taking me to that spa retreat in Daylesford for a couple of days of pampering.'

Liz looked in Hugh's direction as he walked towards the pool and grinned. 'I'm planning on giving him some pampering of my own as well.'

'Okay, okay, enough information,' Evie laughed. 'That's alright though; if I leave really early tomorrow I should be there by Tuesday arvo.'

'How long do you think you'll stay up there?'

'Well, I could be away for a few days if I decide to sell. I may as well get that sorted out while I'm there, but I'll phone you once I've seen the place and let you know what's happening'

After a bit more chat about Hilda and Blackie's situation, Evie said her goodbyes. Promising to come and stay again, she was soon driving down the steep gravel driveway and back onto the busy coastal road.

'Long distance relationships never work ...' Evie ruminated as she automatically drove around another sweeping curve, her new Commodore hugging the road beautifully. 'Dash has his family around him now, he's not going to want to up and move.'

Bass Straight gleamed to her right, the iridescent colour of the water fluctuating dramatically from deepest blue to aqua as it continued it's never ending cycle of ebb and flow. But her vision of giving young Blackie a stable home life persisted.

She'd gradually formed what was now a close bond with him over these last few months – more so since his dad had died – and she couldn't help worrying about his future. She felt sure that the Department would okay her fostering him (after all, it would save them the trouble of finding him another home) and also felt sure that Blackie himself *and* Hilda would be okay with it.

After thinking everything through again she had to

acknowledge the downside of moving interstate – she'd be jeopardising what she felt was the beginning of a good thing between her and Dash.

'No, I think I'll just sell the place and be done with it,' Evie was nodding to herself. 'Then I'll look around for a nice house to buy in Geelong.'

Smiling now she'd made her decision, she reduced speed as she caught up with the 'Sunday drivers' in front of her, taking advantage of the unhurried pace to once more appreciate her surroundings. Having always loved the contrasting scenery all along the Great Ocean Road, she relaxed into what was going to be a slow drive home. The road snaked downwards into a large gully then wound its way upwards again, the massive tree ferns and other lush foliage cooling the air considerably. Up ahead a couple of shafts of sunlight were piercing the thick vegetation, producing a spectacular sparkling effect on the surface of a small creek. Evie smiled, thinking how it gave the whole area a magical quality. Winding her window all the way down, she breathed in deeply, the earthy smell of the rainforest infusing her senses.

'Hmm ... Mother Nature in all her glory,' she said to herself before slowing down to take the next tight, hairpin bend. Awesome views of the ocean were then revealed once more as she carefully navigated the winding road, glancing when she could at the perfectly formed waves slowly rolling towards the coastline.

Arriving back at the flats just before one-thirty, Evie was disappointed to find that Dash wasn't home; in fact no one was home next door. Sighing in resignation, she unlocked her own front door and headed for the bedroom. She felt quite unsettled now, and disappointed that she couldn't talk her plans over with Dash.

Plopping down on her bed in frustration, Evie tossed her bag onto the floor, then using her feet, kicked off her sandals. Being a Leo she was often impatient with herself – whenever she had what she thought was a good idea she wanted to act on it straight away.

But having no idea where Dash was, or when he'd be back, made her realise how little time they'd spent together recently. No wonder they hadn't been able to let each other know what they were doing. Thinking about it more, Evie was a little surprised to calculate that since their weekend away they hadn't been anywhere together; not just the two of them.

'Oh well, he has been doing a lot of overtime at work,' she allowed. 'And with Bushy and Laurie being here, and Marley and Bluey, it's no wonder I've been sidelined I suppose.'

Leaning backwards to fall onto her soft doona, Evie then stared at the ceiling, hating the restless feeling that had invaded her body.

'Of course I've been busy these last few weeks as well,' she reasoned. 'I've done ... what ... three new charts and delivered two others? And Liz and I went to that art show ...'

But a seed of doubt had begun to grow in her mind, and she couldn't help but wonder if Dash was the kind of guy who moved on once he'd gotten what he wanted. Sighing a little, she wondered if she'd ever find a truly trustworthy guy.

Thinking about the last time she had seen him, before she'd left for Point Roadknight, she now realised that he had seemed a bit distant. Even when she'd kissed him he'd just sort of stood there. Then, after analysing their last meeting some more, she realised that he hadn't even said anything about missing her or wanting to get together again. She'd been in a hurry at the time and trying to think of where she could buy some gooseberries, so his now apparent coolness hadn't penetrated through to her 'til now.

'Oh God, don't tell me I've picked another bull-shitter ... when will I ever learn?' She shook her head in exasperation, then after thinking for a bit decided to just wait 'til she next saw him; maybe later tonight, or else tomorrow morning.

'I could be over-reacting to all this ... I'm just not sure now ... when we can get away by ourselves for a while I'll soon be able to tell how he really feels ...' Then, abruptly standing up, she said, 'No, stuff this. I'm not sitting around here twiddling my thumbs 'til tomorrow. If he's avoiding me then so be it. The sooner I find out the better, but I'm not going to sit around waiting for him to call. I'm going to do what I feel like doing and there's no time like the present.'

Having decided to leave for Terrigal then and there, she quickly packed a few clothes and necessities and was ready to go fifteen minutes later.

'I know, I'll leave a message on his answering machine and the phone number of the Terrigal Real Estate office. If he is interested in where I am, then he'll call and I can ring him back later when I get there.'

The long cord on her phone enabled her to take it outside, and after finding some correspondence from the realtor that managed the house, she sat down on the faded floral couch while she rang Dash's number. Listening as it rang, the sound carrying clearly through his open window, she felt a little disappointed that he hadn't rung her yet today. The only message on her answering machine had been from Reen saying that she'd bring Evie back some French perfume.

The bright sun momentarily disappeared behind a small cloud as she listened to the ringing change to his recorded voice. She left a brief message, hating the silly nervous feeling she always got when having a conversation with a machine.

'Oh, um ... hi Dash ... it's me, Evie ... um ... I'm just letting you know that I'm driving up the coast for a few days, to Terrigal ... um ... I'll explain why later ... you can contact me through Terrigal Realty on 02 4385 2956 ... okay ... bye.'

Shaking her head at how stupid she probably sounded, she stood up and walked back inside to get her things, not noticing that one of the pieces of paper had slowly lifted up with a sudden breeze then gently floated back down, coming to rest underneath the old couch.

Six hours later Evie pulled into the parking lot of a small motel in Gundagai, having decided to call it a day. After carrying her overnight bag into the motel room her first action was to ring Dash, but hearing his recorded message again she hung up in frustration without leaving a message.

'Hmm ... he's still not home ... or has he been and gone out again ... hmm ... I wonder where he is?' Feeling tired and confused, she had a quick shower then headed to the pub next door before the meals service finished at eight o'clock.

She made it just in time, and after perusing the chalk-written menu facing her, settled on the 'soup of the day'; her appetite having disappeared along with her normally good mood. Sitting at a table near a large window, Evie patiently waited for her meal, absently turning her head to stare blankly at the cars zooming past on the highway.

Twenty minutes later she was back in her room. Discarding all thought of phoning Dash again, she slowly undressed and got into bed. After her late night at Hugh's, and then with all the driving, Evie felt really tired. Glancing at the clock on the wall as she tried to plump up the thin pillows on her bed, she was surprised to see how early it was.

'God, it's only eight-thirty and I'm going to bed … I must be getting old.'

With that slightly disturbing thought now added into the mix of emotions concerning Dash, it was a while before she eventually fell into a troubled sleep.

Chapter Fifty-Two

After leaving Laurie at Tullamarine in time to catch his evening flight back to Launceston, Dash, Marley and Bluey headed for home. They'd had a great day out and they'd laughed at some of the funny jokes they'd heard over the last two days, taking care not to repeat any rude ones. Bluey sat in the back, laughing as well, even though she hadn't really understood them.

Arriving back at the flats just before eight o'clock Dash was looking forward to relaxing and catching up with Evie over a couple of drinks, so he was pretty disappointed to find out that she wasn't home.

'Bugger,' he swore softly after knocking on her door. 'I thought she'd be here by now ... hmm ... she must have decided to stay the night with Liz and Hugh again ... damn.'

Not having a contact phone number for Hugh's place,

Dash knew he'd have to wait to talk with her another time. He'd been missing their chats and her easy laughter, not to mention the sex they'd enjoyed on their weekend away, which was unfortunately just the once so far. But they hadn't been able to get away anywhere together these last couple of weeks.

'Hmm … not much I can do about it now …' he mused, 'but tomorrow …' a smile now appearing on his face. 'Yep … tomorrow I'll ask her if she's free to get away next weekend.' His spirits were lifted now he had a plan, and he didn't try to stop the flow of erotic images of Evie that the plan aroused in his mind.

Wandering inside he saw that Bushy wasn't home either. That morning he'd said that he wanted to catch up with a mate who was over from the west, adding, 'If I get on the piss I'll probably stay the night at the pub with him, in fact don't worry if you don't see me for a day or two. I haven't seen Mario for years and we'll have a lot of catching up to do.' He'd booked a hire car and left straight after breakfast.

Marley and Bluey had already jumped under the shower together, so he decided to go downstairs and catch up with Blackie while awaiting his turn. He was keen to catch up with the youngster as he hadn't been able to spend much time with him lately with everything else happening.

He'd just about made it to Hilda's front door when he heard his phone ringing, but by the time he got back upstairs he could hear his voice saying to leave a message. Quickly picking up the receiver he realised he was too late – whoever it was had already hung up. It was then that he noticed the green light blinking on his answering machine.

'Damn, I'm an idiot ... why didn't I check this before?' He pressed the play button just as Bluey came running out of the bathroom, freshly showered and in her pyjamas. Hearing Evie's voice he leaned closer, listening intently to what she was saying, not noticing that Bluey was also listening.

'Oh, um ... hi Dash ... it's me, Evie ... um ... I'm just letting you know that I'm driving up the coast for a few days, to Terrigal ... um ... I'll explain why later ... you can ...' when the message abruptly stopped. Looking down he saw that Bluey had pressed the delete button.

'Uh oh ... sorry Poppy ... I didn't mean to stop it. Can you play it again?'

Dash took a deep breath before replying, 'No Blue, you've deleted it.'

'Bluey, what are you doing?' Marley scolded coming out of the bathroom, a large towel wrapped around her. 'I've told you not to touch other people's things. Sorry Dad, I heard the phone ringing and thought you were here to get it. I hope it wasn't something important.'

Taking another deep breath he sighed in frustration. 'It's okay ... it was Evie. She's gone to Terrigal for some reason.'

The brief message had him puzzled. Taking a beer with

him he headed back outside.

'Why's she gone away … and why to Terrigal?' he churned over in his head. 'She sounded a bit strange … why couldn't she explain now … and what is that I can … can what … take a flying leap … go to hell … what?'

It was then that the terrible thought flared into his mind – maybe she and Bushy are together. He knew it was a stupid thing to even contemplate, but he'd been aware of how well they'd gotten on together, and now, seemingly out of the blue, both were away for a couple of nights.

'No, that's ridiculous,' he told himself. But the notion persisted. 'Bushy wouldn't do something like that … and Evie … she's definitely not the sneaky type … no … I'm being paranoid.'

Dash was angry now, mostly with himself for having such thoughts, but each time he tried to erase them another image of the two of them laughing together assaulted his mind. Bluey startled him out of his thoughts then as she slid onto his lap.

'Sorry Poppy, for touching your stuff, but I've promised Mummy that I won't touch other people's stuff *ever* again.'

Dash looked down into his granddaughter's cute, upturned face and as usual couldn't help but smile.

'That's okay Bluey, I know you didn't mean it.' He gave her a hug then said, 'Would you like me to read you a story before you go to sleep?'

'Oh, yes please. Could you read me more of Snugglepot and Coggelpie?'

'It's Snugglepot and Cuddlepie, you silly sausage.' Dash laughed, while he tickled her until she giggled.

Later, after both Marley and Blue had gone to bed, Dash sat out on his balcony and had several quiet beers. He felt calmer now, mainly because he was tired, but his mind continued presenting him with an assortment of assumptions and 'what ifs'. Finally sick of thinking, Dash decided to have another stubbie, hoping that the alcohol would aid him in having a good night's sleep.

Chapter Fifty-Three

Evie had a restless night, but after rolling over again and seeing that it was now seven-thirty, she thought she may as well get up.

'God,' she moaned, stretching her back as she walked towards the bathroom. 'Eleven hours in bed and I still feel like shit.'

She had a longer than usual shower. As the hot water was doing its trick on her stiff shoulders, she was trying to convince herself that Dash would have a perfectly sound reason for being out every time she'd rung.

Twenty minutes later – dressed, ready to go, and sipping the last of her coffee – she rang him. The phone seemed to ring for an interminable time before his answering machine kicked in, but Evie didn't leave a message; she hung up straight away as her anger took hold of the situation.

'Fuck him then,' she said under her breath as she walked out after paying her bill. 'Maybe moving isn't such a bad idea after all.'

Figuring that he must be deliberately avoiding her, she turned the volume up loud on her car stereo. Angry with herself that she'd been sucked in once more by a man who'd obviously only wanted to get his rocks off, she shook her head and stared ferociously through the windscreen, trying to block all thoughts of Dash from her entire psyche.

She drove into the morning sun for an hour or so then finally pulled over to get something to eat and drink at a roadhouse in Yass. She still wasn't very hungry – she never was when she was upset about something – but realising that she'd eaten very little since yesterday thought it best to get something into her stomach.

Buying a toasted ham and cheese sandwich and a cup of tea, she sat mechanically eating and drinking at a small outdoor table; a colourful umbrella fluttering in the breeze above her. Her thoughts were flitting between the certainty that Dash probably wasn't even thinking about her and wondering what state she'd find her house in.

The original tenants were still occupying it after nearly seventeen years. Evie had never raised the rent since she'd owned it. Whenever it had been suggested to her by the property manager, Evie had inquired about the condition of the house. After they'd always assured her the whole property was in top condition she'd always said to leave the rent as it was. She'd figured that as they were saving her money on maintenance she'd pass the savings on to them.

Chapter Fifty-Four

The beer hadn't helped Dash sleep. A variety of nightmares tormented his subconscious, resulting in him finally falling into a deep sleep about five in the morning. Thankful that it was his day off he'd intended to sleep in, but a bit before eight o'clock the persistent ringing of the damn phone finally roused him. Once more though, he was unable to get to it in time before the answering machine kicked in.

Grabbing the receiver, all he heard was the beeping noise. He was wondering why no one else had picked it up when he recalled Marley saying that she'd be leaving early in the morning. She and a few of her mother's group friends were taking their kids to Ballarat to visit Sovereign Hill, the gold mining tourist town. Bushy obviously wasn't home yet either. Trying not to think about *that*, he decided to have a coffee first, then a shower.

'No good trying to get anymore sleep now,' he thought, heading towards the bathroom for his necessary morning piss. Thinking about Evie again, he was trying to imagine what she was doing at that exact moment, then he tried to blot the imagery from his mind.

Dash was feeling really annoyed. He had a couple of quick gulps of hot coffee then stood where he was, frowning out the kitchen window.

'I wonder where in bloody Terrigal she's gone ... and why?'

Frustrated at not knowing what was going on, he banged his cup down onto the kitchen table causing coffee to slop onto his hand, then turned his stereo up loud before storming off towards the shower.

'Bloody women ... just when you think you've got one bloody figured out they bloody go and change the bloody rules.'

His mind wasn't helping him at all either. It just kept on reminding him of all the times lately when Evie had said she had other plans and couldn't stay and chat -and then all the times he'd seen her laughing and listening to one of Bushy's stories. These thoughts then somehow led to his next brainwave ... maybe she was one of those women who just moved onto the next interesting guy whenever they showed up.

Feeling completely frustrated because he was no longer

certain that Evie felt the same towards him as he did her, he angrily turned both shower taps on; the water erupting in a convulsive spurt before transforming into a furious torrent.

'We'd bloody talked about having good communication in a relationship,' he mumbled as he stepped under the steaming water. 'Fuck.'

Five minutes later after cooling off his thinking under the hot shower, Dash was probing his mind, trying to formulate a plan. Rinsing the last of the soap off, the answer slowly manifested in his mind – he'd go to bloody Terrigal himself. The only way he could find out for sure if she'd changed her mind about their relationship was to ask her face to face.

He didn't want to wait 'til she came back because he didn't know how long that would be, and he didn't want to live with the angry, unsettled feeling that had recently taken up residence in his being. If she was with Bushy, he'd smash him one first then leave them to it.

'I won't be hanging around here for long though,' he muttered. 'I'll grab that job in Hedland and be gone.' That decided he was out of the shower and hurriedly drying off.

'No time like the present,' he thought as he dropped the now damp towel onto the floor where he stood. 'Now, first things first,' he thought out loud. 'How am I going to find out where she's staying in Terrigal?'

After getting dressed he made another cup of coffee;

taking it outside to drink and think. Deciding to ask Hilda if she knew anything about Evie's sudden trip, he took his cuppa with him as he descended the stairs.

'No, Evie never said anything to me about Terrigal, Dash; I don't know why she'd suddenly just go off like that.' Her pleasant face broke into a beaming grin. 'You two haven't had a fight have you?'

Dash wasn't sure what to say so just answered, 'Not that I know of … thanks anyway Hilda.' Declining an offer to come on in, Dash slowly made his way upstairs again. As he took the last few steps, his head turned to the left and he spotted what looked like a document of some sort under Evie's old couch. Curiosity got the better of him and he walked over and retrieved it. It was something to do with a house that Evie was renting out … in Terrigal. Not bothering to read it all, Dash's eyes scanned the text for an address of the property.

'Ah ha … got it,' he grinned.

Striding along McKillop Street, his old overnight bag in one hand, he only had minutes left to make it in time. After having secured a seat on the next flight to Sydney, Dash had then rung The Gull bus line and booked a seat on their next airport shuttle bus, leaving the car for Marley to use. The small bus was now in view, plus a group of people obviously waiting to board, so he increased his pace. He'd already organised for a rental car to be waiting for him in Sydney, then he only had the hour or so drive to Terrigal.

Trying unsuccessfully to erase Evie's image from his mind for a while, Dash made himself as comfortable as he could for the hour-and-a-half drive to the airport. Squashed between the window and a lanky, long-haired surfer type whose tanned legs seemed to take up most of the available space, Dash sighed. 'The sooner I get there the better,' he thought impatiently. 'If Evie doesn't want any more to do with me, then so be it, but I won't be staying in Geelong that's for sure.' Closing his eyes, thoughts of their recent weekend away taunted him until he opened them again to stare out the window.

Chapter Fifty-Five

It was a little after one o'clock when Evie began approaching the outskirts of Terrigal. Making a right turn at a roundabout, she was then heading towards the coastline. Turning her stereo off, she then slowly opened her window and inhaled the unmistakable smell of the sea.

'Hmmm ... delicious,' she spoke out loud. 'What a beautiful place ... no wonder old Charles bought an investment property here.'

After cruising along the main streets of the town, Evie spotted the real estate office she'd been looking for.

Fifteen minutes later she was back in her car, a bunch of house keys sitting on the seat beside her. She was angry again after finding out that there'd been no phone call to the real estate agent from Dash.

'Bastard, he must have been home and heard my

message by now.' Slamming the car into gear and driving off, she spoke out loud, 'Stuff him then. That proves he's no longer interested, and that's the last time I ever believe a word any man says to me.'

Forcibly pushing Dash's image out of her mind as she took note of the street signs as she passed them, Evie thought of the conversation she'd just had.

'Well, that's a coincidence,' she muttered, knowing full well that there are no coincidences in life. 'No, it can't be a coincidence, but it must mean something.'

The extremely efficient woman in the office had informed her that the tenants had *just* moved out. Apparently they'd been thinking about moving closer to their pregnant daughter in Coffs Harbour for a while, but had been loath to leave what they'd always considered to be their home. When they found out their daughter had just given birth to triplets though, they had their possessions loaded onto a moving van within days. They'd left yesterday, not bothered about foregoing the two weeks rent they'd paid in advance.

Having then received explicit directions to the house from Ms. Efficiency, it didn't take Evie long to find the correct address and park out the front.

'Well ...' she started, as she looked at what was visible of the house through the open passenger side window, 'not bad ... not bad at all.' It was situated in Hillcrest Street, a delightful part of the town, and as Evie climbed out of the car and stretched her shoulders and neck, she looked around at what could possibly be her new neighbourhood. 'Lovely ... definitely has a good feel ... that's a positive start.'

Slowly walking through the gate and along a winding pathway, she became aware of a very familiar sound, causing her to smile as she breathed in the delightful blend of scents emanating from the many fragrant flowers. Large trees and shrubs shielded most of the residence from the street, so when the rest of the house came into view Evie stopped abruptly, holding her breath for a moment.

'Wow ...' she slowly exhaled. 'This is nice, very nice ... no, it's more than nice ... it's fabulous.'

Stepping up several low flagstone steps to the covered entrance area, she passed a tree from which hung the bamboo wind chime she'd heard, and noted how remarkably similar it was to the one she had at home. Thinking that it had to be a good omen, she then just stood for a moment and admired the intricate carvings on the large set of double doors. They had a Balinese appearance and she loved them. She was feeling excited at the prospect of seeing what the rest of the house looked like, and was unaware that she held her breath again as she turned the front door key, then stepped inside.

'Wow ...' she said again. 'I really love the design ... and I love all the timber flooring.' Gazing around as she slowly wandered through the foyer into a large family room, her eyes were immediately drawn to the wonderful view through the massive windows. Bypassing the rest of the house, Evie made straight for the sliding doors separating her from the huge, encircling verandah; quickly unlocking them.

As soon as she was out on the timber deck she walked towards the protective railing and leant her body against it. She had an elevated view because the backyard sloped downwards, before levelling out into a flat area, enabling her to see over her neighbour's roof. Shaking her head in wonder as she took in the size and beauty of the property, and the breathtaking view of the beach through the trees, she then leant outwards a bit so she could peer over the railing. There was another room under the house. 'Hmm … that might make a good studio for when I get the urge to paint', she thought, before slowly turning around and heading inside again.

The kitchen was next, and Evie thought that although it wasn't modern it was scrupulously clean with heaps of cupboards and bench space, as well as a big walk-in pantry. All the fittings looked top-of-the-line, and the quality factor was still evident. Walking through into an extremely roomy lounge room, she stopped once more and gazed around. Huge windows framed the view in here as well, allowing the late afternoon sun to bathe the room with warm light. The walls were painted in various shades of soft green, giving a multi-dimensional feel, and Evie stood still for a moment and visualised what it would look like with her furniture in place, and a couple of great rugs on the floor.

'I wonder how many bedrooms there are?' she then murmured before continuing her exploring.

One side of the lounge room had French doors opening into a room that she thought would be ideal as a reading area or a study. It had built-in shelving, perfect for her books, and was roomy enough for a desk and a couple of armchairs. Loving the house more with every step, she left the living area intent on finding the bedrooms. She was pleased to discover that all four were situated at the rear of the house, away from the front door and any roadway noise. All were a generous size with built-in robes, and each had a lovely view and access to the verandah.

Next she found two bathrooms and to her delight saw that one of them had a large spa. She eventually found two separate toilets and a large laundry, surprised to see that it had a shower in it as well.

Evie was astonished at the size of the house – it hadn't appeared that big from the outside. It was so light and airy and well laid out; the whole vibe of the place really resonated with her. There'd be no rush to do a chart for this place she realised; just about anybody could tell that the whole property had an extremely positive energy around it.

Her initial elation at realising the house was actually

hers was now starting to fade. An image of her and Dash living there together had taken its place, dampening her spirit.

'Oh well,' she sighed, 'that's life.' Automatically flicking the light switch as she re-entered the kitchen, Evie was surprised when the room was unexpectedly illuminated. Then, after checking the stove, she found that the gas was still connected as well!

'Hmm ...' she smiled, 'I could stay here tonight if I had something to sleep on. Maybe I could go and buy a sleeping bag ... the gas is still on so the heating would work ... plus I have a rug in the car ... I'll need a kettle though, I have to be able to make myself a cuppa.'

Deciding to have a quick look inside the garage first before checking out the shops in the area, she picked up her bag and bunch of keys and headed for the back door.

'Teabags, milk, sugar, chocolate biscuits, a bottle of Champagne ...' Evie was smiling now as she mentally made up her shopping list. Unable to stop her head from scanning the rooms again on her way out, her smile widened. 'Unbelievable,' was all she was able to say.

Trying a couple of different keys in the garage door before finding the right one, Evie then looked at the things the previous tenants had left behind.

'Hmm ... obviously no one wanted this stuff anymore.' An old wooden ladder and a wheelbarrow with a hole in it were propped up against the rear wall, right next to an assortment of different sized, black plastic pots and bases. To her left was a large wooden board with black painted silhouettes of tools, and she noticed that the solitary tool left hanging in its appropriate place was a rusty pair of multi-grips.

There was one item though, that grabbed her attention. After closer inspection, Evie realised it was a brand new mattress, still wearing its clear protective wrapping and the delivery docket. Checking the date, she calculated it had been there for seven months. Not even trying to work out why it'd been left behind, she put her hands on her hips and her head to one side as she wondered how she was going to get it into the house.

'Oh well … all I can do is try I suppose.' She'd just started to move towards the massive mattress when a voice stopped her dead in her tracks.

'So this is where you've come to get away … very nice.'

When Evie turned and saw Dash leaning against the open garage door, nearly all comprehensible thought left her head. With a blank look on her face, all she could manage to think was, 'Where on earth did he come from?'

'Oh … I see … so you're not talking to me now, and you certainly don't look happy to see me; I guess that just about answers my questions.'

As he turned to leave, Evie's brain kicked into gear again.

She was angry now. 'What do you mean I'm not talking to you … you haven't been talking to me. I left a message on your answering machine explaining where I was going, *and* a contact phone number. I've rung heaps of times since, but you never answer your phone.' Before she could gather herself properly and really tell him what she thought of him, Dash spoke again.

'Is Bushy here?'

'Bushy? Why would Bushy be here?'

Dash looked a little hesitant before saying, 'I thought maybe you two had gone off together for a few days.'

'*What* … what a crazy thing to think.' Evie didn't know if she wanted to laugh or hit him.

They stared intently at each other for a minute, unconsciously endeavouring to read the other's mind, before Dash quietly and seriously asked, 'Do you mean that you haven't been deliberately avoiding me?'

'Of course not … why would I do that?' After a few seconds had stretched by, Evie's frown softened significantly. 'Does that mean that you haven't been deliberately avoiding me?'

'Of course not … why would I do that?'

'Well, the fact that you haven't bothered to contact me for one thing,' Evie stated indignantly. 'And I've hardly seen you since you accomplished your mission of getting me into bed. It's as if you've hit the "beam me up Scotty" button.'

Dash couldn't help but start to grin. 'I didn't know you were a Star Trek fan.'

'Of course,' Evie too had started to grin, 'isn't everyone?'

With that they both appeared to release some tension from their previously rigid stance. The magnetism between them had drawn them closer together even while they'd been at odds with each other. They were now face to face.

'Why didn't you ring me?' Evie asked, quieter now.

'I only heard the first bit of your message before Bluey deleted it; there was nothing about a phone number. And you sounded a bit ... distracted. I ended up thinking you'd taken off because you didn't want to see me anymore. Then when Bushy took off for a couple of days, I put two and two together and ended up with you two together.'

'But why Bushy? Whatever gave you that idea?'

'Well, I've seen how good you two get along together. You can't deny there's some sort of an attraction between you, can you?'

'Listen, of course I like Bushy, he's a great bloke, and he's your brother. How could I possibly not like him when he's so much like you? But he's not you.' Taking Dash's rough, unshaven face between her hands, Evie smiled and said, 'I've never felt this feeling that I have for you, ever before. I think about you all the time and the thoughts always make me smile.' She stopped then and said, 'Well, except for today that is. I was so angry and hurt to have been conned I was completely ready to move on again.'

'I'd never con you,' Dash replied. Placing his arms around her he was astonished at the thoughts she'd had. 'I love you,' he looked directly into her eyes. 'You've driven me nuts over the last few days.'

Their eyes locked for a moment, then started to crinkle at their outer corners as they both smiled.

'I love you too, you silly man.'

It was debatable as to who kissed who first, but when they came up for air it was simultaneously. Both grinning from ear to ear, they decided to leave the mattress for now and instead find a pub where they could have a quiet drink. Dash had noticed one on his drive through the town and had found it extremely difficult not to stop and have a quick beer then and there.

'So tell me,' he queried as they closed the garage door,' what are you doing here?'

Chapter Fifty-Six

They talked for hours in the bar of the Terrigal Hotel – about Blackie's and Hilda's predicament, and about how Evie had remembered the house she'd never seen before. After Dash gave it some thought he suggested that they could all move.

'After all, from what you've said the house is certainly big enough and I'm sure Blackie would love it.' He smiled at the thought. 'And I don't think Hilda would have a problem with it either.' Stopping to have a sip of his beer he then went on, 'I'm sure Marley could still do her studies up here somewhere too, and I know she'd like the warmer weather. But what about you ... how do you feel about your life being invaded by so many people?'

'They're not just people ... they're people I love ... and I think it's a fabulous idea,' she answered, now unable to get the smile off her face. 'Liz and Hugh will just have to come up here for holidays; Hugh could even buy a holiday house here somewhere,' Evie said excitedly. 'I have to phone Liz before we go back. I have to let her know that I love the place and she will too.'

After having a counter meal and a few beers they drove back to the house about seven o'clock. The shadows were lengthening as the sun dipped lower in the sky. It had also turned chilly – the previously warm breeze had changed direction and was now coming directly off the ocean.

Dash was quite happy to stay overnight in Evie's house as well, so after they let themselves in they wandered through the empty rooms; switching on the overhead lights as they did so. Dash was also quite astounded at the size of the house.

'It didn't look this big from the outside.'

'That's exactly what I thought,' Evie laughed. 'Come on; give me a hand to close all these curtains.'

The trees around the property had shielded most of the light from the street anyway, but now with the curtains drawn they had total privacy. Dash ignited the gas log fire in the lounge room while Evie unpacked two big bags of goodies they'd bought at the supermarket.

'It feels good to be staying here tonight,' Evie then declared as she again surveyed what was to become her and Dash's new home.

'Yeah, it does feel good,' Dash grinned as he hugged her

tightly then kissed her on her ear. 'Tomorrow I'll drop my rental car off here somewhere, then we can take our time driving back in your car.' Nibbling on Evie's neck for a moment he then murmured, 'I wonder what they'll all say when we tell them our plans.'

'Hmmm ... I don't know ... all I can think about at the minute is you getting that mattress out of the garage and me filling up the spa ... what do you think?'

'I think that's the best thought you've had all day.'

Epilogue

Terrigal, NSW, Australia
December 1998

'Well, that's Christmas over for another year.'

Evie was carefully removing the delicate ornaments from the slightly dried-out Christmas tree, as Dash manipulated the extendable table back to its smaller size.

'Yep, all over red rover,' Dash grinned, as he admired Evie's suntanned legs as she reached upwards for the golden star.

Stepping down off a small ladder, Evie put a tangle of tinsel into a box, then brushed some clinging pine needles off her clothes. 'I wonder what the New Year's going to bring for us this time?' she pondered out loud.

'Well, we'll just have to wait and see I suppose, but I have had a couple of thoughts. How about we go back to France and visit Annie again for our second anniversary? We had such a great time on our honeymoon, and there were lots of places we didn't have time to check out. I reckon another couple of weeks there'd be great.'

Evie's face lit up with pleasure. 'Oh yes, that would be great. What a terrific idea.'

'Yeah, I thought so. But wait, there's more,' he smiled.

'Don't tell me I get a free set of steak knives as well,' Evie joked.

Still grinning, Dash shook his head. 'No, what I was thinking was I remembered you saying that Liz and Hugh were planning a trip to England to visit Lisa next year, so I thought we could all go together. After all, France is just across the channel. We could catch up with Lisa then we could leave them to it and meet up again in a few weeks.'

Evie walked the short distance to where he was standing and wrapped her arms around him. 'Have I told you lately how much I love you Mr. McCallum?'

'Not since yesterday, but I'll let you off this time.'

Kissing her softly on her lips he smiled then said, 'I love you too Mrs. McCallum. So I take it you like the idea.'

'I love the idea. I'll ask Liz later when she and Hugh get here – I know she'll love it as well.'

'Good, that's settled then. How about we go to the beach for a while once we've finished here ... I'll see if Marley and

Blue want to come as well.'

'Yeah, okay, sounds good to me.'

Bluey walked into the room then, a sad expression evident on her freckled face.

'I miss Blackie already, why couldn't he have stayed here with us?'

'Because he wants to live with Uncle Bushy for a while and learn how to fly a helicopter,' Dash explained again. 'Don't worry; he'll be back for a visit soon.'

'I wish I could fly a helicopter, then I could go and visit him,' she said, flopping down into one of the beanbags.

She'd been Blackie's little shadow ever since they'd all moved in together, following him around like a lost puppy. Her constant questions had sometimes been too much for him though, and he'd go to his bedroom and put a 'Do Not Disturb' sign on his door.

'Well, maybe one day you can learn to fly one too,' Dash grinned. 'But how about for now you help me make some sandwiches to take to the beach.'

'Okay. Can I go next door first and see if Tiffany wants to come too?'

'Of course you can. Come straight back though.'

Dash watched her as she jumped up and hurried outside, her curly red hair bobbing as she ran.

'I'm going to miss Blackie too,' Evie said with a tinge of sadness as she removed the last of the decorations, 'but it's a great opportunity for him, and I know Bushy will look after him.' Heading towards the hallway cupboard, her arms chock full of boxes, she added, 'I've never seen him that excited before. He couldn't get the smile off his face, could he?'

'No,' Dash chuckled. 'It couldn't have happened at a better time either.'

They were both thinking about Blackie's decision to leave school after he'd turned sixteen. He'd never been able to settle into the authoritarian system very well, but they'd insisted that he had to have a job before he could leave.

They'd all been lolling around outside on the verandah, after eating way too much Christmas dinner, when Bushy had casually asked him if he'd found a job yet. Hearing that he hadn't, he'd then started talking about a job that was available on the vast cattle station where he was working.

'It's not an easy job,' Bushy had emphasised. 'You'll have to be up at dawn and work all day. It's hot and dirty and the pay's not that good, but if you're interested I can phone Wally and let him know you're keen. You'd have to leave with me the day after tomorrow though; work doesn't stop just because it's Christmas.'

'A jackaroo,' Blackie had kept repeating. 'Wow, that'd be fantastic.'

After his uncle had mentioned that he could probably learn how to fly the chopper when he was a bit older, he'd been speechless with excitement, nearly falling out of the hammock he was lying in.

'Poppy ...Tiffany's coming with us to the beach too,' Bluey said as she ran in the back door. 'She'll be over in a minute. Her mum said she has to be back by five o'clock 'cause they're going to a New Year's Eve party in Gosford later. We're having a party here, aren't we?'

'Yep, we sure are.'

'And then at the end of next year it will be a whole new milenrium, won't it?'

'Millennium, and yes a whole new one ... the year 2000 ... although, actually, it doesn't begin 'til 2001 ... but I'll explain that to you later.'

'Okay Poppy. But I just hope that bug doesn't come here though. I don't like bugs.'

'What bug?' Evie asked as she re-entered the lounge room.

'You know, the one with the funny name; the why two kay bug. I just heard Tiffany's dad talking about it with her and Lachlan.'

Both Dash and Evie smiled and at the same time said, 'It's not a real bug, Bluey ...' then they both paused, looking at each other.

'I'll tell you what,' grinned Dash. 'I'll explain it to you while we get our picnic lunch ready, okay?'

'Okay Poppy, 'cause Lachlan said that planes might crash

because of the bug, and I wondered why they don't just spray it with something.'

Evie couldn't help but laugh. As she watched the two of them heading towards the kitchen she shook her head in wonder, thinking of how much her life had changed over the last few years. Her thoughts returned to Blackie then and she sighed, knowing she was going to miss him terribly, but also knowing that she had to let him go. His early experiences of life had forced him to grow up quickly, and he'd often found it difficult to relate to boys his own age.

'He'll be in his element with Bushy,' she thought smiling, imagining all the things they'd be doing together. 'I just hope we don't have to wait a year 'til we see him again.'

Bushy had been making the long trip to Terrigal for the last three years in time for the festivities, loving the fact that he now had a family he could enjoy the holiday season with. Unfortunately though, he was never able to stay very long.

'There's always work to be done on a station,' he'd say. 'The cattle don't know that it's Christmas.'

He'd been flying a helicopter for a couple of years now, helping with the mustering and looking for strays, and he loved it.

'Nothing wrong with a horse and a good dog, but give me the chopper any day,' he'd grinned. His funny stories about the different characters he'd met or worked with always had them laughing, especially the one about how he'd met Claire, the woman he'd been going out with for the last few months. She was a jillaroo on another station, and they'd met at the last Bachelor and Spinsters Ball when he'd accidentally stood on the hem of her long dress; tearing it at the seam.

'If I'm still with Claire next year I'll bring her along with me,' he'd said. 'You'll like her, she's a good sort.'

Evie was smiling at the recollection of his humorous depiction of the encounter when she heard a knock on the back door. It was Tiffany.

'Hi Mrs. McCallum, I hope I wasn't too long. Lachlan hid my beach towel and wouldn't tell me where it was, so I hid his new book about cricket 'til he gave it back to me. *Boys* ... they're such a nuisance sometimes, aren't they?'

Before Evie could answer, Bluey came running through from the kitchen, Dash following behind with the wicker basket of food and a cooler bottle of drink.

'We're ready. What about you gorgeous?' Dash smiled at Evie.

'I'll be ready in two shakes. You get the girls in the car while I put my togs on and get the towels. Oh, and we'd better take the beach umbrella too. What about Marley, is she coming as well?'

'No, she said she wants to finish her assignment first; it's her last one for the year and she wants to get it out of the way. Then she's going to start on the decorations for the party. She said she'll catch up with us later.'

'Okay, be with you in a minute then.'

Evie had been impressed by Marley's decision to study for her Bachelor of Social Work after gaining her Diploma in Community Welfare. Even though she seemed to have a natural aptitude for the work, the amount of study required had astounded both Evie and Dash. Marley had said many times that she didn't think she'd be able to do it without their help in looking after Bluey.

'Two more years and she'll be finished ...' Evie thought proudly, as she turned to see her back in the mirror as she clipped the clasp of her bikini straps together. 'At least she'll have more time to socialise then.'

After a quick look in the mirror, front and back, to reassure herself that she still looked okay in a bikini, she tied a colourful sarong around her hips then walked towards the linen cupboard to get towels. She smiled as she recalled Marley saying how she was in no rush to hook up with someone new, after her last disastrous relationship. Instead, she'd been going out in a group; friends she'd made at TAFE, both guys and girls. Several of them were coming around later tonight to help celebrate the arrival of the New Year. Evie was looking forward to the party – she loved having the house full of people.

After finding a bottle of sunscreen lotion she headed out to the car, all the while thinking how lucky she was to have such a lovely daughter-in-law.

As soon as they'd parked the car the girls were out and running towards the sand. There was a large crowd on the beach with plenty of people enjoying the surf, but they were still able to find a great spot to dump all their beach paraphernalia. While Dash set up the umbrella, making sure it couldn't fly off if the wind became blustery, Evie ambled over to where the girls were noisily splashing around in a large, shallow lagoon. It had been formed by the tidal sand banks and made a perfect place for the youngsters to swim. After instructing them both not to go wandering off anywhere, she returned to their nearby picnic spot.

'I love it here,' she sighed as she took in her surroundings. 'I reckon it must be one of the best beaches in Australia.'

'Yeah, me too.'

Dash stripped off his t-shirt and sprawled out on one of the large towels. Sitting down beside him they were both quiet for a while, intent on absorbing the fantastic energy created by the sun, sea spray and laughing children. As Evie casually surveyed her surroundings she noticed someone who bore a striking resemblance to her youngest sister.

'Oh, look over there ... that woman looks like Jo, doesn't she.'

Dash sat up to see which way Evie was pointing. 'Where? Oh yeah, she does too, except she's a lot taller than Jo.'

'Hmm ... it's unbelievable how much that couple from

Melbourne offered Jo to buy her business, isn't it? No wonder she couldn't turn it down.'

'Yeah, but she'd spent a lot of time and money getting it running so well; she'd doubled the turnover of the previous owner. Do you think she'll buy another one?'

'No. I think that now she and Tony are back together the travel bug has got her again.'

'Good, they may as well travel while they can. It seems like they're having fun by the sounds of that last postcard.'

Evie nodded her head in agreement. 'Jo always said she wanted to go to Kathmandu. I can't imagine scaling some of those mountains though; it's not something I'd ever try.'

'No, bugger that.'

'I hope it works out for them this time. I really like Tony. I always thought they made a good couple.'

'Have you heard from Bev again?' Dash then asked as he swatted away an annoying sand-fly.

'No, not since she rang last week asking if she could come for a visit next month. I hope she's okay; I'll ring her again tomorrow.'

Shaking her head a little, Evie went on, 'It's been a year now since Pam died, but Bev still seems completely lost. I actually don't think she'll ever get over it. It must be like losing half of yourself.'

'Yeah, it must be, when you consider they'd been together all their lives.'

'At least she has her girls and the grandkids to focus on, not that she sees much of them now. It's a shame, but I can understand why all their kids decided to move away from Geelong.'

'Yeah, me too,' Dash chuckled.

Evie's thoughts wandered back in time to when she and Dash had returned for her mother's funeral, ten months after they'd settled into the house in Terrigal. They'd seen the twins in action again then. Both Pam and Bev had been stridently showing off their first grandchildren to whoever was in range, constantly comparing as to whose was cuter or more advanced or more something.

After Jo had felt the full force of their gushing tirade she'd made her way to Evie's side. 'They're both mad,' she'd said, shaking her head in disbelief. 'I think if they had nothing to upstage the other with their worlds would end.'

Reen and Vince had been at the funeral as well, together with their two girls and the girls' fiancés. Evie and Dash had been surprised to see how much weight Reen had lost. They'd spoken to her later and she'd said how it'd just fallen off her.

'It was like something big changed inside me after I visited Annie in France,' Reen had related.

'Annie laughed when I asked her if Dad had hated me because of what I'd said all those years ago. She said that of course he hadn't, he'd always loved me. She said he knew I was just being a typical teenager and how happy he'd been when he found out I was married, and even more so when he'd read the birth notices in the paper when I'd had the girls.' Reen had gone on to say it was like a weight being lifted from her soul.

It had been Doug that had surprised Dash and Evie the most though. Even though he'd been saddened by his mother's unexpected death, he'd been so relaxed and at ease that Evie had found it difficult to believe it was really him. Erica had been sitting with little Lucy on her lap, one of the prettiest little girls Evie had ever seen, and Doug had been sitting alongside two teenage boys. When Doug had seen them he'd stood up and smiled, saying 'Hi Evie, hi Dash, it's good to see you both again. Liam, Zach ... this is your Aunty Evie and your Uncle Dash.'

Evie hadn't seen either of the boys since they were babies, as they'd both been living interstate with their mothers. They'd chatted for a while before the two boys had gone off to talk to their cousins. It was then that Doug had mentioned that James, his eldest son, still didn't want anything to do with him.

'I can understand it,' he'd said. 'But it still rips me apart. I know it's my own fault though; I didn't want anything to do with the boys after their mothers left me. I've been trying hard for months now to mend some fences,' he'd smiled wryly. 'It hasn't been easy, but it's been worth it.'

He'd shaken his head a little and sighed, 'James is just too angry with me though. He told me it's no good trying to get to know him now when I wasn't there for him before. The thing is ... I understand only too well how he feels. Finding out, and then having to acknowledge to myself, that Dad deliberately abandoned me, hurt so much that it crippled me for a while. I couldn't even get out of bed for a couple of weeks. I only visited Annie in France so I could give her a blast. I wanted to hurt her like she and Dad had hurt me.'

He'd actually chuckled a bit then before saying, 'She's such a lovely person though. She showed me all the photos of me and the birth notices of the boys and explained how it'd destroyed part of Dad when he left us. Apparently he'd been on the verge of picking up the phone and calling me several times. I wish he had, although I wouldn't have been able to keep it a secret. I would've had to tell you and the others, and you know what the twins are like. They've never been able to keep a secret. Annie said that he just couldn't risk it. When I came back I was so fucked up in the head, thank God Erica made me go and see a shrink. It took a fair while but he finally made me realise that I was doing the same thing to my own boys – deliberately abandoning them.'

Shaking his head in disbelief he went on. 'It's strange isn't it, how we sometimes end up doing the same things our parents did to us?'

Evie was again pondering this question when she was

abruptly brought back to reality.

'A penny for your thoughts,' Dash was grinning at her.

'A penny, is that all? Hardly seems worth it.'

'Alright … what about some of these delicious grapes then?'

'Now you're talking … thanks.' Before popping them into her mouth though, she went on. 'I was actually just thinking that by me not having any kids, at least I haven't had to worry about screwing them up in the head somehow. I can fantasize that they would've been wonderful, without all the heartache.'

'Yeah, you do have a point there. I've had so many guilty thoughts about not being there for Marley it's not funny. I think I've just lucked it in that she's so well adjusted though, and such a great mum to Bluey.'

'Yeah, it's like she was born to be a parent,' Evie agreed, then sighing a little, said, 'it's just a shame that Laurie doesn't feel at all paternal yet.'

Dash frowned but didn't say anything for a moment. He was completely pissed off with his brother and the mention of his name threatened to spoil his good mood. Sighing loudly in frustration he grabbed the suntan lotion and began to roughly apply it to his legs.

'I know … I still can't believe it … he knows how hard it was for me … not having a dad. I just hope he comes to his senses soon. Angie idolised him from the start and I know he loves her; he'd been saying for the past year how he reckoned she was "The One".'

Replacing the lid, he then dropped the bottle back into the overflowing beach bag. 'How he could just take off like that now she's pregnant has got me stumped ... and Reg and Jean are furious with him. They'd been so excited to learn they were going to be grandparents again and now they have this to worry about.'

'Well, maybe he just needs time for it to sink in. He's been free to play the field for so long now, it's probably freaked him out a bit knowing he's going to be a dad, but I'm sure he'll get his head around it in time. I really don't believe that he'd completely abandon her.'

'I hope not,' Dash replied angrily. 'She deserves better than that. I just wish he'd contact me though. It shits me the way he's run away; I thought he had more balls than that.'

They both just sat there quietly for a while then, neither wanting other people's worries impinging on their day out together. Fortunately the beach atmosphere had a soothing effect on both of them, so it wasn't long before their moods lifted again.

'I'm looking forward to the party tonight,' Dash said then, wanting to change the subject. 'It'll be great to see Enzo again, and you got on great with Paula when they came to our wedding.' He couldn't help but smile before saying, 'I can't believe she's stuck by the silly bugger all this time. It's about time he finally decided to take her on a decent holiday.'

Evie smiled too. She really liked Paula and was looking forward to seeing her again. Remembering how they'd both shaken their heads upon hearing about some of the situations that Dash and his mate had been in over the years, she couldn't help grinning. 'What time do you think they'll get here?'

'Well, their flight gets into Sydney at three-thirty. By the time they get their bags and hire car ... I reckon they should be here about five-thirty.'

Dash was smiling as he lay back down on his towel, closing his eyes against the glare of the bright sun. Evie was smiling too, thinking of the other people that were coming to the party later that evening. They'd both made several good friends since they'd moved to Terrigal, their next door neighbours being amongst them.

'With Marley's friends as well it should be a good mix,' she thought to herself happily.

A seagull suddenly landed right in front of her, squawking loudly for some food, followed by two more of its noisy feathered friends. As Evie shooed them away, she noticed an elderly lady stop to admire the enormous sandcastle that Bluey and Tiffany were intent on constructing.

Watching the woman's face crease into an amused smile

as the girls chatted on about their creation, Evie unexpectedly had an image of her own mother appear in her mind. Smiling, she stretched her arms up, then out, revelling in the sense of freedom that she always felt at the beach.

'I'm still glad we all decided not to tell Mum about Dad – it wouldn't have served any good purpose,' she smiled. 'No doubt they've sorted it out between themselves by now.'

'Yep, sometimes the less said the better.'

Sitting up and reaching over to take Evie's hand in his, Dash grinned at her and said, 'Come on, it's time we went for a swim.'

The End

Hi, thanks for checking out Six Skene Street; I hope you find it an enjoyable read.

This is my debut novel, and I'm in the process of writing my second, but I believe I first need to give you a little bit of info about myself.

I was born in Geelong and spent my early childhood running free in Portarlington ... as Evie does. I'm now divorced with two lovely sons and daughters-in-law, and three adorable grandchildren. After living in most of the places mentioned in this novel I have returned to reside in Geelong once more.

In my 'spare time' (when not babysitting!) I love to write, have coffee with friends, paint abstracts, have coffee with friends, draw zentangles ... and did I mention having coffee with friends?

I'd love to hear your feedback regarding Six Skene Street, so if you feel inclined you can contact me at:
alisonmorantauthor@gmail.com

Cheers, Alison.